They'd been in the warehouse only minu

when Jill heard a door slam, and the knot coiling in her stomach tightened. Her palms were slick with sweat as she clutched her bag and slowly eased out of her crouch. Dave mimed her silent movement, his lean body tensed like that of a jaguar ready to spring.

Footsteps sounded—the wary, deliberate tread of someone on his guard. When she opened her eyes, she spotted a squat, bulky shadow looming at the end of the corridor. For a split second Jill surrendered to the wild hope that he would pass by. But her desperate fantasy was short-lived.

Slowly the stranger came to life and began to walk directly toward their hiding place....

ABOUT THE AUTHOR

Laurel Pace can't remember a period in her life when she wasn't writing. Her big break came when she was called to write copy in an emergency for an advertising agency where she was employed. This is Laurel's first Intrigue, although she has written for American Romance and will continue to do so. Laurel lives with her husband, Douglas, in Georgia, after having spent years in Davidson, North Carolina.

Deception by Design

Laurel Pace

Harlequin Books

TORONTO • NEW YORK • LONDON
AMSTERDAM • PARIS • SYDNEY • HAMBURG
STOCKHOLM • ATHENS • TOKYO • MILAN

For Nancy,
my favorite American in Paris

Harlequin Intrigue edition published April 1989

ISBN 0-373-22112-6

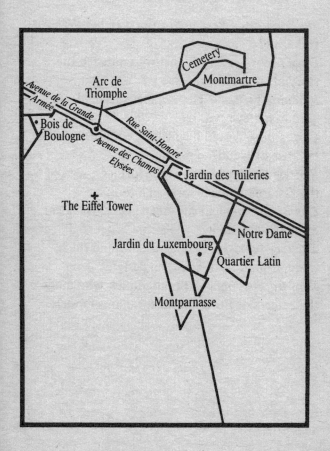

CAST OF CHARACTERS

Jill Fremont—Were her instincts right? Was Cici still alive?

Dave Lovell—A journalist who pursued the story of the century.

Madame Vernier—Her manner was cold, the glint in her eye evil.

Chausson—Would his fashion empire crumble because of fraud?

Simone Nanka-Midou—The former queen of the fashion magazine was in hiding.

Cici Madison—Did she escape her sinking car or go down with it?

Zachary Parrish—Did he mastermind the underground trade in stolen designs?

Sanford Fielding—A photographer who made the careers of Europe's most famous models.

Chapter One

"Any suggestions for a toast?" The young woman's wine-stained lips formed a smile over the rim of her brandy snifter. As she lifted the snifter, it wavered in her unsteady hand, leaving a trail of delicate amber bubbles to bleed into the white tablecloth.

Jill pretended not to notice the spilled Grand Marnier as she lifted her own glass. She gave her companion a smile calculated to ease some of the tension. "Why don't we drink to your next modeling assignment, Cici? You must have been thrilled when Chausson decided to have his spring collection photographed in Bali."

Cici Madison stared blankly for a moment, as if she had not quite understood. Then she caught herself. "Oh, yeah. I'm really looking forward to the trip." Her mouth quivered into another ersatz smile before she tipped the snifter. *"Salut!"*

Jill slowly sipped the liqueur and then carefully placed the glass on the table. "I really appreciate your inviting me to meet you for dinner tonight. Paris is wonderful, but it's nice to get out in the country every now and then." She made an effort to sound gracious. In spite of the small provincial restaurant's pleasant

ambiance and excellent food, however, the evening had
been anything but relaxing. For some reason, Cici remained as taut as a spring, impervious to the soothing
effects of wine or light conversation, and Jill had felt
her own tension level rise steadily during the meal.

"I really hate to call it a night," she began gently,
sliding the strap of her shoulder bag off her chair. "But
I'm afraid tomorrow's a school day."

Cici pushed her glass aside. A frown pleated her brow
as she snatched a large alligator-skin bag from beneath
the table and began to rummage through its contents.
Tossing a pack of Gitanes onto the table, she glanced
first at Jill, then at her watch. "It's only a little after
nine," she protested with surprise. Pressing her lips into
a bloodless white line, she tapped the pack of cigarettes
against the table. Before lifting a cigarette to her mouth,
she remembered to smile. "I'm just not ready to go
back to the city yet. Let's have another drink. Okay?"

"Okay, but I think I'll have some coffee." Although
she could not imagine why Cici would want to prolong
the strained evening, Jill twisted around in her chair to
signal their waiter from across the room. On the edge of
her vision, she watched Cici repeatedly flick the lighter,
swearing under her breath at the tardy flame.

Jill gave her order then turned back to her companion. She chuckled. "Now I wish I had saved some room
for dessert." She broke off and frowned. "Is something wrong?"

The model seemed not to hear. Her dark eyes widened, and focused with an almost ferocious intensity as
she stared past Jill to something across the room.

"Cici? Are you all right?"

Cici blinked at Jill, but her face remained set in a
colorless mask. "I'm fine." Her tight voice mocked her

protest. "I . . . I just thought I saw someone I know. That's all. I must have been mistaken." She forced an unconvincing titter, but her fingers continued to pluck at the stray wisps of fair hair curling from beneath her Panama hat.

Curiosity overrode Jill's usual good manners, and she pivoted in her seat for a look behind her. The diners seated at the three tables clustered near the empty stone fireplace appeared innocuous enough: a gypsy-faced man sipped beer; a portly woman in a snug black suit hunched over a dish of chocolate mousse; and a rather attractive man read *France-Soir* with his after-dinner coffee. When the man's eyes suddenly met hers from over the newspaper's edge, Jill swiveled in her seat.

"Guess I've had too much to drink if I'm startin' to see things." For a moment, Cici's west Texas drawl slipped through her breathy voice like an old petticoat peaking from beneath a designer gown. She fostered a grin, but her eyes drifted involuntarily over Jill's shoulder. "Uh, will you excuse me for a second?" She rose awkwardly from her seat and edged around the table. Bending over Jill's chair, she pointed toward the rear of the restaurant and whispered, "Little girls' room. Be right back."

Jill nodded, but she watched uncertainly as Cici wove her way across the dining room and then disappeared down the corridor next to the service bar. While waiting, she sipped the coffee and tried to make sense of Cici's puzzling behavior.

The waiter must have been keeping a close eye on her, for the moment Jill emptied the tiny cup, he appeared at the table to deposit the check. Good, she thought as she counted out one-hundred-franc notes and arranged them on the black plastic tray. At least there could be no further discussion of another round of drinks if the bill were paid when Cici returned—whenever that might be.

Sliding the check tray aside, Jill glanced at her watch. No, it wasn't her imagination. Cici had been gone an awfully long time. The model had drunk quite a bit, now that she thought about it. Maybe she was sick. Maybe Jill should check on her.

She shifted uneasily in her seat, feeling trapped by the awkward situation. She didn't know Cici that well, really. In fact, until tonight their contact had been limited to the weekly French lessons she taught her. How Cici would react to her barging in on her when she was ill remained the question.

Well, there's one way to find out. Jill's face was grim as she shouldered her bag and pushed back her chair. As she rose, she noticed the corner of Cici's alligator clutch poking out from beneath the tablecloth. Shaking her head, Jill picked up the bag and tucked it under her arm. Thank heaven one of them was sober enough to keep track of mundane things like restaurant checks and handbags. What a fiasco this evening had proved to be! As she made her way across the dining room, she steeled herself to what she'd find.

Three of the waiters had congregated at the end of the service bar. Their voices dropped, and one of them hastily stubbed out a cigarette as Jill sidled past them. Outside the rest-room door, her resolve faltered, and she hesitated. The knob turned easily in her hand, but she knocked softly on the door frame, anyway.

"Cici? May I come in?" Jill cracked the door slightly, admitting a ribbon of light into the corridor. She listened for a second before stepping in.

The rest room was tiny, and unlike many public ones in France, lacked an attendant. The fluorescent tube over the sink flickered and buzzed dully, but even in the scant light Jill could see that the room was empty. *Where was Cici?* Frowning, she retreated into the hall. She started as she turned and almost collided with the stout woman she had seen devouring chocolate mousse. The woman gave her a cold look before pushing her way into the rest room.

At the corner of the bar, Jill paused. As if they sensed her presence, the three waiters immediately straightened themselves and fell silent.

"Pardon, monsieur." Jill gestured toward the now-vacant table as she asked the waiters if they had seen the young woman with the straw hat.

"Elle est partie, mademoiselle," one of them volunteered. *She has left.* When Jill only stared in disbelief, the waiter pointed toward the door at the end of the corridor.

"Partie? Mais, c'est impossible!" Despite the waiter's insistence, Jill could not believe that Cici Madison had excused herself and then secretly slipped out the rear exit. It simply made no sense.

Giving the trio of waiters another dubious look, Jill wheeled into the nubby tweed of an arm. Looking up, she recognized the tweed jacket's owner; it was the handsome man who'd been absorbed in the copy of *France-Soir* while waiting for his drink.

"Excusez-moi, mademoiselle." Straightening his lanky frame, the man mumbled in a voice not quite low enough to disguise his American accent.

When Jill nodded, the man smiled—a slow, wide grin that lit every angle and curve of his face. No wonder most Frenchmen thought all Yanks looked like the Marlboro man, she thought. In spite of her preoccupation, she returned the smile. When she met his gaze, however, she was startled by his eyes; piercing and hawklike, they seemed at odds with his genial expression. There was something hard in those eyes, something as sharp and unyielding as the tempered steel their color favored. She could feel them following her as she hurried down the corridor.

Jill flung open the door and stepped out into the humid night air. Narrowly skirting a stack of milk crates, she peered down the alley. When she spotted Cici's white Ferrari gleaming beneath a streetlight, she rushed toward the corner.

She could see Cici now. The wide brim of the Panama hat was moving along the edge of the car's front seat like a tipsy moon in search of the horizon. In dismay, Jill watched the model slump forward and then sink beneath the dash. Poor thing! She had probably gone out to her car to get a sobering breath of fresh air and had just passed out.

As Jill approached the parked Ferrari, a dislodged trash can lid rattled against the cobbled street behind her. Turning, she recognized the tall American standing in the rear door of the restaurant. Suddenly the roar of a powerful engine sent Jill spinning around in time to catch the Ferrari's headlights flare. The acrid smell of burnt rubber assaulted her nose as the car lurched away from the curb, then sped down the street.

Running to the end of the alley, Jill called after the car in frustration. "Cici!" She might as well have cried out to the distant stars glimmering in the summer sky.

Why had she let Cici finish the bottle of wine? Why had she not stood firm when the model insisted they order after-dinner drinks? She was a teacher, wasn't she? *She*, at least, was supposed to keep her head. Jill reproached herself as she hurried to her own car. But hindsight was useless now. Her only hope was to over-take Cici, allay her embarrassment, and somehow per-suade her not to drive home just yet. None of those tasks was going to be easy.

As Jill pulled the dark blue Peugeot away from the curb, she scanned the narrow roadway leading out of town. There was always a chance that Cici might come to her senses and pull over to the side, but for now the road was deserted, save for an elderly man weaving along on a sputtering motorbike.

Once she had left the huddled village houses behind, Jill stepped down on the accelerator. Although she was normally a cautious driver, the urge to overtake Cici prompted her to drive faster than usual. Not that she stood much chance of catching up to the model's high-powered sports car. Tension locked her fingers around the wheel, and she pressed the gas more firmly.

Jill blinked in surprise when she rounded a curve and spotted the white Ferrari up ahead. As she narrowed the distance separating her from the sports car, she recog-nized Cici's Panama hat, outlined like a halo through the rear window. For her part, Cici seemed oblivious that she was being followed. Jill flashed her headlights off and on, then tooted the horn, but the Ferrari main-tained its maddeningly narrow lead.

"For heaven's sake, Cici!" she muttered under her breath. She could excuse any woman's hesitancy to re-spond to signals from a strange driver, but in the bright light of the full moon Cici surely recognized the blue Peugeot.

Jill flexed her hands as she cut a glance at the illu-minated speedometer and saw the needle edging steadily clockwise. It was not her imagination; Cici was driving faster now. Taking a deep breath, Jill frowned at the speeding white car. What was she trying to do? Get them both killed?

The Ferrari wove across the centerline, and Jill sucked in her breath. The game was becoming dangerous, too dangerous for her tastes. She let up on the accelerator and forced herself to ease back in the seat.

Suddenly Jill's whole body stiffened, and her hand flew up to her mouth. "Oh, my God!" Up ahead, the Ferrari spun out of control at the mouth of the bridge. The car banked for a split second, but its momentum was too great. Like a dancer in a frightful mechanical ballet, the vehicle ripped through the flimsy barrier and plunged down the embankment.

The Peugeot shuddered as Jill jerked the wheel toward the shoulder and stomped the brake. Throwing open the door, she jumped out of the car and ran toward the river. Her eyes remained riveted to the spot where the sports car had disappeared over the edge. She could see the metal barrier clearly now, curled back like a gaping wound.

At the embankment's edge, she almost slipped on loose gravel. Steadying herself on what remained of the barrier, Jill stared down at the river. Although the cab of the Ferrari was still partially above water, it was now too dark to see if it were occupied. In horror, Jill watched the concentric rings widening around the sinking car.

"Cici!" The cry burst from her dry throat. Half sliding, half stumbling, she fought her way down the steep embankment. "Cici! Where are you?"

The water lapped gently at the bank in chilling contrast to the disastrous scene. As Jill struggled through the undergrowth, she could see the taillights growing pale beneath the water's surface. At the river's edge, she stopped. In the shadow of the bridge, she could just make out a straw Panama hat floating on the dark water.

"Cici!" Jill screamed and listened as her voice died out, unanswered, across the water.

Gripped by growing panic, Jill kicked off her shoes and leaped into the river. The cold and oily water stung her body. Fortunately the current was not too strong. Fighting to subdue her emotions, she swam with long, steady strokes. When she reached the now-submerged vehicle, she paddled water, twisting around in hope of spotting Cici. Desperate, she plunged beneath the water's surface.

Jill opened her eyes to a sightless gray limbo. Thrusting her arms in a wide arc, she groped the murky water. Shapeless flotsam flirted with her grasping fingers. Panting, she breached the surface only long enough to grab a breath before plunging under the water once more. This time she pushed deeper, pumping with her legs. When her foot struck something solid and heavy, she turned and stretched both arms into the unseen void.

It was the car! For a second, her hand had grazed the curving windshield. Jill broke once again for air and then dived below. This time she was on target; her hands could make out the edge of an open window. She reached blindly through the window and seized the steering wheel. As the sinking vehicle began to pull her along with it, she had to battle the urge to let go and rush to the surface.

Jill had long since lost all sense of time, but she knew that she must find Cici soon. Still gripping the wheel with one hand, she explored the front seat with the other. Suddenly the car listed to one side. Jill lost her hold on the wheel, and she kicked to regain her equilibrium. She was pushing toward the surface when something fluttered against her arm. She reached instinctively and briefly clasped a length of sodden fabric.

It was a sleeve, but most importantly, the arm within it was moving! The realization sent a spurt of adrenaline through her body. Her lungs were threatening to explode now in their craving for air, but she plunged through the water in a frantic search for the moving target. Her hands snatched at the cold water. When another swatch of clothing—a hem or a shirttail, she could not be sure—ran across her fingers, she latched on to it with an iron grip.

Summoning the last reserve of her dwindling energy, Jill grappled with the twisted fabric in an effort to reel her quarry toward her. In a sudden, desperate maneuver, she relinquished her hold on the wet clothing and lunged for the thrashing body. When her hands closed over Cici's slender arm, a surge of elation bolstered her flagging strength. Her relief was short-lived, however, for the woman slipped away from her grasp. Jill knew that people near drowning often panicked and fought their would-be rescuers, but it was a complication she could ill afford at this point. *Please, Cici! Be calm! Let me help you!* she pleaded inwardly as she struggled to maintain her grasp.

The water was churning around them now, fanned by the victim's flailing limbs. A sharp blow caught Jill in the midsection, forcing a precious gasp of air from her, and she let go of Cici's arm. A dizzy sickness filled her head, but she grasped again.

The moment her fingers locked around a wrist she realized that something was wrong—terribly wrong.

The wrist felt thick, sinewy, matted with coarse hair. This could not be Cici's delicate, rail-thin arm; the limb trapped within Jill's weakening grasp belonged to a man! But who was he? Where had he come from? And where was Cici? The questions assaulted her wavering consciousness like a volley of arrows.

The arm jerked abruptly, and Jill had no choice but to release it. She struggled to orient herself, but the sheer weight of the water held her down. Her chest seemed to swell, strained beyond endurance by her exhausted lungs. Her head was pounding. A cold black curtain passed before her eyes, as the water closed over her.

SHE COULD FEEL THE RIVER sweeping over her body, but her head remained above water. Air was life. As long as she had air, nothing else mattered. Her feet and hands seemed displaced, far away, as if dismembered. She felt gravel scrape her legs, stinging her deadened flesh. Then her mouth was pressed into the dank weeds. River stench filled her nostrils, the smell of stagnation and decay. She wanted to retch, but instead her body rolled limply to face the dark sky. Somewhere far away, up among the invisible stars, she could hear someone calling.

"*Mademoiselle?* Can you hear me?" The voice drew near and then faded.

Jill blinked, straining to bring into focus the clouded form that moved before her eyes. There had been a man kneeling over her. Where was he now? It was so hard, just to see. The world kept pulling away from her. She could barely hold on. Everything seemed so faint now, like the stars and the voice.

"For God's sake, lady! Don't die on me!" The man's voice blurred. When he looked down at her, the place where his face should have been was empty. Helpless, she watched the blackness slowly blot him out along with everything else.

Chapter Two

Jill sat on the edge of the bed and fumbled with a cuff button. Through the shirred white curtain screening the bed, she could hear the sounds of the ward: rubber soles squishing briskly in the paths of rattling stainless-steel carts; hushed voices dispensing greetings along with medications and dressings. How relieved she would be to escape to her aunt's quiet apartment, away from the ceaseless activity and cloying antiseptic smell!

Abandoning the recalcitrant button, Jill shoved her feet into her shoes and slid off the bed. She was looking around the screened cubicle, trying to take inventory of her few possessions, when a shadow loomed behind the curtain.

"Mademoiselle Fremont? Inspector Arnaud is here to see you." The voice was tentative. "If I may help you..."

Jill quickly rolled the screen ajar. "I'm fine, thank you," she told the young nurse, but when she turned to collect her things, the floor felt unnervingly treacherous beneath her feet. "If you could just get the flowers my students sent me, please." She nodded toward the bouquet of lilies of the valley sitting on the side table. Surprised, she spied Cici's alligator clutch, and grabbed it up. Steadying herself against the corner of the bed she followed the nurse past the row of tall white beds out to the corridor.

With the promise to put Jill's discharge papers in order, the nurse ushered her into a windowless waiting room and then hurried away. Clutching the big alligator bag to her chest like a shield, Jill perched on the edge of the green vinyl couch. She sprang to her feet when a portly man charged into the room. Although the previous evening remained cloaked in a fog, she instantly recognized the police inspector's flushed face.

"*Bonjour*, Mademoiselle Fremont!" The man proffered a hand and nodded his balding head.

"*Bonjour*, Inspector Arnaud." Jill loosened her hold on the clutch long enough to give the pudgy hand a brief shake.

"I trust you are recovering from your unfortunate accident." Inspector Arnaud's damp lips automatically slid into an avuncular smile.

"The doctors seem to think so," she assured him. She hesitated a moment, waiting for the police inspector's bland smile to dim.

Inspector Arnaud only continued to beam at her. "I've had your car brought to the hospital, Mademoiselle Fremont."

"Thank you, Inspector Arnaud. Uh, I wanted to ask you about Mademoiselle Madison..." She broke off, her fingers tightening reflexively around the alligator clutch.

Like a mask gliding into place, Arnaud's face suddenly assumed a look of fatherly concern. "I am afraid I have no good news to report. The car was recovered yesterday evening, within a few hours of the accident. But as for Mademoiselle Madison..." He looked down at the toes of his well-shined shoes and shook his head. "She was apparently thrown from the vehicle and swept away. The river's current is deceptively strong, you see, and it may be days—perhaps even weeks—before the remains..."

"'Remains'?" Jill almost gagged on the clinical words. Up till now events had been like a dream.

"I am sorry, Mademoiselle Fremont. Perhaps you should take some small comfort knowing that your friend did not suffer greatly. Our preliminary examination of the wreckage suggests that she was probably killed on impact, so quickly that she would not have known what was happening to her."

Jill was already shaking her head. "Inspector Arnaud, I found Cici Madison near that sunken car, just before someone pulled me out of the water. And she was still alive, still strong enough to fight me in her panic! Surely until you have positive proof to the contrary, you must allow for the chance that she managed to swim to shore." She gestured with the alligator bag in frustration. "She could be wandering around in a daze. She could have passed out in the forest."

The police inspector's black brows rose skeptically. "Please, Mademoiselle Fremont, I know such things are difficult to accept, but there is simply no evidence to support your hopes. And even were we to allow for the remote possibility that Mademoiselle Madison survived and miraculously reached the shore, she would have left tracks among the reeds. We found no footprints. Nothing." He opened his free hand and examined the empty palm before holding it up for her inspection.

Jill stared at the splayed hand, but her thoughts were focused inward. She glanced down at the clutch, the last remnant linking her to Cici, and a bitter pang grabbed the pit of her stomach. *If only I could have held on to her hand . . .*

"Please, Mademoiselle Fremont." Inspector Arnaud's tone had grown annoyingly patronizing. "You have gone through quite an ordeal. Under such circumstances, the senses can play tricks on the mind."

Jill straightened herself. The police inspector was not much taller than she, making it easy for her to meet his darting dark eyes. "Please don't try to tell me that I imagined finding her, Inspector Arnaud," she warned him in a voice as uncompromising as her stare. "I'm certain I touched Cici Madison. And if you don't believe me, ask that man who pulled me out of the river. He couldn't help but have realized that Cici was in the water, too."

The police inspector carefully balanced his hat on one hand and pretended to dust the crown. He cleared his throat before speaking again. "You are, of course, entitled to your opinion, Mademoiselle Fremont, but I am afraid the facts do not support it. The gentleman who rescued you spotted the wreck from the highway. He saw you struggling and managed to bear you safely to shore. However, when we questioned him," he paused and smartly creased the hat's crown, "he mentioned no sign of another survivor."

"But he must have known! Cici could not have been more than a few feet away when I grabbed his arm," Jill insisted.

Inspector Arnaud stepped back into the doorway and glanced down the hall. When he looked back at Jill, he smiled indulgently. "Perhaps you would like to ask the gentleman yourself."

"What do you mean?" Frowning, Jill walked to the door and watched the police inspector gesture with his hat to a man hunched over a pay phone at the end of the hall. The man waved impatiently, still holding the receiver clamped to his ear.

Although Jill retained only the most shadowy impression of the rescuer who had dragged her semiconscious out of the river, there was something vaguely familiar about this man's rangy silhouette. Only when he rang off and turned toward them, however, was she able to place him. As he strode down the corridor, his rugged face moved into focus, erasing any doubts that he was the tall American whom she had seen in the restaurant the previous night.

"Mademoiselle Jill Fremont, Monsieur David Lovell." Inspector Arnaud handled the introduction with officious pride.

"Make that 'Dave Lovell,'" the man amended, adroitly positioning himself between her and Arnaud. "I don't mind admitting that you really had me scared last night, Miss Fremont. When I phoned Inspector Arnaud this morning, I was relieved to hear they were going to discharge you today. Since I was in the area, I decided to stop by and see how you were doing myself. I hope you don't mind the intrusion." His midwestern drawl added an extra note of earnestness to his remark, but it failed to distract Jill from the frank appraisal of his gray eyes.

Jill looked directly into the enigmatic flint-hued eyes. "Not at all. I'm glad to have a chance to thank you. You saved my life."

Dave Lovell deflected her gratitude—and her gaze—with a boyish smile. "I'm just glad I came along at the right time."

"Mademoiselle Fremont wanted to ask you a few questions about the accident victim, I believe," Inspector Arnaud interposed, not without a trace of malice.

Lovell gave Jill a quizzical look.

"Inspector Arnaud insists the driver of the car did not survive the initial crash." Jill fostered an even tone for Arnaud's benefit. "I know that she did, however. When you first reached me in the river, I had just located her and was trying to get hold of her."

Dave Lovell's lean face registered interest but no recognition.

"She was panic-stricken and really churning up the water. You must have noticed," Jill prompted.

"*You* were certainly stirring some water, but I didn't see anyone else," Lovell replied cautiously. "Of course, it was very dark."

"But she was right there!" Jill insisted. She swallowed hard in an effort to subdue her voice. "We were underwater. Maybe you thought she and I were the same person. But this woman had just pulled away from me and I was reaching for her arm when I grabbed your wrist."

Lovell's brow tightened into a dubious frown. "You didn't grab my wrist. I wish you had, though, it would have made dragging you to shore a lot easier."

For a moment, Jill could only gape in speechless dismay. "But I did! I distinctly remember discovering someone else besides Cici in the water. When you jerked away from me, I didn't know what to think." Her heart sank as he slowly shook his head. "Don't you remember?"

"You were practically unconscious when I reached you, Miss Fremont. I'm sorry if I'm not being very helpful," Dave Lovell began, but Jill was quick to ward off any further expressions of sympathy.

"Last night, you gave me more help than I could ask for. I'm very grateful to you, Mr. Lovell. But now, if you'll excuse me, I'd like to go home. I'm awfully tired."

Too tired to fend off yet another attack on the reliability of her senses. She stooped to retrieve her shoulder bag from the couch, desperately needing time alone, time to think.

"If you require assistance, Mademoiselle Fremont, I will be glad to arrange an escort to your home," Inspector Arnaud offered.

Jill pointedly looked past the police inspector, ignoring his smug expression. "Thank you, but that won't be necessary. *Au revoir*, Inspector Arnaud. Mr. Lovell." On her way to the door, she gave each of them a tight smile.

She was bent over the nurses' desk, signing the discharge papers, when she sensed someone's presence behind her. Jill wheeled to find Dave Lovell holding out the bouquet of lilies of the valley.

"You forgot your flowers."

"Oh. Thank you." Shifting Cici's bag beneath her arm, Jill took the bouquet. For some reason, she felt oddly defenseless with her hands full.

Although his mission was accomplished, Lovell seemed in no hurry to be on his way. "Usually you have to stay in the hospital for a few days before anyone thinks to send flowers," he remarked. "You must have a mighty thoughtful friend."

Jill frowned as she tucked the folded copy of the discharge papers into her bag. When she looked up at him, however, he appeared too genuine to be accused of idle prying. "They're from my students," she explained. "Even though I only stayed overnight, word travels fast at the *lycée*."

Lovell nodded thoughtfully. "Uh, listen." He folded his arms across his chest and glanced down the corridor. "I know you're probably sick of being treated like an invalid, but I'd still like to offer you a ride home."

"That's very kind of you, but Inspector Arnaud had my car brought to the hospital." She shook her head reluctantly; she had to admit he was attractive and would've liked to take him up on his offer.

"That's great 'cause I don't have a car. But I'm still a damned good driver." He chuckled, winning a reserved smile from her. "Of course, if you'd prefer to drive yourself…" Pressing his luck, he took a step back from the nurses' station.

Her fingers twisted the strap of her shoulder bag and then loosened their hold. "If you're certain it wouldn't be out of your way," she conceded in a voice far softer than he'd expected. "I live near St. Germain-des-Prés."

I know, Dave thought, but he only shook his head. "No problem at all." He took the redolent lilies of the valley from her and turned toward the elevator.

"I have to confess I was wishing this morning that I could call my aunt and ask her to pick me up from the hospital." Jill had fallen in step beside him, but he had to strain to hear her low voice beneath the ward's din. "Unfortunately, she's on vacation right now."

Thank God for that! Dave congratulated himself, but he only nodded sympathetically.

As they waited for the elevator, she flipped open her shoulder bag and picked through its contents for a few seconds. He took the brief opportunity to study her. She was not very tall, but the navy blue dress she was wearing, one of those drop-waist styles that always reminded him of F. Scott Fitzgerald novels, made her look taller. Her hair was as black as he remembered it from the previous night—although he suspected it looked more like mahogany in the sun—and cut straight to her chin. The haircut had something of the twenties to it, too. Her face was a classic heart shape, set off by a short nose and a pair of extraordinarily direct brown eyes. She was very pretty, especially when she flashed a smile—as she did now when she handed him a ring of keys.

"Dear Tante Yvonne! If she only knew what I had been up to in her car while she's vacationing on Corsica!"

"The Peugeot belongs to your aunt?"

Jill nodded. "I'm living with her this year. You see, I'm teaching English at the Lycée Marguerite de Valois through the Teachers for International Understanding program."

As Dave held the elevator door for her, he once again had to stifle the urge to say "I know." He had not had much time to do a thorough background check on Jill Fremont, but so far she had not contradicted any of his findings. Still, it was too early to jump to any favorable conclusions about her. He needed to caution himself not to be taken in so easily, remind himself that, innocent as this woman might appear, she was involved with a treacherous character like Cici Madison.

After all, Madison had passed the alligator bag to her in the restaurant; he had witnessed that clever little trick himself. His eyes drifted to the big, gaudy thing she now held clenched beneath her arm. No, there were signs all over the place that this woman was not to be trusted. If he could believe that, at least it would make his job easier. And yet for some absurd reason, he wanted to convince himself she was as innocent of guilt as she appeared.

Dave glanced down at the bouquet he was holding. It was not his imagination; the heady fragrance of the lilies had grown stronger, clinging to everything in the elevator. When the door at last glided open, he gulped a breath of the refreshingly antiseptic air.

"Do you live in Paris, or are you just visiting?" Her question interrupted his thoughts as they stepped out of the elevator into the lobby, and for a moment he was caught off guard.

"I moved here about a month ago. On account of my work," he added in hope of short-circuiting any further questions. "From what I've heard, there's an American colony of sorts in Paris. You know many Yanks in town?"

From the corner of his eye, he watched her gaze momentarily shift to the big alligator bag she was carrying. "No, not really."

"This woman who was involved in the accident— what was her name? Cici Madison?—she was an American, right?" This was risky business, he knew, but Jill looked so vulnerable, he couldn't resist chancing it.

"Yes." She broke off and swallowed hard. She looked up at Dave, her eyes bright with moisture. "She was so young, with everything going for her. I just can't believe such an awful thing has happened to her. If only I could have gotten to her in time." She hastily averted her gaze.

Watching her small hands nervously finger the alligator bag, Dave could tell she was struggling to master her emotions. He took a hesitant step toward her and rested his hand briefly on her shoulder. He might be a fool for a pretty face, but there was no mistaking the remorse tormenting Jill Fremont at that moment.

"Cici was a good friend of yours?" The second he posed the question, he felt guilty. Was he so totally without scruples that he could exploit this woman's grief to gain information? Dave resisted confronting the answer to that question.

Mercifully Jill did not look up, but only shook her head. "I didn't know her very well at all, really. She was looking for an American to give her French lessons and contacted me through the *lycée*. I've been tutoring her for about five months. We had met for dinner out in the country last night as a farewell celebration of sorts. School will be out in another week, and Cici wanted to do something special for me before our last lesson. She had left her bag in the restaurant, and I was trying to catch up with her to return it when..." Her voice faltered, and she gestured helplessly with the bag. "When it happened. I should never have let her drink so much!"

"Don't blame yourself," Dave interposed. His hand twitched, inexplicably yearning to smooth the glossy dark head that was bent in front of him.

"I'm trying not to, but I was so close to saving her. At least, I thought I was." She took a deep breath, and he could almost feel the shudder passing through her. Suddenly she straightened herself, her face set once more in a somber, controlled mask. "I see Tante Yvonne's car!" Not waiting for him to respond, she set off across the parking lot at an unexpected clip.

Dave took his time following Jill, giving himself a chance to think. What if her story were just as it appeared at face value and nothing more? Could she really be an innocent party, catapulted by circumstance into Cici Madison's dark circle? And what about the bag? Was her simple explanation for possessing it true? As he unlocked the door of the blue Peugeot, Dave regarded the reptilian monstrosity tucked securely under Jill's arm.

"What do you plan to do with her bag?" He asked the question while he adjusted the driver's seat, hoping he sounded convincingly disinterested.

"Return it to her housekeeper. Cici never said much about her family, but she adored Nana." Jill laid the bag on her lap before snapping the seat belt into place. "Poor Madame Petit was very upset when I phoned her from the hospital this morning. She told me she was trying to get her wits together and organize Cici's things, but everyone has been calling her—police, reporters, attorneys, the design house Cici modeled for. At any rate, I promised to drop the bag off at the apartment tomorrow after school." She sighed, a little shakily, and folded her hands on top of the bag.

Dave's eyebrows rose as he checked the rearview mirror. Tomorrow afternoon. That gave him some time, but only a little.

"By the way, what happened to your car?" Jill twisted in her seat to face him, and he could see she was trying to ease the tension.

"My car?" Dave frowned.

"You were driving a car last night, weren't you?"

"Oh, that car!" He managed a chuckle. "I rented it. Just wanted to get out in the country for the evening. I get stir-crazy in the city sometimes. You know how it is." He had no idea if she did, but he was sure of one thing: if Lying 101 had been a required subject at his university, he would never have gotten his degree.

Jill shrugged and turned toward the window. "Somehow Paris doesn't get to me the way other big cities do," she said and fell silent.

Dave flexed his fingers around the wheel and scowled at the tour bus that had just cut in front of the Peugeot. He was accustomed to asking questions, not answering them, and he didn't like role reversals, especially in this sort of situation. When he dared to glance at Jill, however, he found her staring solemnly out the window. She appeared lost in thought and did not speak until the church of St. Germain-des-Prés loomed into sight.

"Turn right at the corner," Jill instructed him, leaning toward the dashboard. "It's the second building on the right."

Following her directions, Dave turned the Peugeot into an attractive side street and managed to squeeze it into the single remaining parking place.

She was out of the car before he could gather up the flowers and rush around to open the door for her. At the bottom of the building's steps, she paused, clutching the bag in front of her. "I really appreciate your driving me home. If you have time, I'd like to offer you some coffee."

"That would be nice. If it's not too much trouble, that is. I hate to impose on someone who's just gotten out of the hospital." With every Mr. Nice Guy disclaimer, his sense of duplicity grew one hundredfold.

Jill shook her head, and for a moment a tenuous smile dispelled some of the sadness reflected in her face. She took the keys from him and unlocked the front door of the apartment building. As if to taunt his already conflicting emotions, the alligator-skin bag protruded invitingly from beneath her arm as she stooped to check the mailbox.

Inside the elevator, the scent of the lilies rose once more, this time with almost life-threatening intensity. Dave tugged at his tie and loosened his collar. When the car rattled to a stop, he swung back the gate and then followed Jill and the bag down the hall to the apartment.

"Please make yourself comfortable." Jill gestured toward a well-cushioned sofa on her way across the room. She paused by a small mahogany desk and quickly shuffled through the mail. Dave swallowed—audibly, he was sure—as she dropped both handbags on the desk.

"The coffee will only take a minute." Her voice trailed off as she hurried out of the room, leaving him alone with the clutch bag.

Now was the moment of truth, the time for action. But for a second, Dave could only sit on the sofa and stare at the bag, wishing it would levitate and float over to him. Dave stood and walked toward the desk.

"Do you take cream and sugar?" Jill called from the kitchen.

"Just black, thanks."

Dave lifted the bag. For a moment, he simply wanted to hold it, feel its lacquered reptile surface beneath his hands. But time to savor his coup was a luxury he could ill afford. With a quick glance over his shoulder, he snapped it open.

As he had expected it was crammed with stuff Cici Madison would be unable to survive more than five minutes without—Gitanes, designer sunglasses, makeup and enough loose one-thousand franc notes to choke a voracious horse. Dave's hands proceeded methodically as he dug through the mess. The bag was bigger than he had thought, with a myriad of zippered pockets designed to hamper his progress. Something worthwhile had to be here, damn it! He hadn't gone through all this for nothing.

The smell of coffee drifted into the room, blending into a nauseating melange with the pervasive lily perfume. His senses quickened when his fingers brushed the edge of a small volume. Without further ado, he pulled out the book and looked at it. His sweaty palm had left a print on the suede cover, and he brushed the streaks away in annoyance. The smooth pages fluttered beneath his impatient fingers, but even a cursory glance told him that he had discovered Cici Madison's personal calendar!

His eyes raced down the pages. *May 14. 11:45 p.m. L. Pont Neuf.* Who the hell was *L* and why was Madison meeting him or her on a bridge in the middle of the night? He flipped more pages, pausing at an equally ambiguous entry made four days later. *May 18. 11:15 p.m. S. Arc.* Who was *S*? And which arch did she mean? In his excitement, Dave almost ripped one of the pages. Then he hesitated.

He could hear Jill's footsteps now; she was moving cautiously, no doubt to balance a tray. Like a man poised to jump, he confronted his choices. He needed that calendar. It didn't belong to Jill Fremont. Hell, he wasn't a thief; he just wanted to borrow the thing. He would even return it, after it had served its purpose. The rattle of china warned of her approach. In a split second, Dave jammed the calendar into his pocket, snapped the bag shut and rushed back to the sofa.

"I hope it isn't too strong," Jill apologized as she slid the tray onto the coffee table.

Dave accepted the cup she held out to him, but as he sipped the scalding coffee, he was hard-pressed to decide which of them was more uncomfortable. Each attempt he made at conversation felt more artificial than the last. For her part, Jill seemed nervous and distracted, perched on the edge of the sofa like a shy bird about to take flight. Maybe she did have something to hide after all, and his presence was beginning to wear on her. She couldn't possibly know what he had done, he told himself repeatedly. Or could she? Whatever the case, his own eagerness to be on his way remained foremost in his mind. He forced himself to wait until she had finished her coffee before checking his watch. She seemed concerned that he would miss the phony appointment he claimed to have in ten minutes. Dave assured her he would hurry. What difference did another lie make at this point anyway?

"Thanks again for the coffee," he told her from the hallway.

She leaned through the door and smiled briefly. "Thank *you*."

As the elevator carried him and the pilfered calendar down to the ground floor, Dave thought he could detect the faintest scent of lilies.

Chapter Three

A haze hung over the city, as soft and gauzy as the curtains that billowed away from the open doors. Below the balcony, traffic coursed along Rue Faubourg-St. Honoré, but Deschamps scarcely noticed its din. His ears were attuned to the room behind him. He had learned to interpret the most subtle of sounds, each sigh, every faint rustle, even the click of a Limoges cup against its saucer.

When Chausson finally spoke, his voice sounded weary. "You may come in, Monsieur Deschamps. Mademoiselle Soule."

Deschamps nodded to the stout woman standing next to him, then retreated into the room, pulling the balcony doors silently shut behind them. As was his evening custom, Chausson was seated on the green leather Empire chaise. A tray of coffee and anisette was arranged on the marble table in front of him, just as it was every evening. Tonight, however, a row of photographs lay next to the silver tray in place of the designer's favored periodicals.

Chausson was gazing at the photographs, but as Deschamps approached he leaned back and rubbed his eyes. *Even powerful men must age,* Deschamps thought, but his face remained impassive.

When Chausson looked up, Deschamps noticed that the gray eyes were shot with red, the circles beneath them thick and distended. Resting his elbows on his knees, he pressed his forehead into his hands. The wavy gray hair crested over his head like sculpted granite. "And you are convinced Cici was the thief?" He shot his tired eyes up at Deschamps.

"Beyond a doubt, Monsieur Chausson." Deschamps inclined his head ever so slightly toward the husky woman who hung back a few feet behind him. "As you can see for yourself, Mademoiselle Soule's hidden camera has recorded the transaction." He leaned over the coffee table to point discreetly at the photographs. "Cici Madison leaves the bag on the chair. After her departure, her companion waits. Then she takes the bag and also departs."

Chausson's eyes ricocheted among the photographs before locking on Deschamps.

"And then?"

Deschamps heard Mademoiselle Soule clear her throat nervously behind him. "Mademoiselle Madison was involved in an automobile accident on her way back to Paris. She is believed to be dead, and the police are now dredging the river to recover the body."

The designer's left eyelid twitched slightly. "And this other woman?"

"I fear we do not know who she is, Monsieur Chausson," Mademoiselle Soule admitted reluctantly.

"Then *we* must find out," the designer countered, not without sarcasm.

Deschamps instantly recognized the cue. Turning to the portly woman, he nodded. "Thank you, Mademoiselle Soule."

He watched her bulky figure retreat to the hall and waited until she closed the door behind her. Deschamps turned back to Chausson quickly enough to catch the look in his employer's eyes. Only he would recognize how deeply Mademoiselle Soule's ill-fitting suit and unsightly bulges offended the designer.

"Another detective has been assigned to the case?" Chausson asked, anticipating Deschamps's apologies.

"A most effective investigator, Monsieur Chausson. Our best man."

Chausson nodded. Lifting one of the photographs, he studied the grainy image for a moment before tossing it back onto the table. His sigh seemed to fill the high-ceilinged chamber. "Cici! Why, oh, why?" he breathed into his palms. Then he dropped his hands and straightened himself. "How could she steal my designs, Deschamps? How?"

"I only know that the model Cici Madison was the only person—other than yourself and I, of course—who had access to the lambskin cape. The other samples that have disappeared could have been taken by any of several employees; the lambskin cape, however, by only one." Deschamps deliberately kept his delivery straightforward and undramatic. Still, he thought he saw Chausson wince.

For a moment, Deschamps watched his employer wrestle with his thoughts. That he had been fond of the young model had always been obvious. Deschamps had personally found the long-legged Texan unpolished to the point of vulgarity, but he had, of course, never shared that opinion with Chausson. Perhaps in Cici

Madison, the designer had found the daughter he never
had; perhaps, in the way of aging men, he had been
flattered by her unsophisticated awe of him. Whatever
his reasons, Chausson had doted on her, and he was
fighting the suggestion that she would steal from him.

"This other woman, what role does she play?"
Chausson asked at length.

Deschamps folded his hands behind his back and
frowned slightly. "I think, Monsieur Chausson, that
Cici Madison was only a small link in the chain, a con-
duit, if you will. There's a large network of fashion
counterfeiters, as you know. I suspect the handbag that
Mademoiselle Madison passed to this woman contained design sketches or other valuable information."

Deschamps waited in discreet silence. Of all his tal-
ents, he prided himself most on discretion. His discretion had helped elevate him through the house to his
present position as right-hand man to the great designer himself. He was privy, unlike others, to the master's thoughts. Without discretion, he could not have
built the invisible but impenetrable wall around the
House of Chausson. The barrier Deschamps had
erected was so effective that, in a time when bogus
Guccis and fake St. Laurents were as common as flies,
not a single Chausson had ever reached the counterfeit
market. Until now. It was a transgression Deschamps
took personally.

Chausson suddenly pushed the photographs aside
and reached for the decanter of anisette. "We must do
everything possible to avoid scandal, Deschamps. I am
sure you realize the police would only complicate matters for us at this point."

"Certainly, Monsieur Chausson." Deschamps had
mastered the expertly timed pause, and he now used his

skill well. "Of course, we need not involve the authorities. There are ways…" He let his voice trail off. In the silence that followed, the air seemed to sing with tension.

Chausson had walked to the balcony doors and now stood staring down at the street. Outlined against the colorless sky, he looked as vulnerable and helpless as any mortal man. When he at last spoke, he did not turn. "Very well. Do what you must do."

THE CLASSROOM WAS DESERTED, filled with the hush peculiar to schools after-hours. Jill gave the blackboard a few perfunctory swipes with an eraser before turning to the cluttered desk. Although she had missed only one day of school, an intimidating backlog of papers had accumulated in her absence. Pushing aside the Larousse dictionary, she seated herself at the desk and began to sift through her work.

In spite of her good intentions, her mind kept returning, unbidden, to the isolated river bend and the tragedy that had taken place there. The texture, the smell, the very taste of it was imprinted so strongly on her senses, she feared she would never shake its memory, no matter how long or hard she tried. And she would never forget the feel of Cici Madison's wrist wrenched from her grasp for the last time.

Stubbing a pencil against the notepad, Jill stared at the smudgy black hole it bored into the paper. She had put aside her personal aversion to Arnaud and phoned the police inspector that morning, but as she had feared, the police had still found no trace of Cici. Arnaud had reminded her that, with each lapsing hour, her own theory that Cici had somehow survived the accident dimmed appreciably. Jill had not wasted breath to argue with him.

She was having enough trouble battling her own doubts. Perhaps Arnaud was right, after all. Perhaps she was clinging to the hope that Cici was alive just to assuage her own guilt over the unsuccessful rescue attempt. Perhaps she was letting her imagination provide a more comforting scenario than reality could do.

Tossing the pencil aside, she propped her elbows on the desk and rested her face in her hands. No, Cici may not have managed to swim to shore, but she had been alive when Jill had found her in the water, regardless of what Arnaud or Dave Lovell might say.

At the thought of the sandy-haired American, Jill pressed her fingers into her throbbing temples. Arnaud's resistance to her story she could understand, for she suspected the police inspector was bent on neatly wrapping up his investigation. But why had Dave Lovell contradicted her account? Had he lied to cover his own guilt and confusion at being unable to save two drowning women?

Jill frowned into the fingers latticed across her brow. Somehow he hadn't struck her as the sort of insecure man who'd do that. What kind of man was he anyway? He had seemed friendly and concerned, even gallant on the surface, but what really lay behind the cowpoke-in-a-three-piece-suit image? She had come away from their brief encounter with the feeling that his real character had eluded her, even as she felt herself drawn to him. Maybe it had been those intense gray eyes; something in their restless probing had kept her on guard.

She started and looked up when a tap sounded from the doorway.

"I hope I did not disturb you, Mademoiselle Fremont," Madame Fanon, the *lycée* secretary, apologized. "But you have a telephone call, a gentleman who says it is urgent."

Jill tried to control her rampant emotions as she followed Madame Fanon back to the office. Surely it must be Inspector Arnaud calling with news of Cici. Had they at last found her? A knot wrenched her throat at the next question that came to mind.

"Hello?" Her voice quavered as she pressed the receiver to her ear.

"Jill? Hi, this is Dave Lovell. I hope you're doing all right. Did I interrupt one of your classes?" He sounded dubious.

Jill hastily cleared her throat, trying to mask the lump lodged there. "I'm fine, thank you. I was just finishing up some paperwork when you phoned." Why was she so glad to hear from him? "The secretary said there was something urgent," she prompted.

His deep chuckle instantly conjured up the image of his pleasantly rugged face. "Maybe I exaggerated a little bit. The reason I called was to see if you'd like to have a drink with me after school today."

"A drink?" she repeated lamely.

"Yeah. Or coffee. Whatever you like." When she did not immediately answer, he added, "I'd really like a chance to talk with you again."

"Okay," she conceded slowly, but her mind was racing. Perhaps he, too, was disturbed by their conflicting memories of the rescue, and he wanted to discuss it more thoroughly. Jill twisted to one side to peer at the office clock. "Let's see. I have to deliver Cici's bag to Madame Petit, but that shouldn't take too long. I could meet you around six."

"That's too late," Dave shot back immediately. "I have an appointment, and there's no getting out of it," he added in a less demanding tone. "What's wrong with right now? You could just go straight from the bar to see Madame Petit. I suppose you have the bag with you?"

"Yes, but..."

"I could even meet you at the *lycée*, if you like."

In spite of herself, Jill laughed. "You must really need that drink."

"If I said yes, would you agree to be ready in fifteen minutes?"

How badly he wanted the drink was immaterial to Jill at this point. Dave Lovell wanted to talk, and that was reason enough to grant him a small concession. "Make it thirty minutes. Let me tell you how to get to the *lycée*," she began, but he quickly interrupted.

"Don't bother. I already know. See you in thirty minutes." Before she could answer, the phone clicked in her ear.

J. FREMONT, *depart Lycée Marguerite de Valois: 16:51.*

In his notes, Bouton always used military time. He admired its economy, its precision, the hint of irrefutable authority. He finished scribbling and slipped the notebook back into his coat pocket. Flipping up his collar, he pulled into the steady sidewalk traffic to follow the woman and her companion.

The woman was easy to spot; brightly dressed; too absorbed in her companion's conversation to notice anyone trailing her. Not that Bouton would do anything careless, but he was forced to pick up his pace to keep track of her along Boulevard Raspail. In contrast to the people sauntering to cafés for their afternoon aperitif, she and the man accompanying her were striding through the crowd with a purpose.

When his quarries turned into Rue Vavin, Bouton stepped into a corner café to watch them. They were taking their time now, conferring with each other and back-stepping to survey the two bistros at either end of the street. He did not mind the wait, however. In spite of the lingering June sun, he found the day unpleasantly cool; beneath the heavy coat, his chilled body welcomed the steamy warmth of the café.

Finally the woman nodded to the man, and they entered the bistro directly opposite his café.

J. Fremont, arrivée 24, Rue Vavin: 17:12.

Pulling down the pile-lined collar of his coat, Bouton seated himself at one of the tables to wait.

"WHAT'LL IT BE THEN?" David Lovell held her chair for her and then rubbed his hands together. "What do you usually drink?" He was grinning as he slid into the seat across from her.

"Coffee," Jill confessed. "But since you seem to require something more toxic today, I'll have a Dubonnet."

Dave turned to the waiter bearing down on them, stopping him in midstride. *"Deux Dubonnets, s'il vous plâit,"* he ordered in his unabashedly American accent. Ordinarily heavy accents grated on Jill's trained ear, but somehow flawless French pronunciation would have conflicted with Dave's rough-and-ready personality.

"You said you wanted to talk about something," Jill reminded him. She leaned to one side to prop her purse and the canvas tote containing Cici's bag against the table leg.

Dave shrugged and smiled. "Nothing in particular. Actually I just used that as an excuse. I wanted to see you again."

Jill had not expected such a disarming confession, and for a moment she did not know what to say. With commendable timing, the waiter arrived with the drinks, giving her a chance to disguise her surprise.

"Cheers." Dave tapped her glass smartly, and she had to smile.

"In France, we say *salut*." She watched him taste the cherry-red liquid and then cradle the glass between his hands.

There was something paradoxical about those hands. They were big, as befitted a man as tall and sturdily built as Dave Lovell, and not at all delicate. Yet watching the long fingers toy with the glass, Jill was struck by their precision, the lightness of their touch. His whole appearance, in fact, was a blend of contradictions: the sensual mouth, permanently skewed at a contrary angle; the slightly lopsided nose that perfectly balanced the generous forehead; the disorderly sandy hair that shone like hammered copper in the window's light; the gray eyes that could mock and penetrate with equal intensity. As she met his gaze, Jill caught herself and quickly took another sip of her drink.

She managed another smile, coaxing herself to relax. Dave apparently had nothing more to say about the disastrous episode in the river and had contacted her for purely social reasons—an appealing thought, now that she considered it. Jill made an effort to join in the light conversation.

Dave was chatting about his new apartment when he suddenly broke off. "You're still a bit shaken up, aren't you?" he remarked quietly.

Jill glanced up from the empty aperitif glass into his gray eyes, which were as unclouded and direct as the previous day. Now there was an element of warmth in them. "I'm having a hard time coming to terms with some things," she confessed.

Dave nodded thoughtfully. "You shouldn't blame yourself for what happened to Cici Madison, Jill." She felt his hand close lightly around her wrist. "I'm sorry this has been so hard for you." He sounded diffident, unaccustomed to offering consolation. Not giving her time to react, he quickly withdrew his hand and pulled his wallet out of his pocket. "Take your time." Reverting to his familiar casual drawl, Dave nodded toward Jill's drink, which she had scarcely touched.

Trying to shake the curious emotion his brief touch had evoked, Jill pushed the glass aside and checked her watch. "I really need to go. I don't want to keep Madame Petit waiting." She reached for her purse, but Dave was already shaking his head.

Counting out a few bills, he smiled gently. "This time it's my treat. You can pick up the tab next time, okay?"

"Even if it's only coffee?" Perhaps it was the effect of the Dubonnet, but Jill felt herself responding to the balm of that smile.

"Coffee, water, whatever. I already said the drinks weren't the attraction, didn't I?" As he leaned back in his chair, the wallet slid from his grasp. A rain of coins tinkled on the tile floor, and Dave dived beneath the table to retrieve them.

Jill grabbed a stray bill and then scooted her chair aside to help. When she plucked the tablecloth aside, however, she could scarcely believe her eyes. Crouched beside the table, Dave Lovell had pulled Cici's bag from the tote. Worse yet, he had opened it and was in the process of removing the model's suede-covered appointment book.

For a moment, Jill was so taken aback, she could only gape. "Just what do you think you're doing?" she finally managed to gasp.

"I was putting this thing back. It fell out." His normally hearty voice had dropped noticeably, as if he wished to keep their discussion confined beneath the tablecloth.

"No, you weren't. That bag was securely fastened. You've deliberately opened it." Jill could feel anger flooding her cheeks with color. Pushing her chair back abruptly, she stood. She watched as Dave slowly retreated from beneath the tablecloth and rose to his feet.

"I think we're starting to attract a little too much attention." His gray eyes darted warily around the bistro.

"Not half as much as we're going to attract. You were trying to steal from me." In her effort to control her voice, Jill almost choked.

"No, I wasn't. I swear. It was Madison's bag, right?"

Jill's jaw dropped in amazement. "I can't believe this! I catch you with your hand in that purse, and you try to beg off because its owner happens to be dead."

"Look, I'm telling you the truth. I wasn't trying to steal anything from anybody."

"Then what *were* you doing? Just rearranging things?" Jill cut in.

"Damn it, will you listen?" Dave's voice rose in irritation. When a passing waiter glared at them disapprovingly, he reached for her hand and tried to draw her down onto her chair. Jill jerked away and held her ground. "Okay. I admit I had Madison's calendar. See, I'm a journalist. I'm doing a story on American models in Europe, and I guess the temptation was just too great.''

The man had no way of knowing, of course, that Steve had been a TV reporter, but the revelation that Dave Lovell shared her ex-husband's profession—and apparently plied it with the same fervor—only fueled Jill's contempt. Her eyes widened in rage. "You were using me, weren't you? Just so you could get your hands on Cici Madison's private appointment book!"

"I know what I've done looks bad." Dave heaved a sigh and looked down at her empty aperitif glass.

"*Looks* bad?" Jill snorted. "It may only *look* bad to you, but I can assure you you've just pulled the most vile, despicable, underhanded trick ... 'I really need a drink,'" she mimicked his baritone. "No! Make that 'I really wanted to see you again.'"

"Damn it, I did want to see you!" Dave burst out.

"Of course you did. How else would you be able to pry into Cici's calendar and weasel out the gossip some sleazy tabloid is paying you to smear all over its cover?" She snatched up her handbag and the tote.

"Jill, I'd like to talk this thing out." Dave stepped around the table, but her warning look held him at bay.

"Save the energy!" Spinning on her heel, Jill slung her bag over her shoulder and marched out of the bistro.

He was not the first man to lie to her, of course. Jill had already admitted that by the time she reached the corner of Boulevard Raspail. He was not even the most skillful liar she had ever known. No, something more troubling than Dave Lovell's deceit or his crass motives lay at the root of her anger. As she strode through the gate of the Luxembourg Gardens, Jill realized what infuriated her most: her own gullibility; her willingness—against her better instincts—to be taken in by a charming, good-looking man.

But then he had saved her life—with considerable risk to his own. Whatever might have happened in the bistro this afternoon, he had not pulled her from the river and forced the life back into her for the sake of a cheap scandal-sheet story. Walking through the quiet, shadow-dappled garden, Jill grappled with her contradictory feelings.

She was so engrossed in her thoughts as she crossed the terrace that she would not have looked up if a passing dog had not suddenly yapped. Glancing at the little terrier pirouetting on the end of its master's leash, she happened to look at the fountain. She frowned when she caught sight of a man through the water's spray. Although he seemed to be loitering aimlessly, an eerie sixth sense told her that he had been watching her.

Swallowing carefully, Jill watched him saunter along the water's edge. He was now partially concealed by the fountain's statuary, but she could make out the contour of his shoulders, hunched beneath a drab coat that was much too heavy for this time of year. Jill caught herself abruptly. So what if he had been watching her? She herself was an inveterate people watcher, especially in Paris. He was probably just a normal businessman, taking a pleasant shortcut through the gardens on his way home from work.

Hitching her bag more securely on her shoulder, Jill was about to turn down another path when something caught her eye. A bulky figure passed behind the statue of Mary Stuart. Measuring her steps, she inched forward. The dark form glided through the shrubs, fleeting as a ripple on water, and then disappeared behind another statue.

Jill hesitated only momentarily before heading straight for the nearest gate. She had been a little foolish to cut through the gardens this late in the afternoon in the first place. The paths were too deserted; the formal groves and statuary too promising as hiding places for specters, real and imagined. Of course, that man in the ridiculous coat was probably perfectly harmless. All the same, she felt a wave of relief when the roaring traffic of Boulevard St. Michel suddenly spilled out in front of her.

Hurrying up the busy thoroughfare, Jill scarcely glanced at the enticing shop windows. She started, however, when a dark reflection caught her eye. Jill fingered the handle of the tote nervously and pretended to examine the shoes displayed in the window, but she kept an eye on the man in the dark coat. She almost shivered when he passed behind her and then turned down a side street.

He is following me! The thought speared through her mind, frightening her. She licked her lips, adjusting her shoulder strap in a slow deliberate manner. No one was following her; no one had any reason to follow her. This was one of the busiest streets in Paris; there were people all around. Hadn't she passed two *gendarmes* in as many blocks? The reassurances sounded sane, logical and utterly unconvincing, and Jill consciously lengthened her strides.

Her grip on the bag's strap tightened as she approached the side street. With her eyes focused on the plaza ahead, she caught only a movement as she passed the alley—no more than a blur in her peripheral vision, but it was enough to goad her into a trot. She felt the heavy tote bouncing against her leg as she sprinted between a mailbox and an old lady dragging a shopping cart behind her.

Cici's apartment building couldn't be far, just a couple of blocks farther down. At the corner, Jill checked the street sign and realized in relief that she was closer to her destination than she had thought. With a final, quick glance over her shoulder, she turned into the narrow side street. Swinging the tote at her side, she jogged to the familiar three-story building. As usual, the careless *concierge* had left the front door unlocked, allowing Jill to slip inside the welcome security of the foyer.

Through the door's art deco leaded-glass panel, Jill kept an eye on the street for a few seconds. A taxi cruised by, dodging two uniformed schoolgirls on bicycles; a cassocked priest with a *baguette* under each arm hurried along the sidewalk, but no man in a heavy overcoat. Whoever the shady character may have been, he had apparently lost interest in his game.

Sliding the tote strap over her arm, Jill climbed the two flights of stairs. Cici's apartment occupied the entire top floor; only an opaque skylight illuminated the tiny hallway. In spite of herself, Jill glanced over her shoulder as she pressed the buzzer and waited for Madame Petit to respond. Somewhere down below a door opened, emitting the machine-gun chatter of a talk show into the stairwell. When the door closed again the building was very quiet.

Frowning up at the skylight, Jill pushed the bell once more. Where was the housekeeper? Cici had once commented that Nana was a bit hard of hearing, but surely she had heard the buzzer's last protracted squall.

Jill rapped the door sharply with her knuckles. She was startled when it opened of its own accord.

"Madame Petit?" Gripping the doorknob, she took a hesitant step over the threshold.

Jill paused in the entrance hall. An unnatural hush seemed to hang over the place, so tangible she could almost feel it in the air. A shaft of fading sunlight filled the arched doorway leading to the living room, and she instinctively moved toward it. In the archway, she halted, frozen by the spectacle confronting her.

The living room was a scene of utter devastation, not unlike that left in the wake of a bomb blast. Whoever had sacked the apartment had been bent on destruction. Books and papers were strewn everywhere; not content merely to scatter them, the invader had ripped and shredded pages at will. The walls had been stripped of their pictures, the elegant leather couches of their cushions; batting protruded from the slashed pillows. An inlaid side table, a valuable antique Jill had often admired, lay overturned with one of its fragile legs snapped in two. Shards littered the floor, the sad remains of Cici's pre-Columbian pottery collection.

No ordinary burglar would have destroyed with such zeal; this was the work of an enraged madman. The sight was so horrifying that for a moment Jill could only stare. Finally she managed to force words from her dry, constricted throat. "Madame Petit?" But now she expected no answer.

Tightening her grip on the tote, she stepped backward. Whatever had happened, wherever Madame Petit might be, Jill knew she should go no farther. She needed to get help—the police, the *concierge*, anyone—but above all she needed to get out of that apartment.

Only when she turned toward the half-closed door did she see the heavy shadow looming behind it. She lunged for the narrow opening, but not quickly enough. A heavy arm encircled her body, pulling her back, while another arm locked around her neck, stifling the scream swelling in her throat. Jill began to flail and claw at the arm that was squeezing the breath out of her. Jerking her leg back, she brought her heel down onto her assailant's instep. A monster howl rent the air and the grip loosened momentarily. Jill tried to tear herself free. Her arms were outstretched, her hands splayed, straining for the door when the blow landed. She saw the cold marble floor rise up to meet her and darkness fell.

Chapter Four

He was beginning to feel stupid, walking aimlessly up and down the quiet street. If there had only been a few stores or a café, Dave could have found a way to kill time. But the street where Cici Madison's apartment building was located was exclusively residential, save for a small butcher shop near the corner of Boul Mich. How long could a normal man be expected to stare through a window at the sides of beef and split pigs' feet anyway? More importantly, how long did Jill Fremont intend to linger with Madison's housekeeper?

Dave frowned in irritation, pausing to glare at the leaded-glass door again. When Jill had angrily stalked out of the bistro, his first impulse had been to chalk up the whole mess to sloppy investigative technique on his part and write it off. After all, he had managed to photocopy the damned calendar; if Fremont thought he was trying to rifle Madison's bag, so be it. But fifteen minutes and a third Dubonnet later, he had failed to erase the angry confrontation from his mind. In his career, he had often been accused of less-than-polite behavior—even bending the law. He was not a thief, however, and he knew he would not rest until he had convinced Jill Fremont of that fact.

He had hailed a taxi outside the bistro in hopes of overtaking her. The cabbie had turned off Boulevard St. Michel just in time for Dave to glimpse Jill's bright red dress disappear inside Madison's building. He had tipped the driver well and posted himself within easy view of the front door. But over half an hour had passed, and Jill still had not appeared.

Dave had almost persuaded himself to saunter back for another look at the pigs' feet when the door of Madison's building opened a crack. Instantly alert, he walked to the curb, his eyes glued to the flash of red in the opening. Then the door was flung wide, and Jill stepped onto the porch. Dave halted, preparing himself for a scalding reaction, however, she did not seem to see him. As she descended the steps, she clung to the rail; her feet wove unsteadily. Then he saw something red, a much darker crimson than her vibrantly colored dress, smeared across the side of her face. Blood!

In a split second, Dave crossed the street. He reached the building's steps just in time to catch Jill as she sank to her knees.

"For God's sake, what's happened to you?" he demanded. Her small body sagged into his arms and a strangely pleasant feeling rippled through him.

She blinked and reached shakily for the gash on her forehead. "Someone... Dave?" Her dark eyes looked dazed when she frowned up at him. "Someone was hiding in Cici's apartment."

He felt a telltale shudder run through her and pressed her closer. "It's all right," he whispered soothingly into her ruffled dark hair.

"No, it's not," she protested, her voice suddenly stronger. Her hands dug into his chest as she struggled to recover her balance. "Madame Petit! She didn't answer the doorbell. We need to see about her."

Jill had regained her footing, but Dave kept a firm hold on her shoulders. "*You* don't need to do anything right now. Where's the *concierge*?" He glanced at the row of buzzers lining the door.

"Madame Poiteau has the ground-floor flat."

Dave guided Jill into the building and rapped on the *concierge*'s door. He tried to bridle his impatience as he waited for what seemed an interminable time, only to hear slippered feet reluctantly shuffling toward them. At last, the door opened to reveal a frowsy woman scowling at him.

"Call the police," Dave ordered without bothering with introductions.

The woman's glower darkened, hinting at the resistance to come, but when she caught sight of Jill's wound, she drew back. *"Mon Dieu!"* Her hands flew up to her face in horror.

Taking advantage of her shock, Dave ushered Jill through the door. "Mademoiselle Fremont has been assaulted. There's been a break-in upstairs," he explained, and then caught himself. In his excitement, he had forgotten that the old crone might not understand English.

But apparently she did. "The police, yes, right away." Hands still pressed to her cheeks, Madame Poiteau dashed toward the telephone.

While the *concierge* babbled to the police clerk, Dave pulled Jill down onto the sofa. "I'm going upstairs to have a look. Just sit tight. When she gets off the phone, see if she's got any bandages."

But Jill was already on her feet again. "The bleeding has almost stopped," she insisted. "I'm going with you." The determination reflected in her dark eyes warned him not to waste time arguing with her.

Dave fished into his pocket and took out a clean handkerchief. "At least hold this on the cut," he ordered, leading the way out of the *concierge*'s cramped living quarters.

He took the stairs two at a time, slowing only as he approached the top landing, but to her credit Jill managed to keep pace with him. In the middle of the hall, he saw a red smear on the white marble floor, and his anger surged anew. The door to the apartment was standing wide open. Without speaking, Jill tapped his shoulder and pressed a finger to her lips. Although he knew there was little chance the assailant would still be hanging around, he nodded and then cautiously entered the apartment.

Taking care not to touch anything, Dave walked through Cici Madison's living room. Even at first glance, he could see that the intruder had been no common burglar. Expensive stereo equipment, a VCR and a Leica camera all lay within plain sight; he had to step carefully to avoid the broken remains of what must have been a priceless collection of Indian artifacts. No, the person who had broken into Madison's apartment and wrought such havoc had been looking for something special.

"The whole place is like this?" he asked Jill in a hoarse whisper.

Arms locked across her chest, she looked up from the debris surrounding her. "I don't know, I didn't get past the living room. The burglar was apparently hiding in the foyer. I was on my way downstairs to get help when he slipped behind me." She was making an obvious effort to control her voice, but her hand trembled as she gestured toward the hallway.

Instinctively Dave rested his hand on her shoulder for a moment. "Don't worry, whoever broke in is long gone by now. I'll just take a quick look in the other rooms."

As he had expected, the rest of Madison's apartment had received similar treatment. Inspection revealed that the kitchen had been ransacked, the bedroom torn apart. Even the housekeeper's modest quarters had been turned upside down. Dave cursed under his breath when he spotted the curtain billowing from a window opening onto the fire escape, evidence of the intruder's escape route. At least he hadn't discovered any corpses.

When he retreated into the living room, he found Jill hovering near the plundered bookcases. Reading the anxiety reflected on her taut face, he shook his head.

Jill closed her eyes in relief. "I was so afraid Madame Petit had been..." she began and then broke off at the sound of voices from the stairwell. "That must be the police!" She pushed away from the bookcases and hurried to the stairs.

Dave followed her, but hesitated when he stumbled over something half buried beneath an overturned magazine rack. Stooping, he recognized Jill's quilted leather purse. Apparently the intruder wasn't interested in handbags any more than wide-screen TVs or silver-fox coats. Snatching up the bag, Dave hastened downstairs only to collide with two policemen. He started when one of the policemen, a rotund fellow a good head shorter than he, sidestepped to block his path.

"*Bonsoir, monsieur,*" the man said and flashed his badge with a flourish. He had a grim visage.

"Monsieur Lovell is a friend of mine," Jill interposed quickly. "I asked him to accompany me when I went back to check on Madame Petit."

The policeman nodded, apparently placated. He brushed past Dave, with his colleague close on his heels.

"Thanks," Dave murmured under his breath.

Jill stiffened. Although she had described him as a friend to the police, Dave guessed that her personal opinion veered somewhat. "I just wanted to get the policemen off your back," she assured him coolly. "Say!" Her expression brightened slightly. "Is that my shoulder bag?"

"Yeah. I found it in the entrance hall of Madison's apartment." He held up the bag and then ceremoniously slid the strap over her arm. "And I swear, if anything is missing, I didn't steal it."

Jill's mouth twisted to one side as she looked down at the bag. She opened it and gave its contents a cursory inspection. "Apparently I didn't have anything the burglar deemed worth taking."

"Don't feel bad. Neither did Cici Madison. Whoever ripped up that apartment and mugged you left enough expensive goods to fill the Neiman-Marcus Christmas catalog."

Jill nodded. "That's what I thought. What do you make of it?" She dabbed her bruised forehead with the handkerchief and winced.

Dave hesitated. He had his own ideas, none of which he was ready to share with Jill Fremont. "I don't know exactly, but the evidence seems to indicate he was looking for something."

Jill's face darkened as she inspected the blood-stained handkerchief. "I just hope Madame Petit is all right."

"Regardless of what they're after, most burglars like to work in a quiet, undisturbed atmosphere. Chances are this guy waited until he was sure she was gone."

Jill's frown deepened. "She would have been home this afternoon. She was expecting me."

"Something could have come up unexpectedly," Dave suggested.

Jill blotted her forehead gingerly. "I hope you're right," she conceded. "But I can't believe she wouldn't have phoned the *lycée* and at least left a message that she couldn't keep our appointment." Suddenly she wheeled on the stairs. "My tote! Did you happen to see it in the apartment?"

Dave had already pivoted on the stairs. How the hell could he have stalked through the apartment without even thinking of Madison's bag? "*I* didn't see it, but maybe the police found it." *And if they haven't, pray that we get to it first.*

When they reached the landing, they found the policemen sealing the apartment door. Both men shook their heads emphatically when Jill questioned them about the tote. Dave watched closely as she described the big alligator-skin bag. Even allowing for the ingrained caginess of cops, he was certain they were telling the truth when they denied seeing it.

"Perhaps it can be recovered, Mademoiselle Fremont, but normally in such cases..." The shorter of the two policemen shook his head regretfully.

"I understand," Jill assured him. She cast an uncertain look at the apartment door before following the policemen downstairs.

As they approached the ground floor, Dave caught a glimpse of the *concierge*'s gnomelike face peering up the stairwell. When she spotted them, she retreated into the apartment, but not quickly enough to avert the short policeman. While the man questioned Madame Poiteau, his colleague, a thin man with a long, aquiline nose, turned to Jill.

"It would be helpful to our investigation if you could describe the person who attacked you."

Jill bit her lip. "I'm afraid I didn't get a direct look at him. I don't think he was very tall, but he was heavyset. And strong."

The policeman did not look up from his notepad as he flipped through the pages. "Do you recall any identifying characteristics?"

"As I said, I didn't actually see him. I do know that his arms were extremely hairy. They felt like sandpaper around my neck."

The policeman suppressed a smile and scribbled something on the notepad. "Anything else?"

Jill hesitated for a moment. "This may have nothing to do with the break-in," she began cautiously. "But a man followed me through the Luxembourg Gardens on my way here this afternoon. At least I think he was trailing me. And he was slightly below average height and stocky, like the mugger. He disappeared right before I reached this building."

The thin policeman frowned. "Mademoiselle Fremont, if indeed this man were following you, I do not see how he would have had the time to precede you into Mademoiselle Madison's apartment and create such destruction."

"But he could have followed me up the stairs and mugged me, that's certainly possible," Jill countered.

The policeman's dark brows rose dubiously. "Possible, yes, probable, no. In all likelihood, the person who ransacked Mademoiselle Madison's apartment is also the man who assaulted you." He drew a deep sigh. "However, we will keep this additional information in mind. You will be contacted in the event a suspect is arraigned. *Au revoir*, Mademoiselle Fremont. Monsieur Lovell." The man joined his companion.

As both turned to depart, Jill intervened. "*Monsieurs!* What about Madame Petit?"

The squatly built policeman paused in the doorway. "You need not fear for her safety, Mademoiselle Fremont. Fortunately she had left the apartment long before the intruder arrived. The *concierge* saw her leave with her suitcase shortly before noon today."

"She had a suitcase? But she was expecting me this afternoon!" Jill protested.

The policeman shrugged, a little impatiently. "She is an old lady, perhaps she forgot. *Au revoir*, Mademoiselle Fremont."

"Madame Petit did *not* forget," Jill muttered, frowning at the retreating shadows behind the door's opaque glass.

Dave had deliberately remained in the background during the policemen's interrogation. A host of unanswered questions had crowded his mind, and Jill's skepticism only inflamed his doubts. "Maybe she left a message for you with the *concierge*," he suggested.

Jill glanced at him, almost as if she had forgotten he was still there. Her frown gave Dave the uncomfortable feeling that she wished he weren't, but she said nothing as she knocked on Madame Poiteau's door.

The *concierge* opened the door slowly, and peeped out. She was palpably relieved to find only the two Americans waiting for her.

"Excuse me for disturbing you again, Madame Poiteau," Jill apologized. "But I was wondering if Madame Petit might have left a message for me."

"She left no message, Mademoiselle Fremont."

"But you saw her as she was leaving," Jill persisted. "Did she say where she was going?"

Madame Poiteau fingered the hem of her apron uneasily. "As I told the police, I helped her with her suitcase and then I returned to my own apartment, minding my own business."

The *concierge*'s pinched face twitched with uncertainty. *She knows something, but she's afraid to tell,* Dave thought.

With admirable timing, Jill leaned toward the nervous little woman. "Madame Petit is not the sort of woman who simply takes a trip on a lark without telling anyone where she's going. When I spoke with her this morning, the only thing on her mind was her responsibility to Cici's estate. No one is going to convince me that she suddenly decided to take a vacation. Someone attacked me in that apartment this afternoon, Madame Poiteau." She paused as the *concierge*'s eyes darted to her bruised forehead. "I don't care what the police think, I'm not going to feel comfortable about Madame Petit until I've talked with her and assured myself that she's safe."

Despite the hallway's close warmth, Madame Poiteau chafed her arms. "I promised her I would tell no one, Mademoiselle Fremont." She licked her cracked lips and looked down at the marble floor.

"Please, Madame Poiteau." Jill's voice was low and urgent. "This is very important."

The *concierge* swallowed hard. "She said that Mademoiselle Simone phoned and told her she should go away for a while. That is all. I swear it."

"Who is Mademoiselle Simone?"

"Simone Nanka-Midou. She once lived here, before she sold the apartment to Mademoiselle Cici." Madame Poiteau edged behind the door, eager to put an end to the interview.

"Any idea where Mademoiselle Nanka-Midou lives now?" Dave asked, resting a firm hand on the doorknob.

"I did not know these ladies well, *monsieur*. They are models, I am a simple woman. All I know is that they buy the same expensive cars. They have the same fancy friends. They work for the same lady."

"The same lady?"

Madame Poiteau shook her head in desperation. "The lady who gets their pictures in the magazines for all the big money. Please, *monsieur*." She tugged at the door, budging it a scant inch.

Dave felt Jill's hand press his elbow, and he reluctantly released his hold on the doorknob. Madame Poiteau did not waste the opportunity to mutter a quick *au revoir* and then securely shut the door.

"There's no point in badgering her," Jill told him. As she turned toward the door, he tried to read her face. Unfortunately her expression was no less baffling than the question raised by the *concierge*'s cryptic comments. Feeling oddly off balance, he followed her outside and then paused on the stoop.

Given his suspicions about Madison, the rifled apartment did not surprise him. Even the housekeeper's sudden disappearance seemed to fit the scheme of things, now that he thought about it. He was hedging his bets that an investigation of Madame Petit and the mysterious Simone would reveal their involvement with Madison's illegal activity. His cynicism wavered, however, when he considered Jill's role in the bizarre scenario. For some reason, he found her specter from the Luxembourg Gardens profoundly disturbing. That someone else had linked her with Madison and was now watching her seemed highly probable, but what were his motives? The unanswered question raised a host of troubling thoughts in his mind.

Jill, too, appeared gripped by indecision, lingering at the bottom of the steps.

"What are you going to do now?" Dave asked quietly.

Jill glanced down the dark street for a long moment. "Try to get in touch with Madame Petit. Regardless of what the police say, she wouldn't have just packed up her things and taken off at this Simone's behest. And why would she swear Madame Poiteau to secrecy?" She shook her head. "No, something happened after I talked with her this morning, and I intend to find out exactly what."

"Uh-huh. And just how do you plan to find Madame Petit?"

"I'll try to locate Simone, whoever she is." She caught herself and shrugged irritably. "I don't know. Why do you ask anyway?" she countered without turning.

Dave slowly descended the steps, halting just behind her. He sighed, and Jill imagined his husky breath stirring her hair. "Because I don't think you should be wandering around the streets alone tonight. Someone followed you this afternoon, you've just been mugged..."

He suddenly broke off as Jill spun around. "And someone tried to rifle Cici's handbag while we were having a drink together." She glared at him, struggling to revive some of the anger she had felt earlier. In a world increasingly filled with unknowns, here, at least, was one person whose motives were clear; Dave Lovell had tried to deceive her for his own gain, pure and simple. Based on past performance, his expressed concern for her safety should now arouse only skepticism. But as she studied the lean face bathed in the colorless light of the street lamp, she almost regretted her cutting accusation.

Dave hung back on the step above her, but his gray eyes met hers without flinching. "I'm sorry about what happened in the bar this afternoon, Jill. I shouldn't have tried to pull a sneaky trick like that on you, and that's why I followed you to Madison's apartment building—to apologize. In spite of what you think, I really can't stomach dishonesty. At least not between friends."

Jill stretched her neck, adjusting the collar of her silk dress. "I'd like to believe that." She hesitated while her emotions waged a private war within her. "And I really appreciate your support after the mugging. But I wonder, if you had succeeded in taking the calendar, would you have just kept me in the dark and let me go on thinking you were a regular, unassuming Joe?"

"No, because I did snitch the calendar, and I am telling you. I took the bloody thing yesterday afternoon in your apartment, while you were making coffee. I made copies of it later." Jill's mouth gaped in disbelief, but before she could respond, he rushed on. "Damn it, Jill! If it hadn't been for Cici Madison, we never would have met. I was on her trail the night you two had dinner together in that restaurant.''

"No!"

"Yes. But before you accuse me of being a slimy paparazzo, let me remind you that celebrities routinely spend a fortune on press agents, just to keep their names before the public. Of course, the agents are only concerned with the good side. Reporters try to present a more balanced picture. Okay, I admit I felt scummy about taking the calendar behind your back. That's why I made the date with you in time to return it. You just caught me in the act.''

She was silent for a few seconds, prompting him to add, ''You don't have to admire or respect me. Just believe me.''

"I do," she said slowly.

He looked grateful for the reply. "Truce?" He held out his hand.

She looked at the long, tapering fingers; if Dave Lovell were a liar, he possessed the most deceptively steady hand she had ever felt. "Truce," she conceded, shaking it. "But you've got to promise me one thing. You'll never try to deceive me again." She held the big hand firmly in her own, driving her point home.

"I promise." His hand tightened momentarily before releasing hers. He cleared the remaining step as she turned toward the intersection. "I still think you should forget about the housekeeper for tonight and take a cab straight home."

"I'm not going to canvass the streets, calling Madame Petit's name as if she were a lost puppy. And you keep talking as if I were in some kind of jeopardy. I was mugged today because I happened to walk in on the intruder. It was sheer accident." *Wasn't it?* Jill added silently, shooting her eyes at him to gauge his thoughts.

His expression remained maddeningly enigmatic. "Probably. Just like the guy who followed you through the Luxembourg Gardens was probably a harmless middle-aged lecher and nothing more. And Madame Petit probably decided to take a little holiday, just to get away from it all."

Frowning, Jill adjusted her shoulder-bag strap. Her annoyance at the doubts Dave had planted in her mind was superseded only by her gratitude for his company on the dark, deserted street.

He did not take long to interpret her silence. "Look. I'll make you a deal. You promise to play it safe, just for a few days, and I'll help you find Madison's housekeeper."

Jill halted on the corner to face him. "And how do you propose to do that?"

"I have a copy of Cici Madison's calendar, remember? It's chock-full of names and addresses, and we just might find this Simone What's-her-name among them. I can't promise results, but it's worth a try," he added, dangling the bait before her.

Jill's stomach threatened to curdle at the thought of prying into Cici's personal calendar, but at this point her concern for Madame Petit far outweighed her scruples. If Dave Lovell intended to exploit the calendar for a trivial tabloid story, at least she could use it to benefit the missing housekeeper. "Okay." She straightened herself, trying to look more businesslike and resolute than she felt. "When can I have a look at the copy?"

Dave stepped off the curb and threw up his hand at an approaching taxi. When he turned back to her, a wickedly innocent smile wreathed his handsome visage. "Why tonight, of course."

Chapter Five

"You'll have to excuse the mess. I haven't had much time to put things in order." Dave offered the rote apology as he flung open the door and switched on the light.

Jill hesitated on the threshold and then followed Dave into his apartment. At first glance, it was hard to tell if someone were just moving in or just moving out. Newspapers, magazines and papers were stacked everywhere. Although the streamlined furnishings included ample bookshelves, they were almost empty, save for a few volumes leaning haphazardly against one another. Most of Dave's extensive library remained in open cartons shoved against the wall. Except for a framed Chagall poster propped next to the window and a Chicago Bears coffee mug sitting on one of the end tables, the room was completely devoid of ornamentation.

On his way past the sofa, Dave grabbed the Bears mug. "Have a seat while I dig up those copies."

Jill pushed aside the quilted furniture pad draped over the sofa and seated herself at one end. When Dave returned, bearing a folder of photocopies, he jerked the pad off the sofa, threw it on the floor and dropped down beside her.

"Some for you and . . ." Dave divided the copies and placed a sheaf on Jill's lap. "Some for me."

Jill looked down at the pile of copies and felt an immediate pang of sadness at the sight of Cici's looping, backward scrawl. Suppressing the troubling memories as best she could, she began to scan the copied pages of the calendar. It was slow, tedious work. The entries were numerous, some running over others, and Jill had to squint to decipher the notations. Her eyes stung from the effort and her neck ached by the time she had sifted through her share of the copies.

"No luck?" Holding a page up to his face, Dave glanced at her.

Jill shook her head and flexed her tight shoulder muscles. "I couldn't find a single mention of Simone Nanka-Midou. Or even of a Simone," she added, sinking back against the sofa.

Dave sighed as he stacked the pages together. "Neither could I. Cici does refer to someone as *S* in several places. The *S* could stand for Simone."

"That occurred to me, too," Jill concurred. "Unfortunately she didn't list an address or a phone number for this mysterious *S*." Suddenly she pulled herself out of her slump and reached for the folder Dave held. "I just thought of something. Didn't Madame Poiteau say that Cici and Simone were represented by the same agent?" Opening the folder, she impatiently riffled through the pages. "Here it is. Agence Gabrielle Vernier. She would certainly know how to contact Simone."

Dave cast a skeptical eye at the page Jill held up for his inspection. "But would she tell you?"

"All right. I'm sure Madame Vernier doesn't hand out her clients' private addresses to just anyone, but if I explained the circumstances..."

"She still wouldn't give you the time of day." Shaking his head wearily, Dave plucked the photocopy from Jill's hand and returned it to the file. "I hate to shatter your hopes, but I've had firsthand experience with Gabrielle Vernier. When I began researching the story on Madison, she was one of the first people I contacted." He pursed his lips in distaste. "The Dragon Lady does nothing for you unless there's something in it for her. Our phone conversation was very brief and very unpleasant. Believe me, if I thought there were the slightest possibility of wrangling a personal interview out of her, I'd be the first to jump on your suggestion." Sliding the folder onto the coffee table, he stood.

"I'm sure she suspected you were going to write an unflattering story about her client," Jill reminded him as he walked across the room. "In this case, she might react differently. And remember, it's a lot easier to hang up the phone than to turn someone down face-to-face."

"Right. But first you have to get face-to-face." Dave paused in the doorway and shrugged. "Madison scribbled Vernier's private phone number on the first page of the calendar. If you want to give it a try, don't let me stop you. In the meantime, I'm gonna fix a couple of Scotch and waters. How does that sound?" Not waiting for her reply, he disappeared into the kitchen.

Jill turned and stared at the bulging folder lying on the coffee table. So much had happened in the past forty-eight hours—the tragic accident, the mugging, Madame Petit's disturbing disappearance. She felt as if she had stumbled into a perplexing and frightening labyrinth; with every turn she found herself confronted by yet another barrier, yet another unanswered question. Adding to her apprehension was the unspecific yet ominous intuition that Madame Petit might be in danger. And now Dave had just pronounced the one person who could help her find the housekeeper out of reach.

Jill leaned to flip open the folder. She glanced toward the kitchen before reaching for the phone on the end table. Taking a deep breath, she punched out the seven digits. The phone buzzed twice before someone picked it up.

"Vernier." The woman's voice rose lightly on the last syllable.

"*Bonsoir*, Madame Vernier. My name is Jill Fremont."

Before she could get any further, the woman interrupted. "*Madame* is entertaining in the salon and is not to be disturbed."

Jill blinked, taken by surprise that the speaker was not Madame Vernier. This was a servant, no doubt, and one well schooled in screening calls.

"I hate to bother Madame Vernier at home, but this is a personal matter. If you could let me know when it would be convenient, I could phone back."

"You are a friend of *Madame*'s?"

Jill seized the only legitimate claim she could make. "We have a mutual friend, Cici Madison."

The name must have registered with the maid, for she only hesitated for a second. "Please hold, Mademoiselle Fremont."

Please let it work. Jill crossed her fingers, bracing herself for a verbal duel when the maid returned. She almost jumped when an aloof voice came on the line.

"Hello?"

Jill bit her lip to subdue her elation. "Please excuse me for disturbing you at home, Madame Vernier," she began.

"You said this concerned Cici Madison, Mademoiselle Fremont?" Madame Vernier cut in abruptly, almost as if she were issuing a command.

Jill stiffened at the woman's peremptory tone, but she forced herself to remain cool. "Yes." She paused, searching her brain for the most persuasive terms in which to present her request.

Madame Vernier's impatient sigh grated. "I cannot talk with you now, Mademoiselle Fremont, my guests are waiting."

Jill scrambled for what she assumed was her last chance to plead her case. "But this is extremely important...."

"If you wish, you may call at my office tomorrow afternoon at four. *Au revoir*, Mademoiselle Fremont." The phone clicked dead in Jill's ear.

"*Au revoir*, Madame Vernier." Holding the receiver at arm's length, Jill stared at it for a second before hanging up.

"Did you call her?" An old-fashioned glass in each hand, Dave hailed her from the door. Watching Jill nod, he leaned over the sofa and handed her one of the glasses. "Don't tell me. She's meeting you for drinks at Le Drugstore tomorrow afternoon."

"No. At her office. And somehow, I don't think she's planning to serve drinks."

The glass wobbled perilously in Dave's hands. "How the hell did you manage this?"

Jill lifted hers and took a thoughtful sip. "I don't know, actually. She didn't give me a chance to do much talking. She simply said she couldn't speak with me at the moment, but could see me in her office tomorrow.''

"Just like that," Dave marveled. Sinking into the sofa, he regarded her with a look of genuine admiration. "I certainly wish I had your touch."

Jill shook the glass gently, frowning at the diluted amber liquid. "I only wish I could have gotten some information from her sooner. I hate the thought of just sitting around for another day, doing nothing, while Madame Petit might be in trouble."

"You're really worried about her, aren't you?"

Jill felt his warm clasp over her hand, and she glanced at him. Perhaps the mild drink had made her incautious, perhaps the stress of the past two days had left her grasping for any consolation—especially when it was offered by such an attractive man. Looking into the steady gray eyes, however, Jill could find no reason to doubt his sincerity. He gave her hand a firm squeeze before releasing it.

"Tell you what. I've got a detective buddy here in town who's an absolute whiz. I'll give him a call, and ask him to prod those two clowns who investigated Madison's break-in into doing real follow-up work."

"That would be great." Jill looked down at the drink again. "I know you think I disapprove of this story you're doing—not to mention some of your tactics. But I really do appreciate your help this afternoon." She gestured toward the file folder. "You didn't have to offer to help me track down Madame Petit. I guess what I'm trying to say is thanks."

Dave abruptly tossed back the remains of the drink. Although his face was partially concealed by the up-ended glass, Jill thought he looked slightly embarrassed. "You can buy me an aperitif sometime." He chuckled as he reached to slide the empty glass onto the coffee table. "Better yet, work some more of your magic and get me in to see Vernier."

Jill fingered the rim of her glass. "The aperitif will have to wait awhile," she began slowly. "But as for the latter..."

Dave looked astonished. "Am I starting to hear things in my old age?"

"Madame Vernier has never actually seen you, has she?"

Dave shook his head slowly.

"Okay, then I don't see any reason why you can't come with me tomorrow afternoon. But remember, it would just be a foot in the door for you." Jill primly cradled the glass between both hands. "You would have to promise to stay in the background until she's answered my questions. I'm doing this for Madame Petit, not for your story."

Dave appeared too stunned to raise any objections to her terms. "Does she have any idea you're bringing someone with you?" he asked.

Lifting her Scotch, Jill smiled briefly. "She will tomorrow."

"VERY INTERESTING READING, isn't it?"

The man paused beside the couch, stooping slightly to regard her motionless face. She pretended to look past him, tried to ignore the ugly, leering smile. He knew she hated that smile, just as she hated the arrogant way he swaggered around her apartment as if it were his own. Still smiling, he walked to the credenza and poured himself a glass of brandy.

"You *have* taken a look at the calendar?" Turning, he gestured with the lead-glass flask.

"I have," she snapped, no longer able to contain herself. She stood abruptly and tossed the suede-bound volume onto the cocktail table.

The man leaned back against the credenza, warming the brandy snifter in his palms. "Our little bird kept very good records—names, places, dates, everything. I found her code quite charming, didn't you?"

"Her imbecilic 'code,' as you term it, is the work of a child and conceals nothing. Our entire operation is implicated in that calendar!" She glared into the insolent, smiling face and felt her anger mount.

He turned to refresh his glass. "Cici was an amateur, my dear, and her code reflects that sad fact. But now—thanks to our good friend's work—the calendar is ours, safe and sound. The merchandise is scheduled for delivery as planned."

"Your confidence amazes me!" she sneered. Her arms stiffened at her sides, longing to reach out and slap the snifter from his hand. "Your petty thug manages a clumsy purse snatching, and you think the problem is solved!"

"Now, now!" He held up a cautionary finger. "Yves's services are not to be dismissed so lightly. He has proved himself to be a very useful man on occasion."

She looked down at the calendar and chafed her arms, trying to soothe her crawling flesh. "Who was that woman? And what was she doing with Madison's calendar?" she murmured, half to herself.

"We'll find out."

Still clutching her arms, she straightened herself. "You thought we had a clever plan for the housekeeper, but she has slipped from our grasp at the last minute, bearing who-knows-what secrets with her. And now this woman..." She broke off and walked to the empty fireplace.

"You surprise me, my dear. Surely you do not think a simpleminded, old servant can elude us for long. And as for this woman, well, Yves will have to find her, too, I suppose."

She stared into the mantel mirror, her eyes drawn to her own troubled image. Stress had shadowed her face, the legacy of countless sleepless nights, but *he* had always said she was the most beautiful when she was unhappy. Perhaps that was why he had made her suffer so.

"And when he has found them, then what?" she asked, still gazing at her reflection.

The leering face loomed beside hers like a satyr's mask. "Why then he'll take care of them, of course."

IF JILL HAD ENTERTAINED any misgivings about letting Dave accompany her to call on Madame Vernier, he was certainly doing his best to allay them. Dressed in a perfectly tailored tropical wool suit, complete with Givenchy tie, he looked more like a corporate attorney than a tabloid journalist when he met her the following afternoon near the Pont Royal.

Her admiring look was not wasted on Dave. "Dress for success," he muttered, holding up two tightly crossed fingers. "We need all the help we can get."

Jill nodded, flashing him her own crossed fingers. "Let's hope my luck holds out from last night."

Both of them sobered, however, when they reached the building overlooking the Seine where Agence Gabrielle Vernier was located. The building's facade looked modest enough, but when Jill and Dave stepped off the elevator on the top floor, they were greeted by understated elegance. From the Brancusi sculpture to the aubergine silk wallpaper, every element of Gabrielle Vernier's offices bespoke taste and money.

Leaving Dave to admire the Brancusi, Jill approached the receptionist and introduced herself. Having learned French from her Parisian-born mother, she had always regarded her command of the language as her birthright, but for once she was grateful that she spoke as fluently as a native.

The receptionist listened, but her face remained as unmoved as the black marble sculpture. "I am sorry, Mademoiselle Fremont. Madame Vernier is in a meeting." She turned away to greet a bored-looking girl lugging a portfolio.

Jill sidestepped the portfolio that jutted beside the desk like a black leather fin. "I spoke with Madame Vernier yesterday evening, and she is expecting me at four o'clock today."

The receptionist glanced at the desk calendar before fixing Jill with flinty kohl-rimmed eyes. "You do not have an appointment, Mademoiselle Fremont."

From the corner of her eye, Jill glimpsed Dave anxiously watching the proceedings, and her sense of urgency grew tenfold. Bracing her hands on the edge of the desk, she glared at the receptionist. "Perhaps *you* do not have a record of my appointment, *mademoiselle.*"

The receptionist's rouge-caked mouth drew into an angry line, but her gaze shifted inadvertently to the phone. She sniffed before picking up the receiver and punching one of the buttons. After a brief exchange, she looked up at Jill, her eyes black with wounded pride and malice. "Madame Vernier is reviewing slides with Monsieur Fielding, but you may see her."

"Thank you, *mademoiselle*." Jill nodded to Dave as she pivoted toward the suite door.

"Good show!" Dave whispered behind her. He quickly fell silent when the polished door opened, and an ageless faun's face peered out at them. The little man's faded blue eyes darted from Dave to Jill, as if he had just received the wrong order in a restaurant and didn't quite know what to do with it.

"Show her in, Sanford," a demanding voice ordered from the rear of the suite.

The faun stepped back but his washed-out eyes remained focused on Dave. Clearly he had not been expecting two people, and Jill hastened to put him at ease. "I'm Jill Fremont." She smiled cordially and then nodded toward Dave. "I happened to run into a friend of mine on the way here. I hope you don't mind...."

"Not at all." The man's pale face lighted up as he offered a clammy hand. "Sanford Fielding."

Jill gave the translucent fingers a quick shake. Over Fielding's shoulder, she could see a woman seated at the black lacquered desk with her back to the room. She seemed to be staring out the tall windows. Through the gleaming panes, the obelisk of the Place de la Concorde soared in the distance. The woman turned slowly to face her visitors. Barricaded behind her fortresslike desk, she only glared at the interlopers with her fierce dark eyes.

She *was* beautiful; Jill was forced to grant her that. Although she might have been well past fifty, her luxuriant hair was still as black as a raven's wing. Pulled back into a coil at her nape, the hair parted along a white line that dissected her head into two perfect burnished hemispheres. Like her hairstyle, her face seemed composed of geometric elements—the high oblique cheekbones converging into a prominent nose, the sharp jaw, the straight black brows set at an angle. It was a face out of a Picasso, its severity relieved only by a voluptuous crimson mouth.

Looking into those intimidating eyes, Jill immediately thought of Dave's "Dragon Lady" moniker. "I must apologize for the interruption, Madame Vernier, but I promise not to take too much of your time. I'm trying to get in touch with an acquaintance of Cici Madison's."

A trace of surprise flickered across the cubistic features, but Madame Vernier quickly recovered her invincible stare. "My association with Mademoiselle Madison was strictly professional, Mademoiselle Fremont. I doubt if I can help you."

"In this case, I think you can, Madame Vernier. The person I'm looking for is Simone Nanka-Midou. I believe she's also a client of yours."

Shaking her head, Madame Vernier leaned over her desk and flipped through a leather-bound folder. "Simone Nanka-Midou no longer models for this agency."

"If you could just give me an address, or perhaps the name of the agency now representing her," Jill urged.

Madame Vernier's mannequinlike face colored. "I could give you an address, Mademoiselle Fremont, but it would do you no good. Simone Nanka-Midou has long since sold that apartment. She no longer models, and I have no idea where she now lives."

Jill had not been prepared for this turn of events, and she did not know what to say.

As if responding to an unspoken cue, Dave seized the opportunity to step in. "You make it sound as if she had vanished into thin air. What happened to her?"

"Simone could have been Chausson's star, but she was a misguided young woman. She brought her problems on herself." Madame Vernier suddenly caught herself. When they landed once more on Jill, the dark eyes were as penetrating as freshly honed razors. "Cici Madison replaced Simone at the House of Chausson. But then as a friend of Mademoiselle Madison's, you have surely heard that story countless times."

Jill bristled under Vernier's challenging gaze. "No, I haven't," she replied evenly. "Cici and I knew each other only a few months. She hired me to tutor her in French."

"That must have been a difficult undertaking." Madame Vernier's English was as perfect as Cici's French had been flawed. A smile quivered momentarily on the lush red lips. Then she turned to Fielding and nodded, signaling their business to resume.

Jill chose her words carefully. "Cici was a good student. Actually I was trying to locate Simone Nanka-Midou in hopes of finding Cici's housekeeper. I was supposed to meet Madame Petit at Cici's apartment yesterday, but she's suddenly disappeared."

Madame Vernier's short laugh was as brittle as shattered ice. "And probably taken most of the silver with her. It's the rare servant who feels any loyalty to a dead mistress, Mademoiselle Fremont."

Jill's jaw tightened as she fought to control her temper. "I have serious concerns for Madame Petit's safety." When Madame Vernier refused to look up from the sheet of slides she was studying, Jill leaned over the desk, casting a direct shadow over the slides. "I walked into that apartment yesterday, right after someone had torn it apart."

"The servant, no doubt."

"No, Madame Vernier." Jill's sharp voice cut through Vernier's smugness. "Whoever rifled the place didn't take anything, but he was desperate enough to mug me. And if he's still looking for something he couldn't find in Cici's apartment, Madame Petit might be his next victim."

"You would do well to leave such matters to the police," Madame Vernier interrupted as she accepted another sheet of slides from Fielding. "And I really cannot help you. As I said, I know very little about Cici Madison's personal life. I suspect there was not much to know. In spite of her pretensions, she was a simple girl." The violent red lips pursed. "But, of course, you must realize that."

"Cici was young and perhaps a bit naive," Jill countered.

"Young, naive and utterly incapable of handling success. Her case was sad, perhaps, but all too typical, Mademoiselle Fremont. How often have I seen such foolish girls! One day they are too poor to feed themselves, then suddenly they are rich. Or so they think. Like beggars before a banquet table, they do not know what to eat or when to stop." Madame Vernier's mouth curled in disdain as she removed a slide from the sleeve. "With Cici it was cars. First a Maserati, then an Aston Martin, then a Ferrari. Or was it another Maserati? I forget." Easing the slide back into its niche, she shrugged. Her voice sounded weary and disengaged as she went on. "One car after another, one accident after another. Until the silly girl finally exhausted the patience of the gods."

"Cici Madison's death was a tragedy. She wasn't just a pretty image on one of those slides, but a flesh-and-blood woman with hopes and feelings." Jill's words were filled with anger.

Madame Vernier gave her a quizzical look over the transparent sheet she held, but said nothing. She studied the slides for a moment. She pecked one of them with a vermilion fingernail as she handed the sheet back to Fielding. "This one is marvelous! Have Mademoiselle Dumont set up an appointment for her immediately."

From the corner of her eye, Jill could see Dave sidling toward Vernier's desk. Edging next to Fielding, he peered over the little man's shoulder at the sheet of slides. "Whatever your opinion of Cici Madison may have been, Madame Vernier—" she continued, to help distract the porcelain woman "—Francois Chausson certainly seemed to hold her in high regard."

A crimson flush rose above the modeling agent's high-necked dress. "She had the look he sought. The reputation of this agency was built on my ability to place the right girl with the right designer."

Dave grinned as he stepped around the desk. "I'm sure, but from what I've heard, Madison was more than a look. She was an inspiration. A Chausson insider, really. They say he relied on her. Trusted her."

Vernier's lips tightened as her eyes locked on Dave. "Perhaps he did. Now I am sorry, *monsieur*, but I am a very busy woman. I must ask you and Mademoiselle Fremont to leave. Sanford, will you please show our visitors to the door."

Jill did not trust Dave to take the cue, and she was determined to terminate the abortive interview with dignity. Cutting a warning glance at him, she took a step back from the lacquered desk. "Thank you for your time, Madame Vernier."

Fielding was apparently so relieved to have gotten off easily in his role as office bouncer that he hurried to open the front door for them. Smiling anxiously, he escorted them into the reception area. "I had the privilege of photographing Miss Madison many times," he told them in a breathless whisper. "A stunning girl, truly remarkable! But she was a fragile creature, you know, like a gazelle poised for flight. That was her beauty. And her weakness. She was too fragile for this harsh world. Not like Simone."

"What do you mean?" Jill's curiosity was instantly piqued.

The faun's eyes narrowed. "Simone was worldly, perhaps too much so for her own good. She could be quite spiteful." Suddenly the receptionist's intercom buzzed, and Fielding's eyes darted to the front desk. "Ah, me! Gabrielle does not like to be kept waiting," he declared, dropping his voice to a lower key. "But I must tell you. I am very sorry she was not more helpful to you. Sometimes she is... How shall I put it? Distant, yes, very distant." His pale eyes darted back to the suite door as if he expected Madame Vernier to burst on the scene at any moment and berate him for his apology.

"I understand, Mr. Fielding," Dave interposed gallantly. Nodding cordially, he turned toward the elevator.

Only when they were securely encapsulated in the stainless-steel car did Jill feel she could safely breathe the air. "What a thoroughly dreadful woman! As far as she's concerned, Cici was just a commodity to be exploited and then replaced at a whim. I'm wondering if she knows where Simone is and wouldn't tell me, out of spite."

Dave glanced up at the lighted floor numbers. "I don't think she knows."

Jill pursed her lips. "I guess I'm just overreacting, but she really annoyed me. I'm sorry this proved to be such a dead end."

Dave shook his head. "Actually I picked up some useful information. Vernier is cagey, but she does give herself away occasionally. For instance, didn't you think it odd that she got so vitriolic talking about Cici? I mean, it was obvious to me that she hated the kid. Think about it. Vernier takes this unpolished nugget of Texas gold and turns her into the hottest property in Paris. You don't have to be a mathematician to figure out that Madison's commissions alone could keep the agency afloat for quite a while. Does it make sense to you that Vernier would be so critical of such a profitable client?"

Jill was frowning as she stepped out of the elevator. "Maybe Cici was getting ready to change agencies," she suggested when they were out on the street.

"Nope. There are things called contracts that make that sort of thing very unattractive."

"There are also things called lawyers that can make it possible," Jill shot back.

Dave's broad shoulders shrugged. "Okay. You may be right, but my guess is that Madison was about to embarrass the agency."

"How?"

"Oh, I don't know," he said thoughtfully. "Maybe she was involved in some sort of scandal."

Jill regarded him skeptically. "Always on the dirty footprint trail, aren't you?"

Dave halted and leaned back against the rail overlooking the Seine. "More often than you think. Speaking of trails, don't forget that we still haven't found Simone. Or Madame Petit.''

Jill heaved a deep sigh. "Thanks for reminding me."

Dave reached to chuck her lightly under the chin. His fingers felt pleasantly rough against her skin, and she was sorry that the contact was so brief. "Don't despair. We still have a couple of other resources at our disposal. As soon as I find a pay phone, I'm going to call Henri and see what he's learned about the police investigation."

"What if they're sitting on things? Those two policemen seemed to take Madame Petit's absence for granted."

"Then I'm going to call my office and have a researcher pull press clips on Simone Nanka-Midou. Someone like Simone who's been in the public eye doesn't just disappear without a trace." He paused, his gray eyes warming. "And *then* if you don't have any pressing plans, we can have some coffee."

Jill smiled. Battered as she felt after the depressing conversation with Madame Vernier, she was grateful not only for his practical help but for his companionship. "Find a phone. I'll wait for you on one of the benches down there." She pointed to the rows of benches lining the Seine.

As she descended the steps to the riverside walkway, she glanced up at the street to see Dave throw her a jaunty wave. What an impossible man! Impossible to figure out, impossible not to like. Smiling to herself, Jill sank onto an empty bench. They were such opposites: she was a levelheaded, law-abiding teacher, while he seemed to relish skirting the rules. She spent her days conjugating verbs and expounding on French literature; he probably spent his sniffing out celebrities' divorces and sordid affairs and God knew what else. And yet she liked him, more than she had liked any man in a long time.

Drawing a deep breath, Jill leaned back and looked up at the bridge arching almost directly behind her. Against the washed-out city sky, the noble facade of Notre Dame stood out in undimmed splendor. It was a beautiful city, Paris, and even her preoccupied mind could not remain completely impervious to its charm for long—or to the charm of a handsome, appealing man like Dave Lovell. She gazed across the Seine, her eyes lazily following a passing barge.

Her reverie was abruptly shattered when she chanced to glance up at the bridge overhang again. The smile faded from her lips as she recognized the burly figure in the heavy coat. Jill blinked, but there could be no mistake. He was the same man who had followed her through the Luxembourg Gardens, and he was staring right at her.

Chapter Six

When he noticed she had spotted him, he stepped back from the overhang, out of sight, but she knew he was still there. Jill's fingers closed, clawlike, around the edge of the bench seat. Suddenly the quiet riverside walkway seemed unpleasantly deserted, the shadows spread by the heavy tree limbs sinister.

Cramming her handbag under her arm, Jill jumped off the bench. As she hurried up the stone steps to the street, she kept a wary eye on the bridge. A herd of tourists was milling across it now, taking advantage of the camera angle it offered of Notre Dame. She could not make out his heavyset form among them, but she sensed that he could still see her. He seemed to possess the eerie ability to make his considerable bulk vanish at will, only to reappear when she least expected it.

Jill shifted her eyes from the pack of tourists for a moment to scan the street. Quai St. Michel was lined with cafés, restaurants and stores: *Where was Dave? Why doesn't he hurry up?* Jill shook her sleeve back and checked her watch. She had no idea at what time he had dashed off to make his call, but the intervening period now seemed like an eternity.

Two caped *gendarmes* strolled past, close enough for Jill to hail them. She took a faltering step toward them and halted. What would she tell them? That a man had looked down at her from the Pont au Double? That was hardly a criminal offense. And what man? He was out of sight again.

He was clever, all right, but today one factor had definitely tipped the balance in her favor: there was safety in a crowd; and crowds were something Notre Dame never lacked on a sunny summer afternoon. Emboldened by that realization, Jill decided to draw him out, force his hand.

Allowing herself to be swept along by camera-wielding sightseers, she turned onto the Pont au Double. Buttressed by the security of the swarming tourists, she surveyed the throng for the burly figure. In the plaza in front of the cathedral, she paused; here was an excellent vantage point from where she could spot her mark. *Come on, you brute. Show yourself.* She jumped when a hand unexpectedly plucked at her sleeve.

"Excuse me, miss, but do you speak English?" the woman asked uncertainly. She visibly sagged in relief when Jill nodded. "Would you mind taking a picture of my husband and me in front of the church there?" The woman gestured toward a middle-aged man dressed in green plaid pants and an Izod shirt.

"Not at all." Jill accepted the Nikon the woman held out to her. She followed the couple across the plaza and waited patiently while they jockeyed back and forth in front of the cathedral.

"Okay, just a little closer together. That's fine. Smile now."

Jill squinted into the viewfinder and adjusted the focus ring. As the blurred image cleared, however, it re-

vealed not only the broadly grinning Americans but a
now-familiar figure loitering in the background. The
man in the coat was half concealed by a souvenir ven-
dor's cart, but Jill could tell from the lackadaisical way
he was rummaging through the brochures that he was
really looking at her. He apparently knew she had seen
him, for he replaced the travel guides in the rack and
sauntered out of the viewfinder's range.

Before the two Americans could ask for another shot,
Jill thrust the camera at them and hurried across the
plaza. Now that she was holding the trump card, she
was not going to let him quietly slip away, to reappear
when the circumstances were more to his liking. Turning around she frantically scanned the crowd.

"Bitte, gehen Sie rechts!" A hand grabbed her arm,
none too gently, and pushed her to the right.

Looking around, Jill found a blond woman with a
rusty tan prodding her elbow. She managed to pull her
arm free, but the woman persisted. *"Bitte, rechts!
Ordentlich eingehen!"*

As her feet moved in unison with the group the
woman was herding, Jill strained to read the name tag
pinned to her blouse. Frau Koch. *Eurotouristik
Leiterin*, it proclaimed. Hemmed in by the guidebook-
toting German tourists, Jill quickly decided not to resist Frau Koch's misguided efforts to include her in her
tour group.

Not that she had much choice. The group was so
large—at least thirty strong—and so tightly organized,
she had little chance of breaking rank. As they shuffled toward the cathedral's north tower, Jill searched the
plaza for the man in the coat. Although Frau Koch's
instructions were wasted on her, she soon realized they
were headed for the top of the tower, which would give

Jill a superb view of the plaza. Following the example of her companions, she fell into a single-file line as they began to ascend the winding steps.

Never fond of heights, Jill kept one hand running along the wall during the endless climb. Subdued voices echoed behind her, followed by nervous laughter. When a glimmer of daylight at last filtered down to them, a collective sigh of relief filled the stairwell.

As soon as Jill cleared the narrow door, she stepped aside to allow those behind her to pass. Although her height anxiety did not amount to a full-blown phobia, her palms felt uncommonly damp, her stomach queasy. She waited a minute or two before venturing near the parapet.

The view from the tower *was* breathtaking. The forks of the Seine joined at the point of the Ile de la Cité to form the shimmering gray expanse that divided the city in two. To the right stood the Louvre with the Tuilerie Gardens sprawling out behind it. In the distance, the Eiffel Tower pierced the thick air, a modern counterpoint to the ancient cathedral. Lulled by the beauty of the scene, Jill coaxed herself to look down. Her head swam slightly as her eyes swept the plaza in search of the figure in the overcoat.

When she spotted Dave pushing through the crowd, she started. Jill had become so absorbed in her cat-and-mouse game, she had forgotten to keep a look out for him. No doubt he had returned to the park bench and found her gone; given their disaster-strewed past, he probably thought she'd again met ruin. Although she could not see his face clearly, the impatient way he shouldered past the tourists signaled his panic. She threw up her hand and waved, hoping to catch his attention, but her signal went unnoticed. Jill glanced around and found Frau Koch lecturing to a cluster of eager listeners. She was sidling toward the door when she saw something move behind one of the tower's stone gargoyles.

The man in the coat! An icy chill tingled up her spine. He had followed her, was here on the tower with her, had been watching her! Her sense of control shattered, Jill bolted for the door, driven by a primal urge to get her feet back on firm ground. In her haste, she almost slipped on the uneven threshold, but somehow managed to recover her balance.

On her way up the tower, the steps had seemed small and steep; on the way down, they seemed positively lethal. In her panic, however, her feet skimmed the steps two, sometimes three at a time. The click of her heels echoed off the dull silence. The stagnant smell of unmoving air mingled with her nervousness.

Where had all the tourists gone? Only minutes before they had jammed the tower, depleting the oxygen supply and driving the temperature up. Yet now she had passed not a single soul.

Jill abruptly froze, her ears attuned to sounds above her. Someone was coming down the steps—just one person. The tread were so measured, so unhurried, she could only listen for a moment, riveted to the spot. *He* was not frightened; his movements were calculated, controlled, unlike her own haphazard flight. *His* legs did not threaten to stall beneath him, their joints locked in a vise of fear.

As if she were wrenching herself from the jaws of a closing trap, Jill broke into a headlong rush down the stairs. Her hands slapped against the cold stone wall, steadying her hasty progress. When she at last caught sight of the door opening onto the courtyard, she leaped, clearing three steps at a time.

She would not have paused to catch her breath if Dave had not grabbed her arms and jerked her to a halt.

"I've been looking all over for you. What's wrong?" His hands clutched her wrists, anchoring her on the spot.

"I saw him again, the same guy who trailed me through the gardens yesterday. He followed me up the tower...."

Dave looked past her. "What the hell were you doing going up the tower?"

"Never mind!" Jill wrenched her hands free to grab his arm and pull him around. "He should be coming out the door any second. This is our chance to confront him."

Following her lead, Dave broke into a sprint to the tower gate.

A wizened man in a gray canvas smock climbed off his stool to block their entrance. "No, no, *monsieur, mademoiselle. Fermé. Geschlossen.* Closed. No more tickets today."

"We don't want to go up," Dave explained, but the guard only continued to shake his head and shoo them away from the gate. "We're just waiting for someone." He was trying to circumvent the custodian when the man in the heavy coat appeared in the door.

"There he is!" Jill shouted, pointing straight at the man.

For a fraction of a second, the man froze, the expression on his fleshy face startled. As she pushed past the custodian, he seemed to awaken and dashed for the street.

In spite of the low-heeled pumps she was wearing, Jill followed, quickly gaining on her much heavier quarry. As they raced along the Quai du Louvre, she could see his short legs pumping desperately beneath the absurd, heavy coat. Now *he* was the one trying to elude *her*. The thought gave Jill the burst of energy she needed to close in on him.

He surprised her when he turned suddenly and scrambled across the street. She grabbed for the furled tail of his coat and then stepped back, just in time to avoid an oncoming car.

"Oh, no!" Jill was weaving anxiously on the curb, waiting for a break in the traffic, when Dave caught up with her.

"Have we lost him?" He was breathing hard, his face flushed from exertion.

"Not if I can help it!" Jill grabbed his hand and dragged him into the stalled traffic. Horns tooted as the vehicles began to move, but she ignored them. Gesturing impatiently to Dave, she sprinted between two taxis and leaped over the curb. "He's cutting through the Tuileries! Come on!"

The man in the coat had made good use of the time he had gained. Although he was now jogging at a labored pace, he had already reached the Arc de Triomphe du Carrousel. Skidding on the sandy gravel, Jill took a short cut between the precisely intersecting paths.

"Hurry!" she called over her shoulder to Dave. By the time she reached the arch, he had almost caught up with her.

"My God, you can run!" she heard him gasp, but she was too intent on the husky figure lumbering away from them to respond.

Unlike the Luxembourg Gardens, the Tuileries were devoid of close shrubbery and shadowy corners. Laid out around large open plazas, the formal gardens afforded few hiding places. If she had chosen a place to turn the tables on her adversary, she could not have found a better spot.

If only he had not gotten such a good lead on them! Her calves were burning now, and an uncomfortable tightness was beginning to pull at her side, but Jill pushed herself for one final burst of speed. The man was almost limping now, trying to get across the terrace to the Place de la Concorde. She could see his gray felt hat bobbing from side to side as he descended the terrace steps.

At the top of the terrace, Jill stopped and surveyed the traffic converging on the plaza. At least a half-dozen thoroughfares were disgorging cars, trucks and buses around the island that was home to Napoléon's famous obelisk. There was no way he could have skirted that motorized cat's cradle—not in the scant few minutes he had been out of her sight.

"Where is he?" Dave's shoulders were heaving as he grabbed the terrace rail beside her and looked down on the plaza.

"I don't know. He managed to get down the steps before I caught up with him, but he can't have gotten through that mess. He has to be hiding somewhere." Frowning, she lifted a hand to shield her eyes from the waning sun.

"The Métro!" Dave cried suddenly. He gestured toward the subway entrance. Together they raced across the terrace and down the steps to the Métro. With the traffic roaring overhead, Jill felt as if she were descending into the maw of some voracious mechanical monster. They followed the tile-lined tunnel to the trains.

"There he is!" Jill exclaimed the moment she caught sight of a gray hat in the station's crowd.

Dave was already shoving his way through the commuters. He was about to skirt the turnstile when a uniformed man stepped into his path.

"Votre billet, monsieur!"

"Oh, for God's sake, man!" Dave regarded the attendant as if the man had lost his mind.

"Billet. Ticket." The attendant pointed helpfully to the magnetic slot and mimicked inserting a ticket.

"I don't have a ticket," Dave bellowed. "Oh, no!" His voice sank just as Jill reached his side. Together they watched the train pull away from the platform. The man in the coat was in it.

"WANT ANOTHER DRINK?" Dave slumped back against the banquette and stared across the bar into space.

Jill shook her head. "Uh-uh. Two's my limit, but feel free."

"No, I never drink alone." Dave shifted his shoulders against the quilted red leather seat and sighed. "To think how close we came to nailing that guy, and then he got away."

Jill gave him a mirthless smile. "Don't worry. I'm sure he'll turn up again."

"I just hope I'm around when he does," Dave muttered.

"You probably will be. Both times I've seen him, he's shown up right after we've been together. If I didn't know better, I'd almost think..." She broke off abruptly. Reaching for her empty wineglass, she pretended to drain the last sip.

The awkward lapse was not wasted on Dave. "Think what?" He leaned forward and folded his arms on the table, forcing her to look at him.

Jill met his penetrating gaze.

"That I have something to do with him?" Dave supplied, not breaking eye contact.

"I didn't say that," Jill protested. But she had thought it, if only for a fleeting moment. And he knew it.

"You didn't need to, dear." Dave pushed back against the banquette, but he continued to regard her skeptically. When she said nothing, he locked his hands behind his head and looked away. "Look, I know as far as you're concerned my track record isn't the best in the world, but I didn't chase that character the length of Paris today just to throw you off. When I set people up, I try to make it as easy on myself as possible."

Jill irritably shoved the wineglass aside. "Oh, Dave, I don't suspect you of anything..." Her annoyance grew as she searched for the right word. "Underhanded. It's just that, since I've met you, my nice, quiet life has suddenly gotten very weird." She frowned over her shoulder at the pinball machine that had abruptly flared to life across the room.

Dave leaned toward her again. "Poor kid!" His finger grazed her brow, carefully lifting the tip of her bangs. "How's the battle scar?" he murmured, tracing the outline of the white gauze. "You've got it all covered up."

Jill reached up and smoothed her bangs, gently pushing his hand away. Hearing his drawling voice soften that way, feeling him touch her, even having him this close, elicited emotions that she did not want to deal with right now. "I didn't want to make a bad impression on Madame Vernier."

When he chuckled, his warm breath grazed her cheek from across the table. "I think that would have taken more than a bandage. That woman's charity doesn't even extend to her own clients."

"Poor Cici," Jill said sadly. She stared down at the table.

Dave was silent for a few seconds. "There's something I've wanted to ask you," he began. Jill watched him unclasp his hands, then fold them again on the table. "When you were meeting Cici for those lessons, do you ever recall her talking about being in some kind of trouble?"

Jill shook her head. "No. I mean, she mentioned a falling out with her fiancé once, but that was all. And anyway, if she had problems, I doubt if she would have shared them with me. We didn't know each other that well." She watched his tightly interwoven fingers, trying to gauge his thoughts. "What kind of trouble did you have in mind?"

"Oh, maybe problems with Chausson. Like she might have been mixed up in something shady, and word got back to him." Dave shrugged too quickly for Jill to believe he was telling her everything.

"You're holding out on me, Dave," she said evenly. "You're thinking that I might have a clue to the motive for the break-in, aren't you?" His eyes widened just enough to tell her she had hit the mark. "Well, I don't. I've told you everything I know, but I'd like to find out exactly what *you're* getting at."

When Dave looked up at her, the candor in his eyes was simply too genuine to fake. "If I had all the answers, my story would be written." He swallowed and then suddenly checked his watch. "Guess I ought to think about calling it a night," he announced a little too precipitously.

Jill raised an eyebrow. "Just when the conversation was getting interesting."

Dave frowned for a moment; then his face relaxed. "Hey, don't start hurling accusations, this is legit. I have to go to a press conference in the morning, at the House of Chausson, no less. They've called it to announce the designer's plans for opening three new stores in Japan. I expect they'll also make an official statement of mourning for Cici. Maybe I'll be able to read between the lines and learn something."

"Let me come with you."

"You?"

"Yes, me." Jill's voice rose only a few decibels, just enough to make her point. "Look, finding Simone Nanka-Midou is my only chance of locating Madame Petit. When you talked with your detective buddy this afternoon, he didn't have a clue as to where she is. What if those press clips you requested on Simone lead nowhere?" She shook her head. "Simone and Cici both modeled for Chausson. Maybe someone at the design house still knows how to find Simone. I know you think it's a long shot," she conceded, catching the doubtful look on his face. "But it's one I can't afford to pass up. I need your help. Please."

Dave glanced away, and Jill could tell he was wrestling with warring impulses. "Okay, turnabout is fair play. You got me in to see Vernier, I'll take you to the press conference. I'll even get you a real honest-to-God press pass." He paused for a moment, his mouth twisted to one side. "Who knows? If we're lucky maybe the guy in the coat will follow you to Chausson's."

BOUTON HAD BEEN PLEASED to find a restaurant within sight of the bar. Eating helped pass the time, and experience had taught him how unpredictable time could be when a man and a woman disappear into a bar together. He had ordered *couscous*.

Strange how his taste for the spicy dish had never abated. Everything else he associated with his time in Algeria he now loathed, despised with an emotion that more closely approached passion than any other he ever felt. Everything about that heat-baked, wind-blown country now only reminded him of the bitter war that had scarred him, body and soul. Like the old burns that caused him to shiver beneath a midsummer sun, the memories of the Algerian war continued to seep through his mind like a slow-acting poison. Those memories left him hating the past and much of the present. But not *couscous*.

She reappeared before he had finished his coffee. Pushing aside the tiny espresso cup, he opened his notepad and scribbled.

J. Fremont, depart 12, Rue Thénard: 23:20.

Now she was alone. She was probably going home. Would she take the Métro? No, Maubert-Mutualité was the closest station, and she was going in the wrong direction. As she approached Rue St. Jacques, he could see her scanning the passing traffic. That meant a taxi, no doubt. Bouton sighed and reached for his own *portemonnaie*. As he impatiently counted out several bills and stuffed them under the dinner check, he saw her wave to a cab. Buttoning his overcoat against the night air, he hurried out of the restaurant in time to see her climb into the taxi.

Keeping his eyes on the taxi, he hailed the next cab that passed. The driver, a tired-looking man with the drooping eyes of a bloodhound, only shrugged when he ordered him to follow the taxi. Settling back against the frayed seat, Bouton pulled up his collar and waited to see where she would lead him.

Chapter Seven

The pink marble facade of Chausson's Right Bank design house looked even more imposing than Jill had imagined. As she waited for a break in the traffic speeding along Rue du Faubourg St.-Honoré, she experienced an unwelcome pang of misgiving. What if her excursion into the designer's elegant fortress proved as unproductive as her interview with Madame Vernier? Two days had elapsed now since the housekeeper's disappearance, and Jill was still no closer to locating her. When she spotted Dave on the terrace of a café, she forced the troubling thoughts to the back of her mind and hurried to meet him.

Rousing himself from the table where he had been waiting, he waved to her. "Any signs of our pal in the overcoat?"

Jill shook her head, watching him count out change and deposit it on the café table. "No, but the day's not over yet."

"Once we're inside Chausson's, you can relax. *Nobody* gets past their security without a damn good reason." Dave lifted his attaché case onto the table and snapped it open. "Here. This is all yours, at least for the next couple of hours."

Jill looked at the laminated tag he handed her. "Jill Fremont. Worldwide Communications, Inc.," she read. She attached the badge to her lapel and then frowned down at it. "Uh, maybe you ought to brief me on how these conferences run, just so I won't pull any big gaffes. What's my official reason for attending the conference?"

Dave fastened the catches of the attaché case with a flourish. "You're my interpreter."

"Interpreter? You don't have any trouble with the language, Dave," Jill protested, following his path between the café tables. "Your accent is horrible, but you never seem to miss much under any circumstances," she added dryly. "What if someone asks what sort of story we're working on? What should I say?"

Dave chuckled, but when they halted in front of the design house's ornately carved doors, he whispered in her ear. "Just relax, okay? You have a Worldwide Communications press pass, that means you have as much right to be here as anyone else."

Before Jill could raise any further questions, Dave ushered her through the doors. She managed to look unconcerned as they filed past a discreetly forbidding guard and then followed another solemn man down a long hall. Bowing slightly, the man held open a door and gestured for them to enter.

The room was large, its scale magnified by extraordinarily high ceilings. The crystal chandeliers had been dimmed, casting a muted light over the assembled press corps. At one end of the room, an ebony table stood on a low dais. Behind it an enormous oil painting depicting one of Napoléon's victories filled the better part of the wall. Although Jill guessed the reporters numbered well over one hundred, their voices were muted, as if even they were intimidated by their surroundings.

"Is this the inner sanctum?" Jill murmured under her breath.

"Nope, but it's about as close to Chausson as any of the old man's watchdogs will allow humble folk like you and me. Believe me, I'd much prefer a one-on-one interview to this mob scene, but the house simply won't grant personal interviews. No exceptions made, period."

"Well, I guess we'll just have to make the best of this then." As Jill glanced around the room, she unconsciously adjusted the laminated press pass and then checked her watch. "If you don't mind, I'm going to cruise around and see if I can learn anything about Simone."

"Be my guest. I'll hold a seat for you." Dave gestured toward the rows of crimson velvet chairs with his attaché case.

As Jill wandered across the room, she looked back at Dave. He was chatting with a short woman with gel-slicked black hair, but his polite nods and occasional smiles could not conceal the fact that he was supremely bored. Indeed, he looked almost as out of place as Jill felt. The audience was predominantly female, composed of the kind of women who called everyone "darling" and issued dictatorial statements about the season's correct hemline. Surrounded by them, Dave's husky, broad-shouldered frame looked as if it belonged on a battlefield or at the scene of a revolutionary coup. Of course, a lot of top-notch political journalists were women, Jill reminded herself; she was being chauvinistic to question Dave's ability to cover a fashion-related story.

Jill had completed a circuit of the room and was working her way through the crowd when a low, sibilant voice caught her ear. She was certain the name "Cici" had been dropped. Instantly on the alert, Jill sidled closer to the two women.

"Chausson has absolutely no luck with models," one of the women was saying.

"I'd say the poor models have had rather rotten luck with *him*," a cool British accent cut in. "One dead, and the other very nearly so."

"What other model?" Jill asked.

The blond Englishwoman turned to regard her quizzically. Jill could feel the frank blue eyes drift from her face to the laminated press pass and back again. "Why Simone, of course." She blinked at Jill as if she had just informed her that the world was round.

Jill nodded knowingly, trying to keep a lid on her excitement. "Simone Nanka-Midou?"

"Uh-huh." The willowy blonde leaned to clasp her departing companion's hand. "So marvelous to see you again, Grace." Then she turned back to Jill. "You're new, aren't you?" Her smile was jaded, but utterly devoid of malice.

"Very," Jill allowed, grateful for the woman's apparent good nature.

"Laura Shepherd, with *Panache Magazine*." The woman proffered her hand.

Jill introduced herself and returned Laura's genuinely friendly handshake. "I may be a rookie, but I have heard of Simone. What's she doing these days, anyway?"

Laura laughed briefly. "Your guess is as good as mine!"

"Then you wouldn't know where I could find her?" Jill tried to conceal the depth of her disappointment.

The fashion reporter slowly shook her head. "*No* one seems to know. It's as if Simone Nanka-Midou never existed. Although I can't say I blame her for disappearing from the scene. Not after her ordeal."

"What happened to her?"

Laura thought for a moment before answering. "You might say fate toppled her from her throne. You see, Simone was Chausson's first signature model. You can imagine all the hoopla and hype that went along with such a thing. Overnight Simone's name and face were the mainstay of every fashion publication in the world. I'll tell you." Lowering her voice, she swept the room with her world-weary blue eyes. "Cici Madison would never have replaced Simone if it had not been for the accident."

"Accident?" Jill's voice dropped to a conspiratorial hush.

"Simone was crippled in a car crash. That was the end of her career, just like that." The reporter snapped her fingers.

"How terrible!"

Laura gave a short, hollow chuckle. "For Simone," she amended. "But just as surely as one star falls, another one ascends. Exit Simone, enter Cici. God, she can't help but hate that girl!"

"But I thought Cici and Simone were friends," Jill countered.

"That was the story, but I fancy Simone feels a bit differently these days." Laura's blue eyes widened knowingly before darting to her watch. "We'd better fall into formation before His Royal Highness makes his appearance. Hope to see you around, Jill. And good luck." She gave Jill's arm a comradely nudge in parting.

Luck was the one commodity that seemed to be in short supply these days, Jill mused as she squeezed past a clutch of photographers to join Dave. He looked up when she slid into the velvet-covered chair next to him.

"Did you learn anything?"

Jill sighed dejectedly. "Yes, but not what I wanted."

"That makes two of us," Dave interrupted before she could go on. "As far as this crowd is concerned, the burning issue of the day is whether old Chausson has included any pants in his new collection."

Suddenly, as if by prearranged signal, the murmuring around them ceased. Papers rustled, throats were cleared, then a hush fell over the room. Jill craned for a better look at the tall, gaunt man who mounted the dais.

Jill leaned toward Dave to whisper. "Is that Chausson?"

"No, he would never stoop to hold his own press conference. He leaves that to Deschamps, chief of the palace guard."

Jill nodded, but she listened closely as the man welcomed them in a cool, aloof voice. Although he had placed what appeared to be a written statement on the ebony table, he did not look at it. His sharp dark eyes moved steadily across the crowd as he expressed the designer's great sorrow and personal sense of loss for Cici Madison. Pausing only briefly, he then announced the opening of the three Chausson boutiques in Japan, scheduled for later in the year. When Deschamps concluded his delivery, a forest of hands shot up from the floor. The designer's spokesman nodded stiffly, acknowledging various reporters. The questions were predictable: Who would succeed Cici Madison? Would the Japanese stores open in time for the winter collection? Were there plans for further expansion?

Stretching his shoulders, Dave slowly unwound the leg he had swung over his knee and raised his hand. Responding to Deschamps's nod, a woman in front of him stood, but before she could pose her question, Dave was on his feet.

"Monsieur Deschamps, are there going to be any additional security measures taken in Japan?"

Jill could see the taut muscles of Deschamps's neck flex. "Every reasonable precaution will be taken to safeguard the merchandise."

"I'm not talking about merchandise, Monsieur Deschamps. In light of the increasing number of fake Chausson designs showing up on the American market, I was wondering if you have plans to counteract a similar problem in the Orient?"

"Cheap imitations pose no threat to this house, *monsieur*." Deschamps appeared to be having trouble keeping his seat.

"I'm not talking about cheap imitations, Monsieur Deschamps. Isn't it true that a recent raid in Italy recovered high-quality counterfeits of Chausson designs that have never been marketed before?"

"Unsubstantiated rumors, *monsieur*!" Deschamps leaped to his feet and pointed at a reporter in the front row. "Another question, please. *Madame!*"

Dave remained standing for a few seconds before sinking reluctantly onto his chair.

"Wow! You certainly hit a nerve," Jill muttered under her breath.

"I'm not a PR man. I'm a journalist," he told her shortly.

Jill was startled by his curt reply, but before she could comment, the gathered reporters were on their feet, applauding Deschamps, who was already headed for a side door. Dave sprang from his seat. Using the attaché case as a battering ram, he pressed his way through the crowd in an effort to overtake Deschamps. Jill was jostling through the gaggle of photographers, trying to catch up with him, when she saw a uniformed security man step into Dave's path.

"Damn!" Dave turned away from the implacable guard as Deschamps disappeared behind heavy double doors. "Let's get out of here!" Scowling, he marched out of the hall, with Jill close behind him.

"They certainly run a tight ship. I'm sorry you couldn't corner Deschamps," Jill commiserated when they were outside on the sidewalk.

Grimacing, Dave propped the attaché case on his knee and snapped the combination lock. "I got his message loud and clear. Don't mention the *C* word in the hallowed halls of Chausson."

"The '*C*' word?"

"Counterfeit. To hear him talk, you'd think the worse security problem they ever faced was shoplifting! They love to call in the press and garner some free publicity. Just don't bring up any unpleasant topics." Stepping into the street, he threw out his hand to hail a passing cab. When the taxi nosed into the curb, Dave opened the door.

"Tell me more about this counterfeit business. I thought designers were flattered to be copied. After all, they all like to consider themselves trendsetters." Halfway into the cab's back seat, Jill caught herself. "Where are we going anyway?"

"I'm taking you home. With the luck we've had to-day, I don't want you to run the risk of encountering that trench-coated thug," Dave replied matter-of-factly. He nudged her rear gently with the edge of the attaché case.

"You won't hear any arguments from me." She scooted closer to the window. "Now tell me about the counterfeiting. This is something new to me."

"I doubt that. Surely you've seen those Louis Vuitton bags that street vendors sell for fifteen bucks? Or the cheapo Rolexes that quit running after a couple of days?"

"Yes, but practically no one would think they're the real thing."

Dave tilted his head to one side and smiled cynically. "The crummy ones, no. But sometimes copies come real close to looking like the genuine article. Oh, sure, the workmanship isn't as good. The finishing may be a little sloppy; a few details are left off. But some of these knockoffs are good enough to pass. And good enough to sell for more than fifteen dollars."

"Good enough to compete with a designer's products and cut into his business?"

"You got it. The matter gets more complicated when labels and trademarks are forged. A lot of the time, people buy stuff from high-end stores, thinking they're getting a designer bag or an expensive watch. What they're really getting is a quality knockoff, but they're paying the designer price anyway."

"This sounds like a profitable area for enterprising crooks," Jill remarked. "What are the chances of getting caught? Not that I'm considering anything, mind you," she hastened to add.

"Well, the counterfeit process is a complicated one. The fakes are usually manufactured in a factory, just like the real thing. Let's say you wanted to turn out some phony Gucci shoes. You'd find a country where quality shoes are produced and a manufacturer unscrupulous enough to make them without the proper license from Gucci. Then you'd ship 'em to the target market. Maybe you'd hide them in with some other merchandise, stuff them in crates of machine parts or whatever. There aren't enough customs officials to open every single box, so with luck your pseudo-Guccis would make it without detection. Now you're almost home free. You'd just have to arrange to have phony Gucci labels put in the shoes before they were distributed."

"And then I could sit back and rake in my ill-gotten profits," Jill concluded.

"Which would be particularly high if the knockoffs were taken from original designs, something to rival the designer's latest and greatest. Of course, you'd have to get your hands on the designs in the first place." He abruptly fell silent.

A shocking realization suddenly loomed in Jill's mind, spreading through her consciousness like trickling ice water. For a moment, she was too stunned to do more than stare numbly at the back of the cabbie's balding head. Then she twisted around in the seat to confront Dave.

"You can't mean to suggest Cici was involved in a counterfeiting scheme!"

Dave said nothing as he leaned forward and directed the driver to stop.

"That's absolutely absurd!" Jill continued her protest unchallenged. "I mean, she was basically a very generous, good-hearted person. When you asked me if she were in some sort of trouble, I thought you meant...'' She stammered, searching for words. ''I don't know, maybe that she was having an affair with the wrong person or something. But she wasn't a thief!''

''I don't think this is the appropriate place to thrash this out.'' Dave cast an uncertain look at the cabbie, but the man seemed to be more interested in getting to his next fare than in eavesdropping.

Jill was not about to be put off so easily. ''Then we can continue our discussion in Tante Yvonne's apartment.'' Without waiting for his consent, she climbed out of the cab. She held the door until Dave had exited and followed her into the building to the elevator. As if honoring some unspoken agreement, they did not talk until Jill had secured the apartment door behind them.

''I want an explanation.'' Back to the door, Jill faced him and then walked deliberately to the sofa.

''I don't want to alarm you, Jill,'' Dave began, carefully sinking onto the sofa beside her.

She fixed him with a firm gaze. ''I'm already alarmed. A man's been shadowing me all over Paris. I've been mugged, and now you imply the woman whose handbag I was trying to return is a design thief. You have no right to keep me in the dark.''

Dave heaved a deep sigh. ''I have reason to believe Cici Madison was stealing designs from Chausson and funnelling them to counterfeiters.''

Jill shook her head. ''It will take more than your conjecture to make me believe that, Dave. I mean, I'm sure, you pick up a lot of gossip in your business, but this is a serious accusation.''

Dave lifted the attaché case and opened it on the coffee table. ''I'm not a scandal chaser, Jill.''

"I don't mean to insult you, Dave, but tabloids have a reputation for playing fast and loose with facts."

His face was oddly emotionless as he rummaged through the attaché case. "That's one reason I don't write for them."

Jill turned to face him squarely on the sofa. "But you told me . . ."

"I bent the truth and told you I was researching a story on models, but I never said I was doing it for a tabloid. That was your assumption, and I guess I found it convenient to let you go on thinking it. I did follow Cici Madison to the restaurant that night, but not to keep tabs on her social life. I was hoping she would lead me to one of her counterfeit connections."

Jill watched in uneasy silence, her horror growing.

"I know this comes as a shock," he said, reading her thoughts. His smile was tentative, without a trace of its usual boisterous exuberance.

Jill folded her hands in her lap and studied them carefully. "It does explain a lot—why you risked taking the calendar, why you were so aggressive at the press conference. But would it have hurt to tell me the truth?" she chided.

"At first, I wasn't sure I could trust you," he conceded quietly.

"You thought *I* was involved with a crooked scheme?" The assumption seemed so ridiculous, Jill could only gape at him.

"Not for long. But try to look at it from my viewpoint, back before I had gotten to know you."

"I am, and your suspicion seems utterly ridiculous. Why, I'm just a French teacher. I've never even gotten a speeding ticket," Jill argued.

"You saw Cici Madison on a fairly regular basis."

"I tutored her once a week."

Dave dismissed her argument with a contemptuous nod. "That's a terrific cover. Why did you meet her way out in the middle of the sticks for dinner? There's a restaurant on every corner in Paris."

"She chose the restaurant. She wanted to get away from the city, I suppose," Jill countered, a little more urgently.

"Yeah, sure. Why did she give you her handbag?"

"She didn't. I found it after she had left it on the seat."

"Uh-huh."

Jill bit her lip. "I see your point."

"I know better now, of course," Dave went on in a gentler tone. He removed a file folder from the attaché case, and Jill immediately recognized the photocopied calendar. "But in my business, I just can't afford to ignore any possibilities. Naturally a lot of 'em turn out to be false."

"So you're not even sure about Cici?" Jill allowed a tinge of hope to creep into her voice.

"Look at this." Dave arranged two pieces of paper on her knees. "Since we skimmed these copies the other evening, I've read through the whole calendar twice. Entries show she traveled frequently to Milan, London. Most of it, I'll grant you, appears perfectly innocuous. Except for this." His finger underscored an entry.

"'Twenty-six Red Horse Way,'" Jill read. She gave him a puzzled frown. "Sounds like an address."

"That's what I thought, at first. Okay, see this notation? It's the departure time for a flight to Milan. That's where she was on March 26, the date of this entry."

"She went to Italy frequently on assignments. In fact, I remember her talking about this trip. Her boyfriend had planned to accompany her, but they broke up before she took the trip. You haven't told me anything that even remotely proves she was delivering designs she'd stolen from Chausson."

"That's where 26 Red Horse Way comes in. 'Il Cavallo Rosso' is the Italian translation of Red Horse Way. I've checked, and there is no street by that name in Milan. Now if it's not an address, what is it?"

Frowning, Jill picked up the photocopy and regarded it closely. "Maybe she made a mistake."

Dave shook his head slowly.

"She could have been in a hurry and jotted down someone's address on this page. For all we know, Red Horse Way could be anywhere from London to Sheboygan," Jill suggested.

"No. As it turns out, 'Il Cavallo Rosso' is the name of a bar in Milan. 'Twenty-six' is the number of a warehouse located in the same street. And what's interesting about all this—just in case you're wondering—is the stuff the cops found when they raided that warehouse last month." Shoving the photocopies aside, he thrust a newspaper clipping in front of her.

Jill stared at the bold headline beneath the black-and-white photograph. "A cache of phony Chausson handbags?"

"And not just shoddy imitations, but top-of-the-line fakes. Remember, you heard it from the *Washington Post*, not me. Actually, I would have missed the connection if they hadn't included this photo of the warehouse. But there you see it." He tapped one corner of the picture. "It's grainy, but you can still make out the name of the bar."

Jill continued to shake her head as she scanned the article. "I just can't believe Cici could have been mixed up in something like this," she murmured, handing the clipping back to him. The memory of the model's pale young face, her fine brows knit over an unfamiliar French word, rose in Jill's mind to war with the disturbing information Dave had just shared with her.

"I still don't have positive proof," Dave reminded her. "But she always made her entries in the native language: French addresses in French, those in Italy in Italian. There are only two exceptions. This one." He placed another photocopy in her lap. "And this one."

"'166 Mill Terrace.'" Jill blinked at the date. Four days ago. What had happened then at that address? "Have you been able to track it down?"

Dave ran a hand through his hair. "No. The other entries for the week indicate that she planned to be in Paris, but again the translation doesn't correspond to any existing street. I'm afraid it's some sort of code."

"And this time you don't have a newspaper photograph to help you out."

Jill felt her heart sink. She looked down at the copy again before handing it back to him.

Dave tamped the thick folder of copies on the coffee table and then tucked them inside the attaché case. "Look, I know you're upset that I've accused your friend of stealing. I'm sorry. Who knows? Maybe I'll uncover something that will shoot my theory full of holes." He took his time fastening the attaché case. When he looked up, his face was devoid of guile. "You didn't deserve to get sucked into this mess."

"That man who's following me, he has something to do with this, doesn't he? The mugging, all of it..." She broke off and swallowed, trying to ease her painfully dry mouth. Her mind drifted back to the address, 166 Mill Terrace. Despite herself, she began toying with possible meanings.

Without speaking, Dave lifted her knotted fist and lightly stroked her hand. He lifted his free hand to brush the hair from her brow. "We're going to find out who this guy is, and when we do he's going to be sorry he ever bothered you," he vowed in a voice husky with emotion.

His hand drifted down her cheek to her jaw, and Jill felt an almost overwhelming impulse to bury her face in that rough palm. Instead she closed her eyes, the better to wrestle with her confusion. Her relationship with Dave Lovell was hopelessly fraught with contradictions. His entry into her life had coincided with the most harrowing forty-eight hours of her life. He had just saddled her with revelations so startling she was only beginning to come to terms with them. And yet, at that moment, the tenderness he offered seemed the only secure thing in her life.

Jill's eyes shot open, and she jumped when the phone buzzed unexpectedly.

"It's probably Tante Yvonne. She calls from the hotel a couple of times a week, just to make sure everything's okay." Jill roused herself from the sofa and hurried to the foyer. She grabbed the phone, anxious to silence the abrasive buzzer.

"Hello?" She waited for a second, expecting to hear a long-distance operator on the line. Instead a muffled sound clouded the connection, as if someone were holding a hand over the receiver. "Tante Yvonne?"

"Mademoiselle Fremont?" the low, agitated voice said. It was definitely not Tante Yvonne's.

"Oui?" For some inexplicable reason, Jill's hand tightened around the receiver. "Who is speaking?"

"Madame Petit," the woman rasped into the phone.

"Madame Petit! I've been trying to get in touch with you. Are you all right? Where are you?"

The woman cut her short. "I do not have long to talk, it is dangerous for me to linger where I may be seen."

"Tell me where you are, and I'll get help."

"There is no help for me, Mademoiselle Fremont. Even those who appear to be friends cannot be trusted. But I must warn you, Mademoiselle Fremont." Her ragged breath quavered over the line. "Leave Paris!"

Jill swallowed in a vain attempt to dislodge the lump in her throat. "What do you mean?"

"Cici told me to warn you." Her voice had grown more furtive, lowered to a whisper, almost indecipherable. "You can no longer be safe here, Mademoiselle Fremont. Go home, before it's too late."

"What did Cici tell you?" Jill demanded. "Please, Madame Petit! Talk with me! Tell me where you are!"

But Madame Petit had already hung up.

Chapter Eight

"Jill? What's wrong?"

Hand still holding the receiver, Jill heard Dave's voice rise in alarm behind her. As she turned, he read her stunned expression and was at her side instantly.

"It was Madame Petit, Dave," she managed to get out.

"Did she say where she was?" His hands clamped around her arms, reassuring her with their strong grasp, but his voice betrayed a tremor of apprehension.

"No." Jill glanced down at the phone and drew a long, unsteady breath. "But, wherever she was, she was afraid of being seen. I tried to reason with her, but she said there was no help for her, that even friends couldn't be trusted."

Dave's brow gnarled in consternation. "If she wouldn't tell you where she was, why the hell did she call?"

Jill tried to swallow, but her throat rebelled at the effort. "To warn me. She said I needed to leave Paris before it was too late."

"For God's sake, she can't just call you up and tell you to get out of town without offering a reason." Impatience heightened his voice.

"She said Cici told her to warn me, Dave." An involuntary shiver rippled through Jill, and she shot a fearful glance at the phone.

Dave's arm felt sturdy and protective as it encircled her shoulders. He gently guided her to the sofa and pulled her down beside him. "Did she give you any clue as to exactly why Cici was concerned?"

Jill shook her head and then pulled back from him, enough to loosen his embrace but not to free herself entirely. "No, but I think we both have a good idea. Certain people around Cici—I, Madame Petit and heaven-knows-who else—are in jeopardy because someone thinks we know enough to be a threat to the counterfeit operation. Cici apparently realized the danger and tried to caution Madame Petit."

"She would have done better by her friends if she'd kept her hands clean in the first place," Dave muttered bitterly.

"I'm beginning to wonder if Cici had a choice."

"What do you mean?" Straightening himself, Dave let his arm slide off her shoulder.

Jill angled herself to face him on the sofa. "I had a chance to learn a bit about Simone at the press conference. It seems she lost her position with Chausson after a serious automobile accident."

To her surprise, Dave only nodded. "I know. Remember the clips I requested from the research department? They were on my desk this morning when I stopped by the office to pick up your press pass. I took a quick look at them, but most were the usual fashion fluff, and I didn't bother bringing them with me. I do recall a brief item about an accident and Simone's taking a hiatus from her career."

"The hiatus turned out to be permanent retirement. According to the woman I talked with, Simone was crippled in the accident. She's a recluse. No one knows where she is. This reporter seemed to think Simone was consumed with bitterness and resented Cici for taking her place with Chausson." She paused for a second and took a deep breath. "Now what if Simone hated Cici enough to want revenge? What if she framed her successor at Chausson's to make it appear as if Cici were stealing designs?"

"I can see the logic in your argument," Dave agreed cautiously. "But just how would Simone go about framing Cici?"

"I don't know," Jill admitted reluctantly. "But there are several clues pointing to Simone—her phone call led to Madame Petit's disappearance. She could be the friend Madame Petit had learned not to trust. And I'd be willing to bet she's the mysterious *S* in Cici's calendar."

Folding his arms across his chest, Dave nodded. "I guess you're in the same position as I am in my investigation. The most important pieces of the puzzle are still missing."

"Or maybe we have all the pieces, but just haven't figured out how they fit together. I think your instincts were right when you pounced on that calendar." Her eyes traveled to the attaché case still resting on the coffee table.

Interpreting her glance, Dave stretched to flip open the case. He lifted the bulging file awkwardly, as if it were a lead weight, and then deposited it on Jill's crossed knees. "Now what do you propose to do?" Resting one elbow on the back of the sofa, he latched his fingers together and stared wearily at the folder.

"Well, as I see it, I have two options."

"I gather leaving Paris isn't one of them?" Dave interrupted. The trace of a smile flickered across his tired face.

"Not by a long shot," Jill assured him, resting her hands solidly on the file folder. "Either we find Simone, or we figure out what this 166 Mill Terrace means."

"I'm not too optimistic about locating Simone. None of our efforts has turned up any information on her whereabouts, and Henri and his police detectives have drawn a complete blank on her. In fact, the only link with Cici that the police have been able to find is her wrecked car. They've determined no foul play was involved in the accident, but that's about it."

Jill sighed, depressed. Realizing it wasn't productive she perked up.

"Then that leaves the Mill Terrace address." She fingered the folder's cover, taking reassurance in its concrete presence, and opened it.

"I'm game. What next?"

Looking into the haggard gray eyes, Jill recognized the strain that the slow, frustrating investigation had exerted on Dave. She sensed that, like her, he was grateful not to be alone now in his quest. Bolstered by that oddly comforting thought, she began to shuffle through the copies. She paused to squint over a notation and then looked up. "I know one thing. If I were trying to locate anything in Paris involving mills, I'd start in Montmartre."

"I've already thought of Moulin Rouge. You know, 'red horse' in Milan, 'red mill' in Paris. I even spent the better part of a day stalking around Place Blanche, looking for a likely warehouse. I turned up a big zero. There wasn't even a number 166.''

''Moulin Rouge seems a bit too obvious to me.'' Jill ignored the slightly offended look Dave gave her. ''But there are lots of other possibilities. Did you have a look around Moulin de la Galette?''

He shook his head with noticeable reluctance.

''Then that's where we'll start. We'll simply take the Métro to Montmartre first thing tomorrow morning and have a look around. Trust me. If anyone is waiting to get the drop on us, he won't choose a tourist-infested place like Montmartre to do it.''

AS THEY CLIMBED the steps from the Abbesses Métro station the following morning, Jill waved a folded map over her shoulder at Dave. ''I've divided the area into quadrants with a felt tip pen. All we have to do is keep walking in circles until we've covered the neighborhood.''

Dave regarded the map dubiously. ''Don't you think that might look a little obvious?''

''To whom?'' Jill shook her head. ''Remember, we're just harmless tourists, bent on seeing all the sights.'' She paused beneath the wrought-iron art nouveau arch curving over the Métro exit. ''We'll start with the mill.''

''Sounds good to me. From what you've told me, I think I'd really like to see this Moulin de la Galette.''

''Right this way, sir.'' Jill gestured with the map. She headed for the corner, only to pull up short of a group of Japanese tourists posing for a picture. At the curb, they waited for a tour bus to negotiate a tight turn and then crossed the street.

As they started up the steps cut into the steep alley-way, Jill glanced back at Dave and found him frowning. "Sorry, but Montmartre is all hills."

"That's not what's bothering me. Do you see all these tourists?" He shot his eyes toward the gaggle of English speakers they had just passed. "That warehouse in Milan was located in a really out-of-the-way spot. I'm beginning to wonder if a counterfeiter would choose a high-traffic area like this to store his stuff. There are an awful lot of people around here."

"Most of whom are busy snapping pictures and buying souvenirs." Jill twisted her head to one side and studied the map. "Okay. If we take a left here, we can walk right past the mill."

Her argument had failed to erase the doubtful look on Dave's face, but he dutifully followed her directions. By the time they had walked the length of Rue Lepic, however, she was beginning to share some of his misgivings. The narrow sidewalks were so clogged with tourists, eager for a glimpse of the historic district's last remaining windmill, that she and Dave had trouble simply checking the addresses. Even when they branched out to explore the side streets, they encountered a steady stream of sightseers plodding up to the Place du Tertre.

"No 166. And no likely looking warehouses." Dave confirmed her findings when they paused for another look at the map.

Jill wrinkled her nose. "You know, we're not even sure we're looking for a warehouse," she muttered under her breath. "It could be an ordinary house where someone in the counterfeit ring lives. It could be anything."

"We started with mills. What about terraces? Cici's entry read '166 Mill Terrace.'" Hands jammed into his pockets, Dave surveyed the surrounding buildings.

Jill slowly nodded, not looking up from the map. "Back when it was still a suburb of Paris, Montmartre was planted with vineyards, so there are lots of terraces."

"What about one within sight of the mill?"

"We could hike up there and check out the view." Shading her eyes from the hazy sun, she pointed to a stone wall overlooking the street.

Together they climbed the stark incline. Unlike the teaming Place du Tertre, this street had somehow escaped the invasion of souvenir stands, cheap art dealers and restaurants geared to the tourist trade. Instead its cobbled walks were lined with small shops that still catered to the needs of Montmartre's residents. As they neared the terrace, the stores yielded to two- and three-story houses. From behind one of them, Jill glimpsed a brindled terrier racing along a wrought-iron fence, oblivious to the yellow jonquils in its path. The dog's contentious yaps reverberated off the stone walls to pursue them up to the terrace.

"Do you see anything interesting?" Jill turned slowly, taking in the landscape of tile roofs that fanned out around the basilica of Sacre Coeur like a billowing red-and-gray skirt.

"Nothing but..." Dave caught himself. "Come here!"

Jill rushed to his side, her eyes already following the line of his outstretched arm.

"See?" His hoarse whisper grazed her ear.

"Number 166!" Jill's hands gripped the edge of the stone terrace wall as she stared down at the numbers etched over the weathered double doors. Over the building's pitched roof she could just make out the peak of Moulin de la Galette. "We were right! The code is nothing more than a street number within view of the coded place name. Dave, we've found it!"

"We don't know what we've found yet," Dave cautioned her.

"Well, then let's have a closer look." Stuffing the map into her purse, Jill hurried down the cobbled walk with Dave close behind her.

After a false turn that led them into a rear courtyard hung with laundry, they followed another street snaking off below the terrace. Before they even reached the intersection, they could see the warehouse's faded green doors.

"It's almost like a tunnel leading directly to the spot," Jill remarked in a low voice charged with excitement. A feeling of adventure had heightened her senses, fired her imagination. "I wish the place had some windows."

"Maybe it does around back." Arms folded across his chest, Dave regarded the dilapidated building thoughtfully.

"It looks as if the rear is enclosed by a tall fence."

"I may not be much of a runner, but I'm one hell of a climber," Dave contended. When Jill said nothing, he sent a questioning look to her.

Jill swallowed, trying to loosen the sandpaper dryness in her throat. "I'm a bit uncomfortable with heights, that's all," she told him, a little defensively.

"Then wait here while I take a quick look inside the place," he suggested in a gentler tone.

"Be serious! I'd go crazy hanging around outside, not knowing who or what you'd found in there." She shook her head in an effort to throw off her reservations. Before he could protest, she hurried across the street and ducked into the alley.

The fence was even more formidable than it had appeared from the street—at least twelve feet high and crowned with nasty-looking metal prongs. Jill watched anxiously as Dave gave the rusty woven wire a tug before hoisting himself onto one of the steel braces. Following his example, she tested the wire. It left her sweaty palm creased with reddish hatch marks, but the thing felt stable enough. Swinging her bag over her shoulder, she anchored the toe of her Docksider between the mesh, and her stomach did a somersault.

"Just don't look down," Dave called to her.

Head thrown defiantly back, she watched him swing a long leg over the pronged ridge and then jump. She heard him land, with a solid thump, on the other side. The fence shuddered for a moment, recoiling from his violent spring, and Jill fought to keep her hold. When the ripple subsided, she scrambled to the top, not giving herself a chance to stop, much less think. At the top of the fence, she jockeyed herself clear of the prongs, preparing to leap. Taking one last look at the vacant blue sky, Jill closed her eyes and let go.

J. FREMONT, *D. Lovell, arrivée 166, Rue Gaston-Marchand: 13:25.*

Bouton snapped the ballpoint pen and tucked it inside the breast pocket of his overcoat. The phone booth was so close his breath had clouded the windows with a foggy vapor. He felt admiration for their cleverness. Everyone had underestimated the Americans. They were not such a dense group of people after all. Even that horrible wretch, Cici, had surprised them.

He shifted his shoulders beneath the heavy coat, relishing its warmth and the security of his vantage point.

He had to be more careful now, with four eyes watching for him. Fortunately they had been so intent on their mission, eluding them had been a simple task today. And in their carelessness, they had led him to the warehouse itself.

Bouton's ravaged flesh crawled with anticipation. Several minutes had elapsed since they had disappeared into the alley, more time than he would normally have allowed. He could ill afford a confrontation, however, not now—not when he was so close to entrapping them.

He pushed back his sleeve, inspecting with equal dispassion his wristwatch and the discolored skin it banded. They had surely entered the building by now. They would be about their work, unaware of his approach or its consequences. He had let them set their own trap; now it only remained for him to spring it.

Bouton pulled up the pile-lined collar and opened the door of the phone booth. His face ached to smile as he hurried down the steps to the warehouse. Clever they were; but doomed.

"CAN YOU SEE ANYTHING?" Jill rose on tiptoe, straining for a look through the high window.

Hands shielding either side of his face, Dave pressed his nose to the streaked glass. "It's awfully dark. Let me see if I can budge this thing." He took a step backward and tugged at the metal window frame. The corroded casement groaned in protest, but the ancient hinge yielded enough for Dave to squeeze his arm through the crack. Using his elbow as a wedge, he forced the window open. He gave Jill a triumphant grin, but she only glanced nervously around the litter-strewed warehouse yard.

"Let's hurry and get inside."

"C'mon, and I'll give you a boost." Dave locked his hands together and crouched to accommodate her. When Jill rested her knee in his cupped hands, he easily hoisted her to the window.

Waiting for Dave to wriggle through the narrow window behind her, Jill gave her eyes a chance to adjust to the limited light. A row of grimy skylights overhead provided the only available illumination, channeling columns of lint-choked sunlight into the gloom. Jill rubbed her nose, fighting the insidious sting of dust and fiber.

"Well, let's see what we've got." Dave slapped the knees of his khakis as he reached her side.

"Looks like a bunch of mattresses." Jill gestured toward the bastion of blue-and-white ticking that ran the length of the building.

Dave nudged her shoulder. "Don't look so crestfallen. You weren't expecting to find neat rows of fake Chausson goodies awaiting shipment, were you?"

Jill's eyes traveled up the wall of mattresses that stretched almost to the ceiling. "No, just maybe some manufacturing equipment or a workshop." She took a halting step and peered between the rows of mattresses only to find more of the same. "This doesn't look very promising."

"The actual fabrication of counterfeit junk is usually done in a factory that turns out legitimate stuff, too," Dave reminded her.

"So you told me, but why did Cici have this coded address in her calendar? If she were delivering stolen designs, wouldn't she take them to the manufacturer?''

"A counterfeiting operation involves a whole network of crooks. Depending on how well they trusted Cici, the counterfeiters may not have wanted her to get too close to the real kingpins. The fact that they suspect her housekeeper and her tutor of knowing too much should give you some idea of how paranoid these people are. Cici would probably have dropped the designs here without realizing what the warehouse was used for, the same as in Milan." He paused and thoughtfully regarded the mattresses. "This place has the look of a depot to me, someplace where the finished product would be stored prior to shipment and distribution. Besides, can you think of a better place to hide a handbag or a belt or a high-fashion gown from a snooping customs official than inside an ordinary double mattress?"

Jill gingerly poked the bound edge of one of the mattresses. "I wonder if something is concealed inside it," she murmured.

Dave ran his hand along the striped ticking. "It's hard to say. Let's have a look around and see if we can turn up any evidence."

He slipped his arm around her shoulder, guiding her between the rows of mattresses, and she instinctively drew closer to his body's inviting heat field. When they reached the far side of the warehouse, they halted to take stock. A forklift partially blocked the end of the corridor; on the opposite wall a stack of wooden pallets flanked a locked storage room. Some coiled rope and a few common tools hung from pegs.

Relinquishing his hold on Jill, Dave walked to the storage-room door and lifted the heavy padlock. Then he knelt beside the door, pressing his eye next to the frame in an attempt to peek inside. "It's too damned dark to make anything out," he muttered in frustration.

Jill stooped over Dave's hunched figure. "I wish we had a flashlight," she began. She jumped back abruptly, stifling a gasp, when something scurried across her feet.

"It's only a rat." Dave pointed to the naked pink tail just before it disappeared under the locked door.

"Sorry I'm so edgy," Jill apologized with a nervous laugh. "I think I scared the poor rat worse than it scared me. It must be building a nest inside the storage room." She gestured toward a clump of tangled string caught on the base of the door.

Dave was rising to his feet when Jill suddenly grabbed his arm. An idea had flashed into her mind. Still crouching she began to pull the snarled string free. "Look at this!" She held up to the light some fabric entangled in the string. "See those letters?" Her trembling finger traced the two interlocking gold crescents that had been stitched into the soiled fabric.

"They look like two *C*s... My God, Jill, that's the Chausson logo!"

"Exactly! This was part of a large Chausson scarf, Dave, or one that can pass for a Chausson. And you can be certain that rat didn't scuttle down to the couturier district to find it."

"I'm going to break this damned door open." Dave jerked his head toward the storage room as he surveyed the tools suspended on the wall. He selected a large claw hammer and hefted it in his hand. "Too bad there's no crowbar."

"That's something I should have brought, too, along with the flashlight," Jill joked. Excitement had superseded her anxiety, filling her with an almost giddy elation. She flexed her clammy hands, her eyes glued on the padlock as Dave inserted the hammer claw beneath the hasp. Her whole body lurched when a car's engine suddenly rumbled at the front of the warehouse.

"Someone has just pulled into the driveway!" Jill grabbed Dave's shoulder and pointed toward the green double doors.

Slowly stepping back from the storage room, they both watched as a shadow filled the gap beneath the doors. The engine had dropped to an idle now; then a car door slammed, and gravel crunched beneath a hasty tread.

"We've got to hide!" Jill's throat was so tight she was surprised she could still whisper. She pivoted, dragging Dave with her in her headlong rush toward the maze of mattresses. Suddenly he pulled her up short.

"The hammer! I left the damned thing on the floor!"

Dave wheeled and rushed back to the storage room. Jill crouched beside the forklift, her eyes riveted on the double doors. She could hear someone wrestling with a lock; a French curse punctuated the key's probing. Then hinges whined, and the double doors parted a crack. Her eyes darted from the doors to Dave as he flung the hammer on the hook. She could see a green van through the doors now; then a man stepped into the opening.

The alcove formed by the storage room blocked Dave's view of the doors. In a desperate attempt to telegraph a warning to him, she waved. He saw her, and immediately dropped back into the protective shadow of the storage room. Their eyes met across the space separating them, locked in a silent bond of fear. She shook her head emphatically and cut her eyes toward the open double doors. Clamping her lip between her teeth, she waited until the intruder's back was turned. In response to her frantic signal, Dave made his break just as the man climbed back into the van. Jill seized his hand, pulling him down behind the forklift. Together they crawled into the corridor separating two rows of mattresses. Still hugging the floor, they listened as the van rolled into the warehouse. Then the engine died, and the fetid air was very still.

Jill heard the door slam, and the knot coiled in her stomach tightened. Her palms were slick with sweat as she clutched her bag and slowly eased out of her crouch. Dave mimed her silent movement, his lean body tensed like a jaguar prepared to spring.

Suddenly he lunged toward her, flattening her to the wall of mattresses with his outstretched arm. His face was pressed against her shoulder, so close she could hear his rough breathing. But Jill's ears were trained on another, more ominous sound: footsteps, the wary, deliberate tread of someone on his guard.

She felt the muscles of Dave's arm grow rigid, and her own body stiffened with dread. The steps had halted now, leaving a deathly stillness in their wake. An agonizing itch tormented her nose, but Jill dared not move. She blinked hard to gain a moment's relief from the dusty air. She opened her eyes just in time to see a squat, bulky shadow loom at the end of the corridor.

As the man stepped into the shaft of light, his back was toward them. He seemed to be studying the pile of mattresses rising before him. For a split second, Jill surrendered to the wild hope that he would pass by, leaving their narrow corridor uninspected, but her desperate fantasy was short-lived. When the man turned, the breath she held died within her. Helpless and trapped, she could only watch him as he walked directly toward their hiding place.

She could see the heavy, pock-marked face now, scowling over the forklift's hoist. Something about the machine seemed to displease him; his beefy hand groped the steering wheel column, searching for the ignition key. *If he moves the forklift he'll see us.* The realization flashed through her mind like a brushfire out of control.

Her knees almost buckled beneath her when the man wheeled abruptly. His frown darkened, but his brooding eyes were now trained on the double doors. Jill watched him move furtively along the side of the parked van, as if *he* were trying to conceal himself.

Not daring to take her eyes off the man, Jill tapped Dave's shoulder lightly. He turned his head in time to see the interloper slip into the back of the van.

"What's he doing?" Dave's tense whisper rasped in her ear.

"I can't tell," she began and then broke off. "Listen! Do you hear something?"

Dave nodded, the light stubble of his jaw brushing her cheek. "Someone's walking along the front of the warehouse. Now he's stopped." He shifted lightly, his arms still braced against Jill. They listened as the double doors rattled on their hinges. "I don't know who's outside or what he has in mind, but that guy in the van is trying to hide from him. This is our chance to get the hell out of here."

Jill mastered the foolish impulse to bolt for the rear of the warehouse and forced herself to move as stealthily as her cramped legs would permit. Only when the open casement window was in sight did they yield to the primitive urge for escape. Lifting Jill off her feet, Dave heaved her toward the window. He gave her hips a none-too-gentle shove through the skimpy opening and then scrambled after her.

Like a commando storming an enemy compound, Jill rushed to scale the fence. Now was not the time to succumb to her phobia, she told herself as she inched her way up the wire barricade. Unfortunately the pronounced bow that had helped her ascend from the alley with relative ease now worked against her. By the time she reached the top of the fence, her knees were scraped and bleeding, her fingers raw from the struggle. With a recklessness she could scarcely have imagined an hour earlier, Jill flung her legs over the prongs and jumped.

She fell as she landed, sprawling onto the cobbled pavement with bone-jarring impact. Stumbling to her feet, she resisted Dave's efforts to hold her back.

"I'm okay!" she rasped between gritted teeth. "Let's just get away from this place!"

They paused at the mouth of the alley to check the street. Whoever had been prowling around the double doors had either departed or found his way inside. With the coast clear, at least momentarily, they dashed up the street. They did not slacken their pace until they had rounded the corner and put another block between them and the warehouse.

"You could have broken half the bones in your body back there!" Clasping her shoulders so tightly she winced, Dave held her at arm's length. His gray eyes seemed to take in every inch of her disheveled figure in their attempt to ferret out some concealed injury.

"But I didn't." Trying to loosen his hold, Jill shrugged. She grimaced as a sharp pain pierced her right shoulder. "I just got a few bruises."

"And cuts," Dave added severely. Releasing her shoulders, he reached for her hands and turned them over.

Jill closed her fingers over her lacerated palms and gently slid them from Dave's grasp. "I'll live, which is something neither of us may have been able to say if we hadn't gotten a lucky break back there. We need to get in touch with the police right away."

"We're not going to report this to just any cop on the beat," Dave warned her, falling in step with her as they trudged up the hilly street. "Henri is the only person I'm going to trust with a hot one like this. In fact, I don't think I even want to risk talking with him on the phone. You never can tell who might be listening—or who might be on the take."

Jill's sense of trust had taken a marked downward spiral in the last several days, and she quickly nodded her agreement. "So you want to fill him in on the warehouse in person?"

"Just as soon as a taxi can get me to the police headquarters." Dave's mouth was set in a grimly determined line as he scanned the traffic pelting along Boulevard de Clichy. "In the meantime, I think you should go home and get those cuts cleaned up. Put an ice bag on those bruises, too, while you're at it."

Jill reluctantly halted at the Métro entrance. Although she would normally have insisted on accompanying him to police headquarters, her hip was throbbing so painfully she recoiled with each step. "Please be careful." She forced a smile, as much to soften the urgency of her concern as to conceal her discomfort. "I can't handle your getting into any scrapes. I've already overshot my quota of wild surprises for today."

Dave took another stride, joining her on the top step. "*You* be careful." He reached to smooth her bangs and then stepped back.

Primed by the emotional roller coaster of the past twenty-four hours, Jill's senses were sharpened to the quick. Although Dave was maintaining a discreet, albeit slight, distance between them, she was as aware of his tall, muscular body as if it had been pressed against hers. "Call me later, after you've talked with Henri," she said, taking another step down into the Métro entrance.

"Don't worry, I will." Dave looked as if he wanted to follow, but he remained anchored at the top of the steps.

Jill waved and then edged down the stairs. She managed to disguise her limp until she was safely inside the station. Once she was through the turnstile, she paused to examine the Métro map posted on the platform. Montmartre was off her beaten path; she would have to change trains twice to reach the stop closest to Tante Yvonne's apartment. She slipped one foot out of its Docksider and rubbed it gingerly against her swollen ankle. If she had not broken half her bones, as Dave had suggested, she had managed to batter a good many of them, and she was relieved to see a train's yellow light spilling out of the tunnel.

Jill was so exhausted and preoccupied, she had not paid much attention to the other people waiting on the platform. She had boarded the train and dropped into a seat before she noticed a stocky man, half concealed by one of the station's tile pillars. In dismay, she pressed her hand against the window and watched him walk the length of the train. It was him, the man in the overcoat!

Jill slid forward in her seat, gripped by uncertainty. Should she get off the train? The station was practically empty now, and she didn't want to risk a moment alone with him. Suddenly the train lurched forward, making her decision for her. Pushing the window open, she peered back at the receding platform. It was empty now. He had boarded the train with her.

Although most of the car's seats were vacant, Jill stood and walked to the standing area in front of the doors. Two more stops and they would reach the big Barbès-Rochechouart terminal. There would be plenty of *gendarmes* in the station. If she remained calm, she could lead her tormentor right into the hands of the police. She had a plan now; *she* was in control of the situation. That thought helped to steady her jangled nerves.

The train's brakes locked, emitting an agonized metallic shriek. "Pigalle." Jill read the name emblazoned on the next station's wall. She forced herself to breathe deeply as she watched a handful of people disembark onto the platform. The man in the coat was not among them.

Once more, the train rocked gently before picking up speed. When it slowed again, Jill watched the sign designating the Anvers station move past the window. This time only two little boys toting red leather Adidas bags got out, and the train lingered only briefly.

Jill's fingers flexed around the chrome pole. At the next station she would have to act. The important thing was not to hesitate and, whatever she did, not to stray into a lonely spot with him. When the train halted in the

Barbès-Rochechouart station, she was heartened by the number of passengers who rushed the doors. The platform was so crowded, she had to crane for a glimpse of the familiar felt hat.

She wanted him to see her now, wanted to make certain she had him on her trail. From the stairs leading to an intersecting Métro line, Jill looked back and was pleased to find the great hunched shoulders plowing through the throng toward her. Her pulse quickened when she turned and caught sight of a *gendarme*'s blue cape on the platform ahead. She must be cool now, take care not to reveal her intentions until it was too late for him to escape.

Chancing a last glance to assure herself that the man in the coat was still in tow, Jill hobbled up the stairs. The *gendarme* had already reached the end of the platform. He was watching the train gliding to a halt as if he intended to board it. She needed to hurry, but not too fast. The train had stopped now; the *gendarme* had stepped forward, hands folded behind his back. He stood aside to admit an elderly woman, one hand clamped around the train's sliding door.

Throwing up her hand, Jill broke into a limping run. The *gendarme* hesitated, then stepped back with one foot onto the platform.

"*Pardon, monsieur.*" Jill caught her breath quickly. "*Cet homme me suite!*"

She wheeled to point and then slowly let her hand drop to her side. The man who had been trailing her so doggedly, who had been a mere half-dozen strides behind her only moments before, had now vanished.

"*Mademoiselle?*" The *gendarme* regarded her quizzically.

"Non, non, pardon, monsieur." Still staring down the platform, Jill stepped back from the slow-moving train.

How had he managed to disappear so quickly? If she were not such a levelheaded person, she'd have suspected the man possessed magical powers. Jill watched her frowning image blur across the windows as the train accelerated. Like a curtain drawn back from a stage, the departing train swept along the platform, revealing a cast of waiting travelers on the opposite side of the tracks. Jill's heart sank when she recognized the man in the coat, standing at the very edge of the platform.

They were face-to-face now, with only a few meager feet of track separating them. He seemed to be gazing at nothing in particular, his dull eyes fixed on some unspecified spot in space. Drawn by a perverse fascination, Jill studied the jowly features. So this was the man who had stalked her in her waking hours and haunted her dreams. She felt her anger rise. She wanted him to look her in the eye, this hulking beast of a man. He had no right just to stand there, playing the innocent commuter.

Suddenly the expressionless eyes opened wide, and a look of undisguised terror flashed through them. The fleshy mouth gaped, shaping itself around an unvoiced scream. Jill could only watch in horror as the heavy body lurched, then fell straight into the path of the oncoming train.

Chapter Nine

"Someone pushed him." Jill's voice was flat, drained of its usual vitality. Bathed in the merciless fluorescent light, her face looked drawn and colorless.

Dave swung a chair around and angled it next to the table with its back facing hers. Sinking quietly onto the seat, he rested one arm on the back of the chair. His free hand reached to stroke her hair, but she seemed not to notice. "I believe you, but the police can't do much if you didn't get a look at him."

"He must have been directly behind the man in the coat. I guess he just pulled back into the crowd after he pushed the man onto the tracks." Jill frowned at the scarred table. Her voice was scratchy, strained. "It's so frustrating. I feel exactly the way I did after the episode in Cici's apartment. To think that I was right there." Her hand grabbed the air and then dropped onto the table. "And I still can't describe him." She looked up at him suddenly, her dark eyes pleading for understanding.

"You still may be able to help." Dave's hand settled on the back of her neck and gently kneaded the strained muscles. "Henri would like for you to take a look at the dead man, just to see if anything about him reminds you

of the mugger. I hate to put you through any more un-
pleasantness, but . . ."

Jill planted both hands firmly on the table and shook
her head. "If there's even the slightest chance he's the
mugger, I want to see him."

A tap at the glass-paneled door caused them both to
turn in their seats. Dave stood and extended a hand to
the wiry, dark-haired man who had just entered the
room.

"Jill, I'd like for you to meet Inspector Henri Dessenier. Henri, this is Jill Fremont."

"Mademoiselle Fremont." Henri nodded cordially,
but the appreciative look that glimmered momentarily
in his ice-blue eyes was not wasted on Dave.

"Dave tells me that you would like for me to see the
corpse." Jill was already on her feet. Although she was
obviously near exhaustion, Dave was glad to see a trace
of her old spunk.

"If you will come with me please, Mademoiselle
Fremont."

As they followed Henri down the hall to the morgue,
Dave gave Jill's shoulder an encouraging pat. He was
struck by how small her hand felt when she reached to
squeeze his own, much larger one. That hand could fool
a person who didn't know her well, lull him into thinking she was fragile and easily shaken. But Dave knew
better. Jill might be a good head shorter than he—and
God knew how many pounds lighter—but no one could
ever say she wasn't tough.

She didn't flinch when Henri pulled the sheet back to
reveal what was left of the man in the coat. Dave's eyes
traveled from Henri's jaded, dark-jawed face to Jill's
frowning countenance. Although he was not a
squeamish man—in his chosen career, he had covered

too many gory scenes to indulge such weaknesses—he avoided looking at the mangled figure lying on the slab. He was relieved when Jill at last shook her head and stepped back from the table.

"No, he can't possibly be the man who was hiding in Cici's apartment," she said firmly.

Henri's finely etched dark brows rose questioningly. "You are sure, Mademoiselle Fremont?"

"Yes. The man who mugged me had very hairy arms." Jill's finger delineated the corpse's out-stretched arm. "This man's arms are as bare as a baby's."

Henri cocked his head to one side and regarded the unnaturally white forearm. "The medical report indicates that the victim had suffered third-degree burns over eighty percent of his body at some time in his life. That would account for the lack of hair. And the fact that he wore a coat most of the time. As you can guess, the tissue damage was very extensive." He pulled the sheet over the corpse. "Very good, Mademoiselle Fremont. I thank you."

When they were outside the morgue, Jill posed the question that had been building in Dave's mind. "Who was he?"

"Maxim Bouton is the name given on his driver's license." Henri cleared his throat as if he were preparing to deliver a lecture. "Age, fifty-six. According to our preliminary findings, he was born in Lyon, the son of a mechanic and a shop clerk. Honorably discharged from the army after serving in Algeria, where he was injured in a tank explosion. That would account for his severe burns."

"No wonder he endured wearing that heavy coat in this weather. Poor man. Any clue as to why someone would want to bump him off? Or why he was following Jill?'' Dave ventured to ask.

''As to your first question, I do not have any conclusive evidence. But as for the latter—'' Henri inserted a dramatic pause ''—it seems he was paid to do so. You see, my friend, Maxim Bouton was a private investigator. We found a notebook in his pocket. He has been observing you for some time, Mademoiselle Fremont. His last entry recorded your arrival at the warehouse address in Montmartre.''

''Who was he working for?'' Jill demanded, struggling to keep her voice down.

Henri regarded her carefully for a moment. ''The House of Chausson.''

''Chausson? But why?'' Jill gasped.

''Ah, that is but one of many questions I cannot yet answer, but we will learn in time.''

Dave knew Henri well enough to take comfort in that discreet assurance. ''Thanks a lot, Henri.'' He pressed Jill's waist, guiding her toward the elevator, but she balked.

''What about the warehouse in Montmartre, Inspector Dessenier?'' she asked.

''We will make a thorough investigation tomorrow.''

''Tomorrow? But that gives the counterfeiters a whole day! They could move the merchandise or...'' Jill frowned, struggling to overcome her fatigue enough to make a lucid argument.

''There are certain legal procedures we must follow before we can search private property, Mademoiselle Fremont—just as in your country. I assure you, the investigation is being handled with the greatest expediency.'' Henri smiled, but Dave could not tell if he were amused by Jill's vehemence or put out with her for telling him how to do his job. "You should go home and try to rest, Mademoiselle Fremont," he concluded with a polite nod.

"Henri's right. You're so exhausted, you're about to drop in your tracks," Dave coaxed in a low voice.

Jill's eyes lingered on Henri's retreating figure, but she allowed Dave to summon the elevator. She was spent now, too tired to question or argue as he escorted her out of the police prefecture and hailed a cab. Once they were encapsulated in the darkness of the taxi's back seat, she settled into the crook of his arm. Her eyes were closed; some of the tense furrows had eased from her face, and for a moment Dave thought she was asleep. Then her eyes opened narrowly, but she did not move.

"Thank you." She touched his hand that was resting on her shoulder.

"I haven't done anything," he protested. "If only I had taken the Métro with you this afternoon!"

Her fingers brushed the back of his hand, ruffling the light matting of hair there. She glanced up at him before closing her eyes again. "You're here now. That's all that matters."

And that *was* all that mattered—to him as well. The thought sobered him, made him grateful for the long taxi ride through the deserted streets. So much of his adult life had been given over to action; he seemed always to be in motion, racing to keep pace with ever-changing events. There had been little time for quiet reflection, and even less of it to share with another person. He wanted to thank Jill Fremont for changing that, if only for a moment. Instead he bent his head and tenderly kissed her smooth dark hair.

When they reached the Left Bank apartment building, Dave gently roused Jill and then dispatched the taxi driver.

"What time is it anyway?" She frowned as she dug through her handbag.

"After midnight." Dave took the keys from her unresisting hands and unlocked the door. "Time for you to have a nice nightcap and then get some sleep." He was glad to see the lighted elevator car waiting for them and wasted no time piloting her into it.

"I hope you have some milk and sherry on hand," he said as he opened the apartment door for her.

"There should be plenty of milk in the refrigerator, but you'll have to dig around in the sideboard to see if Tante Yvonne has any sherry." Jill's hand fluttered toward the oak cabinet in a tired gesture.

Dave intercepted her before she could reach the kitchen and pivoted her back toward the hall. "I'm perfectly capable of pouring a shot of sherry into a glass of milk. In the meantime, you need to take care of those cuts and bruises."

Jill absently glanced down at her scarred palms. "I'm too numb to hurt anymore," she protested, but she dutifully walked to the bathroom.

Dave squatted in front of the cabinet and rummaged through the decanters until he found a bottle of Harvey's Bristol Cream. True to Jill's word, the tiny kitchen's fridge contained an unopened bottle of milk. As he filled a saucepan and placed it on the gas flame, he tried to sort through the bizarre events of the past day: Madame Petit's frightening phone call; their discovery of the suspicious warehouse in Montmartre; and, most disturbing of all, the murder Jill had witnessed in the

Métro station. His journalist's intuition told him there
had to be a connecting link somewhere. But where?

Dave forced himself to smile as he carried the steam-
ing cup of sherry and milk to the living room. After her
ordeal, Jill did not need to be reminded of the growing
multitude of unanswered questions. He was pleased to
see that she had kicked off her shoes and stretched out
on the sofa.

"Sip this slowly." Dave slipped a pillow behind her
head and then cupped her bandaged hands around the
mug.

Jill tasted the drink carefully and then sank back onto
the cushion. "Ever think about becoming a doctor instead of a reporter?"

"Nope. Lousy bedside manner."

"Says who?" Her hand reached up to encircle his
wrist and pull him down beside her.

"My ex-wife, for one." Dave had let the revelation
slip out without thinking. Now he could only wait to see
how she would react.

Jill's hand did not move against his wrist. "I didn't
realize you were divorced. What happened?" she asked
quietly.

"I was working for a small paper in Illinois when I
got an offer from the *New York Times* to join their bureau in Buenos Aires. I wanted to go, and Joanna
didn't. So I went, and Joanna stayed."

"That sounds awfully simple." Her soft voice was
free of accusation—and far too sincere for him to avert
with facetious word games.

Dave sighed, trusting himself to ease back on the sofa
slightly. "Oh, I suppose we weren't that well suited for
each other to begin with. Back when we were in school
together, the future looked so rosy. We thought we were

in love, and like a lot of people suffering from that disease, we tended to ignore practical matters. It took a couple of years of marriage for us to realize that, as much as we might like each other, we didn't like the same kind of life at all. Joanna thrives on country club parties and well-fertilized lawns. I don't. I'm sure she always hoped that I'd become the editor-in-chief of a small-town paper. Not only would I have been a lousy editor, Jill, I would have suffocated. At any rate, we had been drifting apart for some time, but neither of us had had the courage to end it. We ended up letting the *Times* make the decision for us.''

''What happened to her?'' Jill asked, looking down at his wrist.

''She's married to an auto exec in Grosse Pointe and has two little girls. It's the kind of life she's suited for, and I imagine she's really happy.''

''And you? Are you happy?'' Jill glanced up to regard him quizzically.

For once, Dave did not have an immediate rejoinder. After a few seconds, he said carefully, ''I'm doing the only thing I could be doing and still stand to get up in the morning.''

''I think I understand what you mean.'' Jill's shoulder grazed his leg as she shifted her knees on the sofa.

Now that she was no longer facing him, Dave felt emboldened to ask, ''Ever married?''

''Once upon a time.'' Jill lifted the mug to her lips, releasing his hand to steady it.

Dave was painfully aware of the intervening silence. ''I'm sorry I asked,'' he said at length.

Jill's bandaged finger hesitantly traced the rim of the mug as she shook her head. ''Don't apologize. The divorce was final only last year. I suppose I haven't quite gotten the hang of talking about it yet.''

For a moment, Dave studied her solemn face. ''You don't have to answer this, if you don't want to,'' he began haltingly. ''But I'd really like to know. What went wrong?''

The small, gauze-swathed fingers tightened around the mug. ''A marriage is like a garden, Dave. It doesn't matter what sort of grandiose plans you have for it. If you don't cultivate it—both of you—it won't flourish. In our case, we expected the garden to grow all by itself, or at least Steve did. He had always poured a lot of energy into his work. He'd just gotten the eleven o'clock news anchor spot in Jacksonville the year we married.''

Dave groaned softly. ''He was a reporter?''

''A television personality,'' Jill corrected. ''To be fair, I can't say I didn't know what I was getting into. Even back when we were dating, he was constantly on the go, at the station at crazy hours, making public appearances all over the place. You couldn't flip on the TV without seeing him yucking it up at a county fair or turning on the charm at a fund-raiser. The trouble was, after we married, the dating stopped, and there wasn't very much left to take its place. Unless you call mumbling something to each other while you're brushing your teeth a 'relationship,' '' she added before taking a quick sip of the drink.

''I don't. Did you tell him to straighten up?''

Jill shook her head wearily. ''How could I? It was all so important to him. Then, too, I was hurt—so hurt that I wanted to show him I could treat him the same way,'' she confessed. ''I started volunteering for more committee work at school, took on some private students in the evening, got involved with the local Alliance Française.''

"And pretty soon you weren't even seeing each other when you brushed your teeth?"

"No, but my strategy worked very well. I hurt him." Her laugh was brief and uncharacteristically bitter. "Looking back, I shouldn't have been surprised when I found out he was having an affair with one of the station's weather announcers. She was certainly spending more time with Steve than I was at that point. And that was that. We divorced. He got engaged to Diane, and I came to Paris for a change of scenery," she concluded hastily. He watched the muscles tighten beneath the smooth skin of her face as she swallowed and then bit her lip.

"I didn't mean to upset you, asking about the divorce."

Jill managed a shaky smile. "Honestly, I'm not usually this maudlin. I can imagine what you must think."

Dave lifted his free hand and let it meander down her cheek to cup her jaw. "I think," he began, drawing her to him with his eyes. "I think that Steve really blew it."

He took the mug from her hands and placed it on the coffee table. Bracing himself against the cushions, he leaned over her. He was keenly aware of her palm's texture, of the rough stubble of his own chin as her hand traced his jaw. He turned his face, just enough to kiss the soft skin exposed between the bandages. When her hands clasped behind his neck, he followed their direction. Her lips tasted sweet, a tantalizing blend of warm sherry and a flavor that was uniquely Jill.

"I won't leave you tonight," he whispered, letting his lips rest against her cheek for a moment.

"I don't want you to." Her hands squeezed his neck tightly before loosening their hold.

She looked at peace now with her eyes closed and her soft hair billowed out on the cushion. His own body should have been crying for sleep by now, but for some reason he felt oddly alert. He wanted to keep watch over her as she drifted off, protect her from intrusions and unpleasant dreams.

When the phone rang, he sprang to grab it before Jill awakened. She stirred on the sofa, prompting him to cup his hand over the receiver.

"Hello?"

"Dave? I thought I would find you at this number."

Dave chose to ignore the hint of smugness in Henri's voice. "What's up?"

"We found Madame Petit."

Dave twisted the phone cord for a glimpse of Jill's sleeping form. "Where was she?"

"In the Bois de Boulogne."

"Did you learn anything from her?"

"I fear not, my friend. You see, she was dead."

Chapter Ten

"I just can't believe Madame Petit is dead. That poor woman!" Jill stared at the front of the gray metal desk without blinking. The image of the housekeeper's round little face, smiling through a cloud of coffee vapor as she interrupted Cici's French lesson to serve refreshments, rose in her mind. Jill had no idea who had murdered Madame Petit, but the killer had to be a monster devoid of feeling.

Standing behind her chair, Dave closed his hand comfortingly over her shoulder. "Maybe Henri will have some news on the investigation. When I talked with him last night, he assured me that his people won't sleep until they've made an arrest."

Jill looked up at him, resting her hand over his for a moment. She jumped up, and they both turned when the glass-paneled door suddenly swung open behind them.

"*Bonjour*, Dave! Mademoiselle Fremont! The clerk said you were here to see me." Henri smiled, but his eyes lingered on the file he was carrying as he hurried past them to his desk.

Dave eyed the open file pointedly. "I hope that's the case you've built against the counterfeiters."

"To build a case I need hard evidence." Hands braced on his desk, Henri glanced up.

Dave frowned, and Jill could tell he was bristling at Henri's comment. "We gave you the warehouse, buddy. What do you expect, signed confessions?"

"The warehouse is nothing," Henri announced bluntly.

"But that's impossible!" Jill blurted out, and then hastily lowered her voice. "Dave and I found a scrap of cloth with the Chausson logo on it, right outside that storage room. What on earth was a piece of designer fabric doing in a mattress warehouse?"

"All I can tell you, Mademoiselle Fremont, is that we found nothing out of the ordinary—no scraps, no counterfeit goods, nothing but mattresses," Henri replied evenly.

"Then they moved the stuff and cleaned up the place last night, before you and your people had a chance to get there," Jill countered. "And whoever stored the mattresses there could still intend to conceal counterfeit goods inside them."

"If that were the sole foundation for suspicion, Mademoiselle Fremont, we would be forced to keep every bedding warehouse in Paris under surveillance."

"Who leases the warehouse?" Dave's question bore an impatient edge.

Henri's neck tightened inside his starched white collar. "A Swiss-based consortium of bedding distributors. We're still in the process of checking various connections, but so far it appears to be a perfectly legitimate enterprise."

"This outfit wouldn't happen to do business in Milan, would they?"

"They do business all over the continent, my friend," Henri replied, sliding open the desk drawer to pull out a pack of cigarettes. "I know what you are thinking, but we have uncovered no links with the warehouse that was recently raided in Milan."

"Don't forget about Cici Madison," Dave reminded him.

"I know how obsessed you are with this model's calendar, Dave, but the warehouse addresses in which you put such stock are pure conjecture on your part." The unlighted cigarette wavered, poised in one corner of Henri's mouth.

Jill felt her own hackles rise. "For God's sake, Inspector Dessenier, they're codes! And if they're not, then why did Cici Madison write only those two entries—of all the notations in her calendar—in English?"

"They could simply be erroneous addresses. If you would check all the other addresses in her calendar, I imagine you would find a few mistakes among them, too."

"She was planning to meet someone at the warehouse, but she only refers to him—or her—as *L*. Why would she use a code for the name?" In her exasperation, Jill had to fight to modulate her voice.

"Unfortunately we cannot ask her." Henri sounded utterly unperturbed. "Let me remind you, however, that Mademoiselle Madison frequently substituted an initial for a full name. *J* for Jill Fremont, for instance."

"Just what are you trying to insinuate?" Dave cut in.

"Nothing, my friend. I simply want to caution both of you not to jump to conclusions too quickly."

"I thought you would be interested in pursuing every lead," Dave said, making an obvious effort not to sound too surly.

"Come now, David," Henri chided him. "You know I am always willing to work with you. In this business, one needs all the help he can get." Not taking his eyes off Dave, he twisted a match from its book and swept it across the edge of the desk.

"We'll keep that in mind. Come on, Jill." Still glaring at the detective, Dave held the door open. "I think we need to let Henri get back to work. *Au revoir.*" The glass panel rattled as he slammed the door behind them.

Only when they had reached the sidewalk outside the police prefecture did Jill vent the frustration that had been building inside her during their conversation with Henri. "I can't believe he's so skeptical of every clue we've turned up on that warehouse. What does he expect a bunch of counterfeiters to do, post a sign over the door that says Phony Knockoffs, Inc.? And now that Madame Petit has been murdered, you'd think he would want to jump on every possibility."

Dave shook his head in genuine bafflement. "I don't understand his reservations, either. Henri is usually gung ho for the thinnest thread of evidence, but he seems to discount our entire theory."

"I don't care what he says. Cici's calendar is the key to the whole counterfeit scheme," Jill told him firmly.

A slight smile played on Dave's weary face. "You're as convinced of her guilt now as I am, aren't you?"

"I don't know if I would have chosen the word 'guilt,'" Jill replied thoughtfully. "I still don't believe Cici would have been party to an operation that murdered people. She loved Nana, and she would never have willingly done anything to cause her harm. In fact,

I think we have evidence that Cici was trying to protect innocent people. She apparently told Madame Petit that I should be warned under certain circumstances.''

"Unfortunately no one warned Bouton."

The unpleasant reminder halted Jill in her tracks. "Why was he following me, Dave? If Chausson were having every one of Cici's acquaintances watched, the private detectives would be stumbling over their own feet."

Dave shrugged uneasily. "I'm afraid only the House of Chausson can answer that one."

Although the streetlight had changed, Jill hung back on the corner. "If only we could find a way to get to Deschamps!"

"Maybe we can," Dave said so slowly that she was certain he had thought the matter through earlier. "I know for a fact that Chausson is doing a big photographic shoot at the foot of the Eiffel Tower this week. Deschamps is almost certain to be there. Of course, if we try to crash the set, we run the risk of getting tossed out on our ears."

"Compared to our close call yesterday, that seems a relatively mild risk." Jill gave him a grim smile. "The House of Chausson owes me an explanation, Dave, and I won't rest until I have it."

LONG AFTER SHE HAD FINISHED reading the brief news item, she continued to stare at the newspaper. She could feel his eyes on her, preying on her strung nerves, waiting for her to react.

"Anything of interest, my dear?"

Without looking up she could imagine the sardonic smile that would have accompanied his remark.

"Do you realize what this means? Murder, they are calling it! Murder!" She leaped from her seat and threw the paper onto the floor. It landed not far from his feet. She watched his passionless eyes travel the length of her tensed body as he stopped to retrieve the newspaper.

For a moment, he pretended to read. "'A death in the Métro. *Possibly* a murder.' Pity the papers must print such rubbish. But then how else can they satisfy the public's demand for violence and scandal?" He shook his head slowly, his long fingers pressing neat creases into the newspaper. "If I did not know you better, I would think you did not appreciate the great service Yves had performed for us."

"There are many witnesses in a Métro station, too many." She turned abruptly and walked over to the table, unable to tolerate the cold probing eyes any longer.

Murder she could countenance; when her pain had been greatest, she had longed for her enemy's blood with a rapacity that knew no bounds. No, it was not the killing that disturbed her, but rather the way in which he talked about it, coolly and with no more hatred than one felt crushing an insect.

"The man had to be eliminated." His voice was brusque and impatient. "Fortunately Yves was on the premises, and heard him prowling about the warehouse. He had no choice but to dispatch him as swiftly as possible."

"Do you know who this Bouton was?" She seized the back of one of the chairs, her fingers locking through the finely hewn fretwork.

"One of Chausson's plodding bloodhounds. But even if he were merely a curious fool, what does it matter at this point?"

Still clutching the chair, she turned to glare at him. "It matters because he had to have learned about the warehouse from someone! You and your precious Yves! How sick I am of your constant reassurances that everything is going as planned! Do not worry, you tell me, Yves will take care of Madison's housekeeper and the tutor. And what has the great Yves done? Murdered a man in full view of hundreds of commuters!" Her voice was growing strident, but she was powerless to restrain her unleashed fury. "Mark me. This Bouton could have learned about the warehouse from only one of two people—the housekeeper or the teacher."

Watching him walk toward her, she felt a sense of dread rise within her like a creeping sickness. When he leaned across the table, she stepped back in spite of herself. Splayed on the gray marble surface, his soft hands reminded her of dead squid in a fishmonger's window.

"The housekeeper did not tell him," he said very slowly and deliberately.

She stiffened. "I see. And the teacher?"

He cocked his head to one side and regarded his outstretched hands for a moment. "Give Yves time—" he pushed himself away from the table and smiled "—and he will make certain she never reveals our secret again."

DESPITE HER BRAVADO, Jill was relieved the following day when they approached the photographic set erected at the feet of the Eiffel Tower and found it swarming with people. Besides a substantial cadre of technicians, stylists and fitters, a crowd of passersby had gathered to watch the elegant models pose against the dramatic backdrop. Although numerous security guards were in evidence, even they seemed to have adopted a reassuringly casual attitude. Jill and Dave hovered on the periphery of the set, waiting for the right moment to infiltrate. When the caterers arrived, bearing fresh coffee and pastry for the weary crew, they took advantage of the crush to slip beneath the cordon ropes.

"I wonder if Deschamps will remember you from the press conference?" Jill whispered at his elbow.

"We're about to find out."

Adjusting his jacket by the lapels, Dave appeared to brace himself. Jill could see Deschamps's domelike head bent over a table at the rear of the set. It was anyone's guess how he would react to the arrival of uninvited—and certainly unwelcome—guests. She was thankful to have surprise on their side.

"*Bonjour*, Monsieur Deschamps." Dave skirted the table and pulled out a chair for Jill in a single fluid motion. Not taking his eyes off Deschamps, he sank into the chair beside her.

Deschamps looked up from his test photos like a raptor whose prey has just been snatched from its talons. His flinty dark eyes regarded the two interlopers with unconcealed antipathy.

"I think we've met before, but let me introduce myself. Dave Lovell with Worldwide Communications. This is Ms. Jill Fremont." Dave offered his hand and let it hang in the air for a moment before dropping it at his side. "Sorry to pop in on you like this—" he glanced at the pile of photos "—but there are a few questions we'd like to ask, and you're a hard man to reach."

Deschamps's thin lips drew back into an unfriendly smile. "I do not grant interviews, Monsieur Lovell."

Dave rested an arm on the table and leaned to one side. "I know." His eyes followed a stylist hurrying silently past them. "That's why we didn't ask for one. We just have a few questions about some mutual acquaintances of ours. Let's start with Maxim Bouton." He turned suddenly to face Deschamps, and Jill was please to see a fleeting crack in the hostile mask.

Deschamps, however, was a master of the quick recovery. "Let us not engage in tiresome games, Monsieur Lovell. You and I both know that Bouton is dead." His bony hand lifted one of the test shots and carefully placed it to the side.

"Why did you put him on my trail, Monsieur Deschamps?" Jill demanded.

When Deschamps only stared at Jill, Dave slammed the table with his open hand. "It was because of Cici Madison, wasn't it?"

The gaunt neck stiffened. "I am not free to discuss such matters."

"Don't hand me that bull, Deschamps," Dave cut in. "We want some answers. Your thug was terrorizing Ms. Fremont until she saw him murdered yesterday. I don't know what the hell is going on, but it certainly has the makings of a very embarrassing news story for Chausson. If I were you, I'd think about bending the rules and discussing things before someone jumps to the wrong conclusions."

Deschamps's face tightened and his lips twitched as he turned slightly toward Jill. "You were one of Cici Madison's contacts, Mademoiselle Fremont. You came under suspicion after one of our security people witnessed a clandestine exchange between you and Madison."

"In a restaurant in Chevreuse?" Jill interposed, pinioning Deschamps with her intense dark eyes. "But surely you understood my relationship with Cici Madison. Until she hired me as a tutor, I had never laid eyes on her. I ended up with her handbag strictly by accident.''

"You should not interpret this as a personal attack on your character, Mademoiselle Fremont. Rather consider it an effort to prove your innocence," Deschamps asserted coolly. "Bouton was assigned to monitor your activity as part of a larger surveillance operation. He discharged his duties with scrupulous care—up to the very end. Let me remind you that, in a security breach of this nature, every precaution must be taken. Monsieur Bouton was simply doing his job."

"Even if it meant having me assaulted when I tried to return the bag to Cici's housekeeper?" Jill's voice was low—and all the more challenging.

For the first time, Deschamps was visibly shaken. "I know nothing of an assault, Mademoiselle Fremont."

Jill's face hardened. "Perhaps you prefer to call it a mugging or a purse snatching, but someone attacked me in Cici Madison's apartment and took that handbag of hers."

"Monsieur Bouton had nothing to do with such a thing!"

"I know the assailant wasn't Bouton," Jill shot back. "But you've just admitted that he wasn't the only detective working for you."

Deschamps's lips pulled into an inflexible line. "I do not know who attacked you and stole Cici Madison's bag, but I can assure you that this person did not work for the House of Chausson. I swear it."

Dave searched the skeletal face for a chink in its facade. In spite of his skepticism, however, he was almost certain that Deschamps was not lying. "If that's the truth, then it means someone wanted Madison's bag

worse than you did, Monsieur Deschamps," he put in.
"But who?"

Deschamps's hand curled like a shriveled claw on the
table. "I wish I knew, Monsieur Lovell. I wish I knew."
He looked up abruptly, his eyes traveling past Jill and
Dave. "She looks magnificent, Sanford."

Jill turned in her seat to find Sanford Fielding with a
model and two fitters in tow. "Miss Fremont! Mr.
Lovell!" The faded denim eyes ricocheted from Jill to
Dave. "What a surprise to see you here." The diminu-
tive photographer was obviously taken aback to have
encountered Gabrielle Vernier's worrisome guests
again; Deschamps's choleric expression could only have
alerted him to the danger of being unwillingly drawn
into another confrontation.

Jill moved quickly to allay his fears. "We were just
leaving, Mr. Fielding." She stood to signal her good intentions, and Dave followed suit.

"A pity you can't stay. This is Britta's first shoot,"
Fielding indicated the model with a tip of his silvery
head, "and she is simply marvelous to watch."

"Maybe some other time," Dave mumbled in what
Jill could only assume was a stab at humor.

As they picked their way between the photographic
lights and reflectors, Jill glanced back at the model and
her coterie of fitters. "Maybe we should hang around
a bit. You never can tell, but someone here might have
some information on Simone."

Dave checked his watch. "Feel free to, but I really do
have to run. One of the customs officials involved in a
big bust of fake Cartier watches in Marseilles is in town,
and we have an appointment in half an hour. I'll call
you tonight." Jacket slung over his shoulder, he was
already jogging toward the row of taxis lining the Quai

Branly. He threw up his hand in a hasty wave just before ducking into one of the cabs.

Jill waited until Sanford and the model were a safe distance from Deschamps before daring to approach them again. The little photographer was busy directing last minute adjustments to the model's gown, but he looked genuinely pleased when he spotted Jill.

"So you've decided to stay after all?" He smiled as his pale hands plucked at the model's tumbled mane of hair.

"I'm always interested in what's new in fashion." Jill sidestepped the seamstress kneeling over the gown's hem to join Sanford.

"*Everything* is new in fashion. When it becomes old, it isn't fashion anymore," Fielding declared philosophically. "Always a new silhouette, a new color, a new face."

"I suppose careers are brief in this business." Jill took a deep breath, testing the water. "You know, I'm really curious about what happened to Simone Nanka-Midou. Did you ever work with her?"

"Oh, my goodness, yes! I photographed her many, many times. She had a most elegant neck."

"Her accident was a real tragedy." Jill paused, hoping that Fielding would pick up the cue.

The translucent skin furrowed across his brow for a moment. "Simone was finished before the accident, Miss Fremont."

"What do you mean?" The photographer's remark had thoroughly piqued Jill's curiosity.

Fielding gave her a worldly smile. "Simone's career had already passed its peak, but she—like many beautiful women, if you will pardon my saying so—was unwilling to admit the inevitable. She became very bitter, very self-destructive. Simone wanted to blame some-one for her fate—Cici Madison, Chausson, anyone but herself."

"She bears a grudge against Chausson?"

The white brows rose like two wispy exclamation points. "But of course!" He turned to nod at one of the assistants hovering at his elbow. "I'm sorry, but the cameras are ready. Will you please excuse me, Miss Fremont?"

"Certainly." Jill smiled cordially, but her mind was reeling from the damning evidence Fielding had just laid in her lap. If Simone Nanka-Midou had managed to coerce Cici into stealing designs from Chausson, she would have found a perfect way to wreak ruin on both of her perceived enemies.

"Mademoiselle Simone has many enemies, but she is a good woman." The raspy voice intruded on Jill's thoughts like a fingernail skidding across a black-board. She turned to look down into a pair of dark, yet bright eyes glaring out of a dried apple-doll's face.

"You knew Simone Nanka-Midou?"

The seamstress's eyes shifted to the satin bandeau she held in her wrinkled hands. She cocked her head to one side, frowning over the seed pearl she was basting into place. "I know her well. You must not believe every-thing you hear, *mademoiselle*."

"About Simone?"

When the seamstress looked up at her, her eyes were as sharp as the needle she wielded. "About anyone." She gave the bandeau a shake. "Especially about Si-mone."

Jill swallowed, trying to appraise the little woman's oblique comments. "I'd like to hear what you have to say about her, *madame*," she began.

Still frowning over her handwork, the seamstress cut a wary glance around the crowded set. "I will talk with you," she said after a long pause. "But not here." Her head jerked curtly, beckoning Jill closer.

Jill felt as if she were making contact with a spy as she bent over the wizened head. "Twenty-four Rue Cochin. After six today. Ring 'Simenon.'"

"I will be there, Madame Simenon," Jill promised, slowly drawing back from the little woman.

The cracked lips quivered, but Jill could not be sure she was smiling. "What is your name, *mademoiselle*?"

"Fremont. Jill Fremont."

"*Au revoir*, Mademoiselle Fremont." The woman's unexpected cackle reminded Jill of rustling dry leaves. Just as abruptly, she was quiet again, bent over her work as if Jill were not there.

What a strange woman! But then nothing that had happened in the past week had fit the normal pattern of day-to-day life. As much as the seamstress's cryptic comments about Simone Nanka-Midou, Jill was intrigued by the shriveled little woman herself. Like a throwback from an earlier century, she would have fit in well with the mobcapped women who had knitted beside the guillotine during the Reign of Terror.

As it turned out, the apartment building where Madame Simenon lived was just what Jill had expected: an old, soot-stained structure huddled at the edge of a narrow street. As she pressed the doorbell, cooking odors filtered down to her from the open windows, along with shrill voices and the tinny undertone of a radio. Dave would have made an appropriate comparison, no doubt, likening the gritty setting to some black-and-white movie they had both seen.

She had tried to call him on her way to Madame Simenon's apartment, but he had not yet returned to his office. It was probably just as well, she reflected. If the seamstress's veiled hints proved to be no more than an old woman's ramblings, he would be spared the pursuit of yet another inconclusive lead. Still, when the buzzer sounded, permitting Jill into the unlighted corridor, more than a few misgivings crossed her mind.

Several seconds passed before her eyes adjusted to the gloom. Blinking, she saw that a door had opened, ever so slightly, at the far end of the hall. She could distinguish Madame Simenon's wrinkled face, peering through the crack like a troll glaring out of its lair.

"*Bonsoir*, Madame Simenon." Jill took an uncertain step forward. When the seamstress said nothing, she added, "You remember me? Jill Fremont?"

"I remember you." Madame Simenon gave a brief, wheezing laugh. "Come in, Mademoiselle Fremont." She gestured and stepped back behind the door.

Jill followed the pinch-faced little woman into the apartment. It was a tiny place, on much the same scale as Madame Simenon herself. A settee and two upholstered chairs were crammed in front of a window with chintz curtains; an old-fashioned treadle sewing machine occupied one corner, while a bulky television set took up most of another. Through two open doors, Jill glimpsed a bedroom and a minuscule kitchen.

"So you want to know about Mademoiselle Simone." Shaking her head, the seamstress dug a wrinkled handkerchief from her apron pocket and coughed into it.

"I'd like to hear what you have to say about her." Jill chose her words carefully as she eased into a sagging armchair.

Seated on the tapestry-covered settee, the seamstress's feet barely grazed the floor, but she looked at Jill with an air of authority. "I first met Simone Nanka-Midou at the House of Chausson. I have always sewn for him. He pays better than most." She rubbed her fingers together before thrusting her hand into her pocket.

"Was Simone modeling for Chausson at the time?" Jill prompted.

Pulling a tobacco pouch from her pocket, the seamstress looked at it pensively. "Yes. Ah, those were the good days for our Simone! There were some who called her the most beautiful woman in Paris. The world was at her feet."

"I suppose this was before Cici Madison arrived on the scene?"

Neatly creasing a cigarette paper, Madame Simenon shrugged. "Simone was still the top girl, even after Mademoiselle Cici came to town."

Jill looked down at the carpet with its violent swirls of maroon and gold paisley. "That was before Simone's accident?"

The seamstress carefully sprinkled a line of tobacco along the creased paper. "Before the bad times." Holding the paper up to her lips, she paused for a second. "There are many who say that Simone hated Cici and Chausson, blamed them for her misfortune. People will always gossip."

Jill's eyes followed the tip of the woman's pink tongue as it glided along the edge of the cigarette paper. "But you don't believe them?"

Madame Simenon scooted forward on the settee and snatched a book of matches from the coffee table. Twisting a match from the folder, she frowned. "Simone is a strong-willed woman, and she had her differences with Chausson. But how could she hate him? He was like a father to her. As for Mademoiselle Cici, she was very much like Simone in many ways. You see, Simone was born in Senegal. When she came to Paris, it was her first time in a big city. She had always been a poor girl. Just like Cici." The seamstress struck the match and held it to the cigarette. She took a quick puff before adding, "Of course, Simone learned very quickly. Still, she was always a kind lady, especially to the little people like me. No, there was only one person she hated."

Pressing her hands against the chair's threadbare arms, Jill leaned forward in her seat. "Who?"

"Lebrun." Wrinkling her nose in disdain, she paused to pick a fleck of tobacco off her lip. "Lebrun was the one she hated, more than a woman can hate an old lover, even."

"He was her lover?"

"I think not, Mademoiselle Fremont. To be honest with you, I do not know who he was. An actor or a muscle man perhaps, something like that. I am not sure. I only know that Mademoiselle Simone wished him dead."

"Dead?" The word tasted cold, heavy on Jill's tongue. "But why?"

Leaning toward the coffee table, Madame Simenon tapped her cigarette against the green glass ashtray. As she settled back on the settee, she gave Jill a weary smile. "Perhaps you should ask Mademoiselle Simone yourself."

"You know where she lives?" Although they were alone in the tiny apartment, Jill's voice dropped to a whisper.

"Of course. I still sew for her. After the accident, she did not wish to see many people. I think, truly, she did not wish many people to see *her*. She does not tell me everything, but we have remained friends."

Jill mustered the courage to ask the big question. "Do you think she would mind if I called on her? She may be able to help me sort out some things."

Madame Simenon's lined face contorted for a moment as a hacking cough tore through her frail body. She tapped her chest with her fist and then smiled. "You are a nice lady, Mademoiselle Fremont. I do not think our Simone would mind. But—" she held up a bony finger "—you must not tell other people how to find her. People like that silly photographer from New York."

"Sanford Fielding?" Jill smiled at the seamstress's blunt characterization of Fielding.

The little woman nodded as she pushed herself up from the settee. "They are all vultures, those kind. Waiting to pick the meat from the bones of the dying."

Leaving a trail of smoke in her path, Madame Simenon shuffled into the bedroom. When she returned a couple of minutes later, she carried a folded piece of paper in her hand. "Simone lives in an old farmhouse near St.-Germain-en-Laye. There is no address really, just a house in a meadow. Follow those directions and you will see it." Her bright eyes narrowed as she smiled. "You may tell her that we spoke."

Jill accepted the piece of paper as if it were a precious treasure. "Thank you, Madame Simenon. You've been very helpful. And very kind."

She had found Simone Nanka-Midou! The thought filled Jill with such elation that she could scarcely keep from running down the street to the Métro station. On the short train ride to Tante Yvonne's neighborhood, however, troublesome thoughts intervened to dampen the initial thrill of her discovery.

What was she going to do next? A mere four hours ago, she would have immediately said, "Tell the police." Now, however, she was not so sure. Although she was still convinced that Simone Nanka-Midou had played a significant role in the events of the past several days, she had been swayed by the seamstress's account of the model's tragic downfall. Without substantive proof of any wrongdoing on Simone's part, Jill was hesitant to violate the reclusive model's privacy.

She had reached one unshakable conclusion by the time she arrived at her aunt's apartment building: she would do nothing until she had discussed the matter with Dave.

Jill paused in the foyer to collect the day's mail. When she opened the box, a glossy color postcard fluttered to the floor. As she picked up the card, she smiled at the photo of an azure-blue sea dotted with white sailboats. Tante Yvonne had already gotten a light tan and was eating too much. The hotel was very peaceful, with employees who knew how to pamper an old lady. Jill grinned at her vivacious aunt's amusing—and totally inaccurate—characterization of herself.

She would be sure to send Tante Yvonne plenty of postcards when she finally got around to taking her own vacation. Her smile dimmed when she remembered someone else who would also be on her vacation mailing list. What would she write on a postcard to Dave? "Having a ball, wish you were here"? Is that where their relationship was leading, to a few clichés scribbled on the back of a retouched photograph? Waiting for the glass-encased elevator to descend, Jill could think of no logical alternative. After the postcards, there would be Christmas cards across the Atlantic, maybe an occasional letter. After a time, the letters would grow briefer, the intervals between them longer, and then...

Jill slammed the elevator's wrought-iron gate. Biting her lip, she stared down at the mail clutched in her hand. This was ridiculous, she told herself as she shuffled through the blurred envelopes. She had known him for less than two weeks, and what she did know indicated that their worlds were poles apart. By his own admission, Dave had let his marriage go down the tube when the *New York Times* beckoned. He was charming, funny and good-looking—had all the ingredients to attract a woman—but behind the lopsided grin and those irresistible gray eyes lurked the heart of a nomad. Jill trusted her instincts enough to believe that Dave cared about her, but he would always care about her from afar—from Beirut or Manila or wherever the winds of fortune took him.

Suddenly Jill blinked, yanked back to the present by the envelope she had just uncovered. Frowning, she held it up and scrutinized the address. "Mlle. Jill Fremont. 9 Rue Jacob." The plain white envelope looked as if it had been folded in three at some point; it bore a Paris postmark, but no return address.

An ominous feeling gripped Jill, one she could not brush off as she ripped open the envelope. Standing beneath the elevator's harsh light, she unfolded the white paper. A single sentence had been typed on the page, but it leaped out at her with a shock of recognition.

Prends garde de Lebrun!

There was no signature, but whoever had typed that cryptic note had warned her to beware of Lebrun.

Chapter Eleven

"Henri should have a rundown on the letter this evening." Dave squeezed her shoulder as he bent over the sofa and placed a plate on her knees. "You really should try to eat something."

Jill picked up the sandwich and nibbled one corner. She chewed slowly, taking far more time than the tiny bite warranted. Swallowing with some difficulty, she slid the plate onto the end table. "There's something about that letter that really gives me the creeps."

Dave gave a mirthless laugh. "I guess so. If an anonymous writer had warned me to beware of someone I'd never met, I'd be pretty shaken up, too."

Jill frowned at the uneaten sandwich. "I wasn't talking about the message itself. I mean, *that's* spooky enough. But everything about the letter is weird. Did you notice how it was addressed?"

Dave shrugged as he walked over to the living room's double windows. "Whoever sent it knows you're living with your aunt. It was addressed correctly."

Jill smiled grimly. "That all depends on who sent it. In France people normally place a comma between the number and the name of the street. Whoever typed the envelope left out that comma."

Dave parted the curtains to peer down at the street. "It could have been a typo."

"There was another mistake, in the message itself. The person who wrote it used the preposition *de* instead of *a*. It's like saying 'beware from' instead of 'beware of.'"

Letting the curtain fall back into place, Dave glanced over his shoulder at her. "Everyone makes grammatical errors. Even the French."

"Look, I know you think I'm being pedantic, but this is simply not the kind of error a native French speaker would make. It's a mistake . . . that Cici used to make."

Dave adjusted the curtains carefully. His broad-shouldered silhouette was outlined against the sheer panels, thrown into relief by the streetlight outside. "Cici couldn't have sent that letter, Jill," he said in a quiet voice. "It was postmarked just yesterday."

Jill grasped the arm of the sofa with both hands. "Maybe she wrote it earlier and asked someone to send it. That's possible. She gave Madame Petit that message for me, didn't she?"

"Yes," Dave agreed reluctantly. "But before we start jumping to conclusions, I think we ought to see what Henri's people turn up. Police technology can work miracles these days. They can trace everything from the acid content of the paper to the make of typewriter the note was written on."

"But will they be able to tell us who sent the letter?" Jill grabbed a throw pillow and clutched it protectively against her chest.

Dave abruptly seized a cord and lowered the blinds. Sliding his hands into the rear pockets of his jeans, he walked over to the sofa. "In time, maybe."

Frowning, Jill picked at one of the pillow's tassels. "And maybe not." Tossing the pillow onto the floor, she gestured angrily toward the folders stacked on the coffee table. "Look at all the information you've gathered. You could write a book on Chausson and his circle."

She flipped open one of the folders and spread the press clips across the table helter-skelter. "Here's a picture of Chausson when he was younger, playing polo with Prince Philip. Chausson accepting the Legion of Honor. Here's another one of him with Vernier and some model named Koko." She held the picture up and grimaced. "According to the caption, he and Vernier were engaged then. One big, happy family. Oh, I like this one. Cici and Vernier *and* Chausson on the Riviera. That must have been back when everyone was speaking."

Jill dropped the clips in a pile on the coffee table. "We know what Chausson and his pals eat for breakfast, yet we still don't have the faintest idea who's really behind the design theft or who committed those murders. Now we have another name to add to the list—Lebrun. There must be hundreds of Lebruns listed in the Paris phone book, and God knows how many who aren't. And this one might not even live in Paris."

"Henri has access to a whole network of police records," Dave insisted.

"Assuming that Lebrun has a record." Jill shook her head. "I don't know about you, but I'm beginning to lose faith in orderly investigative technique."

Dave rested a knee on the edge of the sofa. The cushion sank, tilting Jill toward him. "I'm sorry," she murmured. She could feel his hand gently lift her hair and then settle on the back of her neck.

"Why? You've been through so much. Most people in your place would have been on the first plane back to Jacksonville last week." His fingers massaged the base of her neck, setting a tingle running through the stiff muscles. Sinking onto the sofa, Dave continued to ply her neck while his free arm pulled her into its crook.

Jill breathed deeply, letting the long sigh bear away some of her tension. The even rise and fall of his chest felt reassuring beneath her cheek, and she snuggled more deeply into his embrace. "Lebrun is the *L* in Cici's calendar. I'm as sure of it as if I'd written it myself. But who *is* Lebrun?" With the substantial, muscular arm coiled around her, she felt secure enough to utter the dreaded question.

Dave's fingers ceased their caressing for a moment. "Someone we're probably not going to like very much, if we ever meet him." He slipped his hand under her chin and lifted her face. "You know, that was a pretty damned foolish thing you did this afternoon, going to that old lady's apartment by yourself."

Jill pursed her lips. "I'm a grown woman, Dave. I don't need a bodyguard to protect me from an eighty-year-old seamstress."

"It could have been a setup," Dave reminded her, giving her chin a light chuck.

"But it wasn't." She squirmed, straightening herself slightly. "And if I hadn't talked with her, this message about Lebrun would have made even less sense."

"You did find Simone. I expect Henri will be paying a call on her very soon."

"Yeah." Jill twisted around and leaned back against his comfortable bulk.

"'Yeah.'" Dave mimicked her dubious tone. "After scouring Paris for a lead on Simone Nanka-Midou, is that all you can say?"

Jill locked her hands over his arms, holding them securely around her waist. "I can't help but feel ambivalent about her now, Dave. According to Madame Simenon, she's been the victim of a lot of malicious gossip. Maybe she didn't set Cici up after all. Madame Simenon asked me not to reveal Simone's whereabouts to anyone, and now I've told the police."

"You had to tell them, Jill. Simone may have been one of the last people to see Madame Petit alive. She may be able to shed some light on this Lebrun character. Regardless of how sympathetic Madame Simenon made her appear, her name has cropped up too often in this case for you to grant her the luxury of holing up in her farmhouse, undisturbed."

"You're right," Jill conceded. "I just wish I could have gotten to her first and explained the circumstances."

Dave settled his chin on her shoulder. "I have a couple of interviews in the morning, but we could still drive out to Simone's home and have a talk with her in the afternoon. You might feel a little less in the dark about this Lebrun if you could ask her about him personally. Who knows? She may be willing to share some details with us that she's withheld from Henri."

Jill cut her eyes up at him. "Just a minute ago, you were arguing in favor of leaving everything to the miracles of police technology."

"How could I do that when you keep digging up such tantalizing clues?" He ruffled her bangs playfully—in an effort to distract her, Jill could tell. "You know, if you keep up the good work, you might get promoted from interpreter to senior investigator.''

"If you keep up the good work, you might even learn to speak French someday," Jill retorted. But as she settled back against his chest, she hoped that day did not come too soon.

"HOW CAN YOU have allowed it to come to this?" Her voice was choked with rage. Her fingers tightened, nails digging into the flesh of her palms, and for a moment she imagined how it would feel to close her hands around his throat and squeeze the life from his despicable body.

"Control yourself." He kept his back to her, took his time with the decanter of brandy. When he turned, he offered her a glass along with an insolent smile. "Drink this. It will calm you down."

Her hand shot out and knocked the glass from his grip. It shattered into a spray of glistening shards on the polished floor. "How can I be calm with this teacher prowling behind my back? And do not tell me that Yves will take care of her. I am sick of hearing that, sick of waiting while he does nothing!"

"Nothing, you say?" He raised an eyebrow, admonishing her with his expressionless eyes. "Perhaps you would have preferred to handle Chausson's detective and the housekeeper yourself?" He paused, and she could tell he was listening to her labored breathing. "No, I think not."

"Listen to me." Her voice was so hoarse that she could almost imagine she was listening to someone else speak. "We cannot afford to wait any longer. The teacher has learned Madison's secrets, and now she suspects us.''

"That's absurd," he began, but she cut him off.

"Do not deny what I know in my heart. I swear to you, it is only a matter of time before she arrives at my door, demanding payment for her silence." Her eyes followed him, stalking his languid movements as he returned to the credenza.

"Jill Fremont will remain silent. That I promise you." He held the glass up to the light and watched the trickle of brandy welling inside it. "But we will not have to pay her to do so."

THE DRIVE to St.-Germain-en-Laye was a pleasant one, made more so by the mild, sunny weather. Watching the countryside passing outside the car window, Jill was struck by the dazzling variety in the shades of green. In places, the late afternoon sun had burnished the meadows to a rich gold hue, while the moss clinging to the ancient trees dimmed to a near black. It was a landscape straight out of an Impressionist painting, almost beautiful enough to make her forget the purpose of their journey.

"We passed the château over a half hour ago, and I'm still looking for an unpaved side road. I wish Madame Simenon had been a little more specific."

Jill took her eyes off the road for a split second to see Dave frowning over the seamstress's nearly illegible directions. "Let's drive a few more kilometers, and then backtrack," she suggested.

Turned toward the window, Dave shook his head. "Pull over right here and turn around. We just passed the thing."

Jill eased the Peugeot onto the shoulder and then pulled into the opposite lane. As she turned onto the overgrown dirt lane, she marveled that Dave had noticed it at all. To the casual driver, the mouth of the road was almost completely concealed behind a screen of vines and underbrush.

"Simone certainly likes her privacy," Dave remarked dryly.

"And from the looks of this road, no one ever disturbs it." Jill glanced up at the overhanging trees that seemed to close over the car like a gradually narrowing tunnel. The encroaching forest gave her the sense of being swallowed, and she was relieved when the trees began to thin, opening onto a field.

True to Madame Simenon's prediction, the house stood in the middle of the meadow. It was a rambling two-story structure with a thatched roof that jutted over the half-timber facade like a bushy shock of hair. A barn and various smaller outbuildings were scattered around the house. Over the crumbling stone wall flanking one side of the driveway, Jill could see a vegetable garden and a few stunted apple trees.

She angled the car around a boarded-up well and then braked. For a moment, Jill and Dave sat in the car, silently regarding the old house. Although no signs of life were visible behind the closed doors and drawn curtains, they both sensed that their arrival had not gone unnoticed.

"At least she doesn't have a pack of snarling guard dogs," Dave remarked as he opened the car door.

Jill climbed out of the Peugeot and slammed the door, setting off an angry volley of barking from the house. She gave Dave an ironic glance over her shoulder as they picked their way through the muddy yard to the house. The barking grew louder and more furious, reaching a crescendo when Dave rapped the iron knocker against the door.

The dog was coming closer. On the other side of the door, Jill could hear its sharp claws clicking against the stone floor, its paws sliding frantically in their eagerness to reach the intruders. The barking had altered to a gasping series of yelps, punctuated by rumbling growls that vibrated through the door. When the door opened a crack, she stepped back, expecting a bare-fanged monster to lunge for them.

"Silence, Hercule!" The voice was soft, but commanding, with the vaguest hint of an accent.

The door opened wider, revealing the speaker and her panting mastiff. *So this is Simone,* Jill thought. She was exceptionally tall with long graceful hands and the elegant neck about which Sanford Fielding had raved. Although she was dressed in a loose-fitting white caftan that swept the floor, her willow-slim figure was apparent beneath the soft fabric. Her black hair was slicked back from her forehead into a severe knot, giving her face the royal cast of an Ashanti princess. Even without makeup, her strong cheekbones and heavily lidded eyes were startling.

"What do you want?" She posed the question abruptly. Sensing his mistress's irritation, Hercule bared his teeth menacingly.

Jill quickly introduced herself and Dave, taking care not to mention that he was a reporter. There was something in Simone's unfriendly dark eyes—not to mention those of her salivating dog—that prompted Jill to launch into a rapid explanation of their visit. "Since you had phoned Madame Petit prior to her disappearance, I thought you might be able to tell me..." Jill was saying when Simone interrupted.

"Mademoiselle Fremont, I can tell you nothing. I contacted Madame Petit to offer my condolences. I suggested that she might want to go away for a while, to recover from the strain. That is all.'' The dark eyes did not flinch.

"The *concierge* said Madame Petit was very upset when she left,'' Jill said evenly, not taking her eyes off Simone's.

"That does not surprise me. She was very fond of Cici Madison and mourned her death deeply.''

Jill frowned slightly, looking for a chink in the flinty gaze. "Do you have any idea what Madame Petit meant when she phoned to warn me of danger?''

The thin shoulders shrugged beneath the caftan. "The world is full of dangers, Mademoiselle Fremont.''

"Like Lebrun?'' Jill shot back.

The regal neck stiffened. "I do not know what you mean.''

"I think you do, Mademoiselle Nanka-Midou,'' Jill said quietly. "Who is he?''

Simone's perfectly sculpted jaw was set, and she edged the door slightly. "I will not discuss Lebrun.''

"Please,'' Jill began. She took a step forward, but Hercule's murderously curling lip stopped her in her tracks.

"I have answered enough questions already, Mademoiselle Fremont. With the police one cannot say no. You are not the police. I do not wish to be disturbed.'' Before Jill could respond, Simone pushed the door firmly shut.

Jill stared at the closed door for a moment before turning to Dave. "She knows something, Dave. I'm sure of it. If only I could have persuaded her to talk!''

Dave looped his arm around her shoulders and lead her toward the parked car. "You couldn't very well force your way into the woman's house and threaten her. Maybe Henri had better luck.''

"I hope so." Jill tried to mask the dejection creeping into her voice. Although she knew her expectations had been unrealistic, she had hoped, in the back of her mind, that Simone Nanka-Midou would prove to be a source of vital information. The former model's stony resistance had left her feeling dispirited and out of sorts—and completely at the mercy of the faceless Lebrun.

Dave, bless him, seemed bent on cajoling her into a brighter mood. "Tell you what. When we get back to Paris, why don't we go out and have a real meal, soup to nuts? We might as well salvage something from the day."

Jill managed a smile. "That sounds like a good idea."

Freeing her shoulders, Dave elbowed her gently. "Hey, I'll even drive. Gimme the keys."

Jill halted on the stone walkway to dig her keys out of her purse. As she handed them to Dave, she chanced to glance over his shoulder at the farmhouse. What she saw left her frozen in her tracks. The curtain of an upstairs window was parted to reveal a man peering down at them. The moment she spotted him, he let the curtain fall back into place. But that brief glimpse had been enough for Jill to recognize the brooding gypsy face.

"Is something wrong?" Dave frowned at her and started to turn, but Jill quickly grabbed his arm.

"Let's get going," she said, tugging him toward the car. "I'm starved, aren't you?"

"Well, no, not really." Dave hesitated, taking his time getting into the car. "Are you sure you're okay?"

Jill heaved an exasperated sigh. "Yes, I'm fine. Now let's get *out* of here."

Only when Dave had wheeled the car onto the dirt road and the farmhouse had disappeared from sight did she poke his arm eagerly. "I saw him!"

Dave's brows knit in the rearview mirror; he shot a doubtful glance at her and then braked. "Saw who?"

Jill gestured impatiently toward the dash. "Don't stop here! He may come after us." She scooted around in the seat to check the road behind them.

Dave reluctantly shifted the Peugeot into gear. "Will someone please just tell me what the hell's going on?"

Jill smacked the back of the seat triumphantly. "I saw a man peeping out of Simone's upstairs window. He was the same man I saw in the restaurant in Chevreuse the night of the accident. Cici got very agitated when she spotted someone in the restaurant, and now I understand why. He could very well be Lebrun."

"Hold on a minute. I thought Madame Simenon said Simone hated Lebrun. If that's the case, what's he doing in her house?"

Jill shook her head impatiently. "Madame Simenon didn't claim to have all the facts, but she alluded to their having been lovers at one point. Didn't you think Simone got awfully defensive when I asked her about Lebrun?"

"Well, yes."

Jill rapped the dashboard with her knuckles. "Whatever the case, I recognized that man from the restaurant. His showing up in Simone's house two weeks later simply can't be a coincidence."

Dave let out a low whistle. He braked the car at the end of the dirt road and then swerved out into the road. "Henri's going to go through the floor when he hears this one."

"Maybe we should stop somewhere and call him," Jill suggested.

Dave glanced up at the darkening sky. "It's getting pretty late. Rather than waste time trying to find a pay phone out here in the wilderness, I think we should just concentrate on getting back to Paris as quickly as possible."

"I suppose you're right." Jill folded her arms across her chest and forced herself to ease back against the seat. "It's just so hard to be patient when you know a murderer is on the loose. You know, Dave—" she hesitated, chafing her arms lightly "—something else just occurred to me. Remember after the accident how we couldn't agree on what happened in the water? I thought I had grabbed your arm, but you didn't remember that happening."

She watched his reflected image nod in the windshield. "Well, maybe I did grab a man's arm—only it wasn't yours. If this man I recognized is someone Cici had reason to fear, is it so farfetched to think that he could have forced his way into her car that night, overpowered her and engineered the wreck to look like an accident?"

"You're suggesting she was murdered?" When Jill nodded, he let out a long breath. "Why?"

"Maybe she wanted out of the sordid counterfeiting business."

"At this point, nothing would surprise me." Suddenly Dave frowned at the rearview mirror's bright reflection. "For God's sake, man, dim those things!"

Jill squirmed around in the seat and squinted at the approaching lights. She could see now that a truck, not a car, was bearing down on them. She sucked in her breath as the headlights loomed directly behind them.

"This is dangerous. Why don't you slow down and let this idiot pass?"

"Good idea. I'm in no mood to duel with a drunk driver." Dave eased off the gas and pulled toward the shoulder.

The truck slackened its speed and made no effort to pull around them.

"Come on!" Dave irritably rolled down the window and motioned the truck around them.

They both started when the Peugeot lurched unexpectedly.

"He bumped us!" Jill exclaimed, now thoroughly alarmed. She twisted around in the seat again just in time to see the burning lights sink beneath the bumper. "Look out!" Her neck popped as the truck rammed their car once more, this time with noticeably more force.

Dave's face was grim as he clamped both hands on the wheel. "Is your seat belt fastened?"

Jill commanded her voice to remain steady, with mixed success. "Yes."

"Okay, then hang on." Dave pressed the gas, and the Peugeot surged forward.

Jill drew a deep breath as the truck's lights receded. Her stomach sank when the piercing beacons began to gain on them once more.

"Don't worry. There's a hill coming up. That'll give us an advantage," Dave tried to reassure her through tight lips.

True to his prediction, the menacing headlights gradually faded into the background as the Peugeot soared ahead on the incline. Through the open window, they could hear the heavy vehicle's gears grinding, but the truck was no match for the lighter car.

"We need to find a cop." Jill's eyes scanned the blank darkness in vain.

"Tell me. Where are they when you need 'em?" Dave straightened his leg, anchoring the gas pedal to the floor.

As the headlights appeared over the crest of the hill behind them, Jill bit her lip. "Do you think we can outrun him?" Hands braced against the seat, she glanced at the lighted speedometer dial.

"I'm sure as hell going to try."

She could hear the throb of the powerful engine picking up speed as it cleared the hilltop. The bright lights sliced through the gloom like lasers. Suddenly the lights cut to the side.

"Thank heaven, he's decided to pass us." Over the back of the seat, Jill watched the truck pulling up on their left.

Her relief was short-lived. As soon as the truck had overtaken the Peugeot, it swerved, smashing into the side of the smaller vehicle. Jill's head was slammed against the door as the car careered onto the shoulder. She gasped, not trusting herself to look down into the chasm gaping below the shoulder's right edge.

Dave held the wheel steady, easing off the gas enough to keep the car from spinning out of control. He was gaining momentum, preparing to pull onto the highway again. But before he could edge the Peugeot onto the road, the truck sideswiped them again.

There was a crash, then the agonized squeal of tires ripped across rough tarmac. Jill heard her own scream tear through the night air as the car flipped over and rolled down the embankment.

Chapter Twelve

His body was being slung through a huge centrifuge, one that scattered head and limbs and torso in a dozen different directions. Then came the bone-jolting impact, the sound of steel being crushed, of glass reduced to countless atoms. The stillness that followed was as black as the starless night.

Pinned against the mangled door, Dave listened to his own ragged breathing and told himself that he was still alive. But what about Jill? He tore frantically at the restraining harness, trying to free himself so he could reach her. She was lying crumpled against the opposite door; her head hung limply to one side and her eyes were closed.

For some reason, his left arm refused to work, leaving his hand to paw helplessly at the harness catch. With great effort, he wrenched his trapped body enough to reach the catch with his good hand.

"Jill?" Dave's hand trembled as it touched her forehead. When she did not answer, he ran his palm beneath her nose. A faint puff of warm air brushed his skin. "Oh, God, Jill!" Overwhelmed with relief, he let his head sag against her cheek.

A familiar sharp smell brought him bolt upright. Gasoline! The tank must have ruptured in the crash. Forcing his arm behind Jill's back, he groped for the harness catch and ripped it open. Her head lolled back, and Dave caught it with his enfeebled arm. A numbing pain shot up to his shoulder, but he ignored it as he fought to pull her along the seat.

Jill's face was contorted; a fitful moan escaped her lips. He had no idea how badly she had been injured, but he was certain of one thing: another minute or two in that car and it wouldn't matter.

Letting her rest on the seat for a moment, Dave pressed his shoulder against the door and succeeded in budging the misshapen steel panel a scant inch. The thing was wedged shut, held in place by the massive tree that had stopped the car's tumbling descent. His only hope was to crawl through the open window.

When he thrust his upper body through the narrow opening, a savage vise closed around his battered ribs. Cold sweat washed over him, along with a blackness that filled his head, threatening to overpower him. Inching his way free, Dave fought to hang on to his consciousness. He landed clumsily, setting off a fresh stab of pain in his arm.

Dave staggered to his feet and reached through the window for Jill. She was frowning now, trying to focus her half-closed eyes. "Where...Dave...?" Her hands fumbled ineffectually, trying to grasp his arms.

"Come on, kid. You can make it," he coaxed her. He gripped her shoulders with his functioning arm and edged her over the gearbox. "Good!" Jill was on her knees, struggling to climb through the window. As soon as her shoulders had breached the opening, he staggered back, pulling her with him.

He got her to her feet, but her wobbly legs threatened to collapse beneath her. Almost lifting her off the
ground, Dave dragged Jill away from the wreck. The
shock of the explosion sent them both sprawling into
the underbrush.

Dave rolled onto his throbbing side and held Jill close
to him. He could feel the fierce heat against his face as
soaring flames engulfed the Peugeot. Jill stirred, pulling her head from the protective curve of his arm. She
squinted and lifted a hand to shield her eyes from the
conflagration's blistering light.

Suddenly Jill twisted to face him. She touched his
brow and drew back, grimacing at the dark blood on
her fingers. "You're hurt! Oh, Dave!"

Dave abruptly clapped his hand over her mouth,
holding her flat against the earth with his own weight.
He felt her stiffen as she too saw the source of his alarm.
Through the screen of thick bushes, his eyes followed
the man warily circling the wreckage.

He was dressed in black clothes and a knit ski helmet
that concealed most of his face. His dark figure moved
like a featureless shadow against the blazing background. Dave could tell he wanted a closer look at the
front seat of the car, but the violent flames held him at
bay. Now he had stopped near their hiding place, close
enough for Dave to see the pistol he held cocked in his
right hand.

The boots stepped carefully, backing toward them.
Another three, maybe four paces, and the muddy heels
would graze Jill's arm. Dave's body was taut, coiled like
a spring. His eyes traveled from the boots to the gun as
he weighed his options.

The man took another backward step. Dave held his
breath, poised for action. He felt Jill cringe as a shaft

of light suddenly penetrated the bushes, cutting across their crouched bodies. When the light struck the heavy boots, they stopped in their tracks.

"Hallo?" The flashlight beam skittered back across Jill and Dave's hiding place.

The boots were in motion now, thrashing through the bush with the abandon of a man in full flight. Still holding Jill to the ground, Dave looked up to see the darkly clad figure dash up the hill to the road. He recognized the growl of the truck's engine as it rumbled to life. Easing up onto his knees, he could just glimpse the taillights as the big vehicle sped away.

The flashlight beam was zigzagging through the darkness now, unsure of where it should focus. When Dave stood, however, it landed squarely on his face. Blocking the light with one hand, he blinked. *"Un accident! La femme est blessee!"* He stooped over Jill, but she was already weaving to her feet. "The lady is hurt," he repeated as the flashlight advanced on them.

The man holding the flashlight channeled the beam on Jill and gasped, *"Mon Dieu!"*

"I'm okay," she assured him in a shaky voice. "But he needs immediate medical attention. He's bleeding." She pointed to Dave's head.

The flashlight slashed across Dave's forehead and then recoiled. "Cybele! Come quickly!" the man cried over his shoulder. When Dave took a step forward, the flashlight anchored its beam on his chest. "Do not move, *monsieur*!" the man cautioned him nervously. "It will only make your injuries worse!"

"Look, I can walk. I've just banged up my arm and a few ribs. My head's fine." He gestured with his good hand, winning a look of even greater alarm from the man.

Fortunately the man's wife proved to be less cautious than her husband. When she reached the scene, her sharp eyes appraised the situation in a glance.

"We must take them to a hospital," she announced. "By the time we summon the police he will only have lost more blood."

"We do need to call the police," Dave reminded them. "That fellow driving the truck forced us off the road."

With promises that the police would be summoned from the nearest telephone, the couple, who had now introduced themselves as Monsieur and Madame Clary, helped Jill and Dave stumble up the hill to their car. Two children, a boy of about eleven and a girl who was slightly younger, obediently bailed into the rear of the Renault wagon to make room. From behind the seat, they regarded the battered passengers with wide-eyed curiosity.

"What a vile thing to do!" Madame Clary commiserated from the front seat. She glanced back at Jill and Dave and shook her head in dismay.

"Did you happen to get his license plate number?" Jill asked hopefully.

The Clarys exchanged rueful looks.

"I am afraid not, Mademoiselle Fremont," Monsieur Clary apologized. "When we saw the burning car from the road, we had no idea that this man had deliberately caused the wreck."

"No, you wouldn't expect that." The Clary family was so obviously distressed over the accident, Dave felt obligated to reassure them. "I don't suppose you got a very good look at him."

Both Clarys shook their heads.

"He was wearing dark clothes," Madame Clary offered helpfully.

Dave sank back against the seat. The pain in his arm was constant now, a dull, numbing ache that filled the entire limb. His whole body felt bruised, pummeled into submission by the jarring crash and the latest turn of events.

Jill found his free hand lying on the dark back seat and clasped it tightly. "We know who he is, Dave," she whispered. "The police will get him." Her face was partially concealed by shadow, but what he could see looked worn, ravaged.

Squeezing her hand with what strength remained in him, Dave took comfort from her quiet assertion. Now more than ever, he shared Jill's conviction that the man watching them from Simone Nanka-Midou's window was dangerous, and that he had tried to kill them. That he had almost succeeded was something Dave did not want to think about right now.

When they reached the hospital, the Clarys insisted on escorting Jill and Dave into the emergency room. The couple seemed satisfied when a platoon of white-uniformed medics took over and whisked the accident victims into examining rooms.

Common sense told Dave that he needed to submit to the X rays and the inevitable cast that followed, but he hated it nonetheless. Even more, he resented being separated from Jill, resented submitting to the routine questioning of the bored policeman whom the Clarys had summoned.

If it took the last shred of energy he possessed, he was going to find a way to call Henri. With this thought in mind, Dave closed his eyes as soon as the nurse had administered a painkiller. As soon as her brisk steps had petered out at the far end of the ward, however, he struggled to sit up. He rummaged in the drawer where they had stowed his wallet until he found a *jeton*. Then he swung his legs over the side of the bed. The moment his feet touched the floor, he felt a massive weight on his shoulders, threatening to buckle his knees under him.

Groping his way along the wall, Dave staggered down the dark corridor. Somewhere behind him, he could hear a nurse's startled voice call after him, but he didn't stop until he reached the pay-phone nook.

"Dessenier." When Henri answered he sounded groggy and very far away.

"Henri, it's Dave. I'm in the hospital. Some guy..." He choked on a wave of nausea. Cold sweat trickled down his face, and he leaned against the cold wall. "Some guy tried to run us off the road and kill us." He was vaguely aware of his immobilized arm sweeping air, of the receiver clattering off into space, as he collapsed in a heap on the floor.

"THANK YOU for rescuing us this morning." Nestling the large cup of *café au lait* in her hands, Jill smiled at Henri. Her face had regained much of its rosy cast, and her eyes were clear and lively. Except for a purple lump bulging beneath one side of her bangs, she looked amazingly fit.

Henri's blue eyes narrowed, following the curling ribbon of smoke wafting in front of them like a serpent's ghost. His nostrils flared as he inhaled deeply. "After David phoned me in the wee hours, I wondered if you would both survive until morning. Perhaps you should eat more." He gestured toward the empty plates that were pushed to one side of the small table.

Dave glanced around the café where the three of them had arranged to meet that afternoon. "Give me a break, Henri. You know damned well I didn't call you last night to whine about the crummy hospital food and that idiotic gown they made me wear."

"I know, my friend, I know." Henri's words emerged in puffs of blue smoke, followed by a jaded laugh.

"Did you pick up Simone's friend?" Dave frowned and irritably pulled at the Velcro strap securing his arm sling.

Henri's chuckle dissolved into a hacking cough. "No."

"Why not?" Dave and Jill demanded, almost in unison.

Henri stubbed out one Gauloise before shaking another one out of its pack. "I do not have enough evidence to charge anyone with anything."

"You don't?" Jill's voice fell, along with her face. She looked so downcast, Dave wanted to take her in his arms and comfort her. The thought that he had only one good arm with which to do it only added to his frustration.

"No." Henri's roughly sculpted lips pulled to one side, and he shook his head. He tamped the cigarette against the scarred table before lighting it. "After I spoke with you this morning, we paid another visit to Simone Nanka-Midou's farm. We questioned her and the man. His name is not Lebrun but Serge Bastide—a movie extra and professional stuntman. As far as we can tell, he has never used an assumed name, nor has he ever been involved in criminal activity. Except for a few traffic violations, his record is as clean—how do you put it—as a whistle? Bastide swore that he had not left the place in the past twenty-four hours, and Simone

corroborated his story. Based on the tire tracks we examined in the dirt road, I believe them.''

"Maybe he parked the truck somewhere else and
walked to and from the farmhouse." Jill's desperate
tone suggested she was grasping at straws.

Henri fanned the cloud of pungent smoke envelop-
ing their table. "He did not walk fifty kilometers, Mademoiselle Fremont. The truck that caused your
accident has been located, and that is how far it was
abandoned from St.-Germain-en-Laye. It had been
stolen from its rightful owner the very evening of the
accident," he added, anticipating their next question.

Dave twisted in his chair, trying to angle the cumbersome arm cast out of the way. "Okay. We know that the
guy living with Simone isn't Lebrun. And maybe he isn't
the bastard who forced us off the road. But that still
doesn't explain the warning Jill received."

Henri ground the cigarette into the black plastic ashtray. "There are many Lebruns with the sort of back-
grounds that make them worthy of investigation."

"Any of 'em look particularly interesting?" Dave
winced as he hitched his shoulder to lean across the table.

Henri shrugged and flipped open the pack of Gauloises. "A few."

Dave regarded the lean, swarthy man sitting across
the table from him. Henri knew more than he was telling, a lot more. "Look, pal, this isn't just a story I want
to impress my editor with anymore. Twice someone has
tried to warn Jill. People are getting strangled and
pushed in front of trains. And last night some maniac
tried to kill us. Right now, I couldn't give a damn about
all those phony handbags and watchbands, but I do care
very much about her life and mine. Put yourself in my

place, Henri. You'd want to know who was after your neck."

Henri lit the cigarette carefully, watching Dave out of the corner of his eye. When the bright ember flared, he shook the match before tossing it aside. "If I knew who was driving that truck last night, I would do more than tell you, *mon ami*. I would arrest him. However, I do not know."

"But you have an idea?" Dave gave the table an angry rap with his good hand.

Henri's long fingers meshed over the ashtray, and he thoughtfully twisted it to one side. "There are many possibilities. My job is to pursue all of them. In the course of an investigation, one must take precautions that nothing is done that might hamper a successful arrest. You understand what I am saying, I think."

Dave shook his head impatiently. "You don't have to talk to me like a cop, Henri. We've known each other a long time. You can trust me not to blow the cover off your investigation." His hand clenched and then opened in frustration. "I want to know who this guy is."

"So do I," Henri shot back. Suddenly he pushed the ashtray aside and looked at Dave. "I know you do not like to take advice, my friend, but I will give you some anyway. Go home and write your story. There are enough fake Gucci bags and Hermes scarves to keep your readers happy. Forget about Chausson."

Dave kept his eyes trained directly on Henri. "If I didn't know you better, I'd think you were telling me to back off."

Henri straightened his lapels as he rose. "Be careful, Dave," he said in a deceptively even voice. He counted out a few bills and dropped them beside the ashtray.

Tucking his wallet into his breast pocket, he looked down at Dave. "If you wait to write your story about Chausson, you may be waiting a very long time. *Au revoir.*" He smiled briefly at Jill before turning and walking out of the café.

Jill had been watching the exchange in silence, but now that they were alone, she placed a hand on Dave's wrist. "He's not going to help us anymore, Dave. We're on our own."

Dave frowned at the small hand clasping his sleeve. "Maybe he's right, Jill. Maybe we should just leave it to the police. They're still keeping an eye on your apartment, you know. That should make you feel pretty safe."

"Watching the apartment didn't keep that man from crowding us off the road last night." Her hand tightened its hold. "He had a gun, Dave, and he intended to use it."

Dave pulled his hand free and ran it through his hair. "Damn Henri!" Jill's insistent gaze was making him uncomfortable, compounding his own growing sense of helplessness. "I just don't know what we can do," he admitted reluctantly.

"Go back and talk with Simone," Jill said without hesitation. "She has to open her door sometime. I'd be willing to stand on her porch until the thing rots out from under me, if that's what it takes to find out who Lebrun is."

Looking into her small, determined face, Dave had no doubt that she meant what she said. Anyone who thought a near-fatal accident would be enough to dissuade Jill Fremont was dead wrong. She had courage—perhaps too much for her own good. As much as he shared her urge to tackle matters head-on, he felt obligated to steer her out of harm's way.

"Let's suppose Simone will talk about Lebrun. Then what?" Dave asked quietly. When she said nothing, he leaned back in his chair. "I think we should sit tight and give Henri a chance to pull things together."

She let him wait several moments before she finally nodded. "All right." But when she looked at him, Dave had the uncomfortable feeling that she was disappointed with him.

SHE WAS UNACCUSTOMED to deceiving people, and the practice didn't sit well with her—not that Jill had actually lied to anyone. When she had phoned her aunt long-distance to break the bad news about her car, she had briefly described the accident. Poor Tante Yvonne had been so relieved to hear that her niece had escaped serious injury, Jill had seen no point in mentioning the gun or the frightening warning about Lebrun.

Fooling Dave would have been harder. He was a born skeptic and seemed to have an uncanny knack for reading her thoughts, to boot. For that reason, Jill thought it best to avoid seeing him until she had carried out her plan. The following morning when he called, she told him she had some work to catch up on and quickly concluded the conversation. Dave seemed taken aback by her abruptness. He would have been even more appalled if he had seen her pick up a rental car later and set out in the direction of St.-Germain-en-Laye.

Dave had not abandoned the chase, she told herself during the lonely drive, not by a long shot. All of his talk about leaving things to the police had been strictly for her benefit. Although she could appreciate his concern for her, she had no intention of sitting on the sidelines and waiting for Lebrun to strike again. If Dave refused to include her in his investigation, he gave her no choice but to act on her own.

In spite of her determination, she felt a faint tremor of uneasiness when she turned onto the rutted dirt road leading to Simone's farmhouse. Somehow the place had seemed less isolated the last time she had been there; the late afternoon sun had dispelled some of the forest's oppressive gloom, and Dave had been sitting beside her. Still, there was no turning back now—literally. The road was so narrow, Simone's farmyard was the first place that afforded enough room to turn the car.

At least she would be spared the ordeal of hammering on Simone's door and hoping for a response. When Jill turned into the driveway, she immediately spotted the former model, bent over some low plants in her garden patch. At the sound of the car's engine, she straightened herself. Her eyes followed the white rental car as it pulled into the yard and then braked.

Jill hesitated only long enough to assure herself that the ill-tempered Hercule was not around before climbing out of the car. "*Bonjour*, Mademoiselle Nanka-Midou." Now that she was here, she might as well take a direct approach.

Simone met her at the garden gate. Today she had abandoned her elegant caftan in favor of jeans and an oversize cotton sweater, but her bearing was still that of a queen or a goddess. "I told you I did not wish to be disturbed, Mademoiselle Fremont." Her beautiful face was as hard as the wall's gray stones.

"And I don't wish to disturb you," Jill replied. "But someone tried to kill me last night, and I think you're the only person who can help me find out who he was."

It was such a dramatic statement, Jill was not sure how Simone would react. The limpid dark eyes studied her for a moment, widening slightly when they noticed the bruise on Jill's forehead. Simone's full lips parted and then closed; the slim hand clasping the basket of fresh beans flexed nervously. She seemed gripped by hesitation, unable to decide what she should do. "You were seriously injured?"

"No, but I could have been." For the first time, Jill recognized a trace of empathy in the dark eyes. Who more than Simone Nanka-Midou could appreciate the chilling finality of a near-fatal automobile crash? "I need to know about Lebrun," she pleaded in a hushed whisper.

Simone looked down at her basket and sighed. "Let us go inside the house," she said at length. She unlatched the gate and then beckoned for Jill to follow her.

As Simone led the way up the mossy stone path, she walked with an odd, rolling gate, as if the flimsy basket she carried were too heavy for her. Jill realized with a start that the limp must surely be the result of the tragic accident that had ended the model's career.

Simone deposited the basket by the door and then swung it open for Jill. Hercule was dozing by the empty fireplace, but he only snuffled drowsily when the two women entered. Apparently the big mastiff sensed that Jill's presence was sanctioned by his mistress, at least for today.

Simone seated herself in a fan-back chair next to the hearth. She smoothed the legs of her muddy jeans and waited for Jill to sit. "I will discuss Lebrun, Mademoiselle Fremont." She spoke slowly and deliberately. "But first you must tell me what you know of him."

"Very little. But someone has warned me to beware of him." Jill folded her hands in her lap and recounted the events leading up to the automobile crash. "I think Lebrun was the man who forced us off the road and then looked for us with a gun," she concluded.

Simone listened without comment, her face a solemn, unmoving mask. "And you think he committed these other murders? Madame Petit and the detective?"

"Yes, I do. I don't have any proof, but I'm almost certain Madame Petit had him in mind when she phoned to warn me. Mademoiselle Nanka-Midou, I didn't know Cici Madison as well as you did, but I can't believe she would steal from Chausson of her own accord. I think someone tricked her, forced her, did *something* to make her take designs. And I think Lebrun is connected with those people."

The mastiff stirred and rested its ponderous head on Simone's foot. She absently stroked its ears as she went on. "Lebrun is capable of such things. I first met him at a party in New York, actually. I was in town for my first magazine assignments. Up until then I had only done runway work in Paris. I was Fielding's big discovery that year. My face was on every cover—*Vogue, Bazaar,* all of them." A bitter smile flickered on her lips and disappeared just as quickly. "But that is of no concern to us now. Lebrun was living in the United States at the time. He was a boxer—not a very good one, I think—but he wanted to get into movies. Or so he said. He is a coarse man, and I never liked him, but he came to my apartment a few times, always with other people. Twice he asked me to deliver packages to a friend in Paris, and I agreed, but only twice."

She abruptly withdrew her hand from the dog's head and clasped it tightly on her knees. "When I saw him later in Paris, I was surprised. He was very familiar, said he wanted to make a deal with me. He asked me to steal designs from Chausson, Mademoiselle Fremont. I refused, of course. Then he threatened me. He said I had smuggled drugs for him, in the packages I had carried from New York. He told me that I was already implicated in the eyes of the police, and that things would not go well for me if I turned to them."

"What did you do?" Jill asked. As she waited for Simone to answer, she listened to the monotonous rhythm of the mantel clock's pendulum.

Simone drew herself up in the chair and let out a deep breath. "I went to the police. Lebrun was arrested. There was a trial, but in the end they could prove nothing, and he was acquitted." She paused to examine her long hands knotted in her lap. "The accident occurred several months later. Brake failure, they called it. The brakes of a new Mercedes do not fail, Mademoiselle Fremont."

"Surely there was some kind of investigation."

"The results were inconclusive." When Simone looked up, her face seemed to have aged beyond its years. "I will go to my grave knowing that Lebrun damaged those brakes, but I will never be able to prove it. He is a dangerous man, Mademoiselle Fremont."

Coming in the wake of Jill's own accident, the shock of Simone's story was all the more immediate. For a moment, she could only stare at the empty fireplace grate and try to digest the troubling information. "I know the police have questioned you in connection with my accident. Did you tell them all this?"

Simone's short nose flared in contempt. "With Lebrun, the police are useless. I have seen that already."

Jill could offer no argument to counter Simone's harsh assertion. Instead she decided to share a disturbing thought that had been building in her own mind. "Do you think Lebrun could have engineered Cici Madison's accident? Maybe she was trying to extricate herself from his plot, and he decided to punish her. I mean, the police never have recovered her body. Who knows what really..."

Simone cut her short. "I cannot speculate about such things, Mademoiselle Fremont." Her long neck stiffened, signaling that she had revived enough painful memories for one day.

For several moments, only the clock's syncopated ticking disturbed the silence. Jill was the first to speak. "I'm afraid, Mademoiselle Nanka-Midou, and I don't know what to do. I don't even know what he looks like, where he lives, anything. It's as if he were a phantom. Do you know if he lives in Paris now?" She knew she was pushing her luck, but she held her breath, waiting for Simone to respond.

The former model hesitated, wrestling with some private demon. "His name is Yves Lebrun. The last I heard, he was working in a gym in Montparnasse. *Le Physique* it was called, I believe. He lived in a room over the gym. There. I have told you all I can."

Jill leaned forward on the settee and impulsively clasped Simone's hands. "Thank you, Mademoiselle Nanka-Midou."

The slender hand that closed around Jill's was cold, almost icy. "Be careful, Mademoiselle Fremont. Be very careful."

Chapter Thirteen

Dave plowed his fingers through his hair and walked over to the window. He had long since dispensed with the orderly custom of timing his vigils, just as he no longer bothered considering how many minutes had elapsed since his last attempt to call Jill. Sooner or later, she would answer his call or miraculously appear in the street below. And if she didn't . . .

Dave suppressed the sickening panic fermenting in his stomach and pivoted back toward the phone. The knock at the door caught him in midstride.

For a long moment, Dave could only stare at the small figure framed in the doorway. "Where the hell have you been?" he finally blurted out. "I've been worried out of my mind."

Jill cleared her throat. "I drove out and had a chat with Simone today."

"You *what*?"

Jill peered past him into the apartment. "May I come in?" When Dave stepped behind the door, she walked past him. "I just told you, I talked with Simone."

Dave closed the door, anchoring it shut with his back. "We drive out there to get the royal cold shoulder, total your aunt's car in the process and almost end up with our heads blown off. And you're telling me you went back for more!"

When Jill turned, her face was unnaturally calm, almost serene. Only a certain tightness in her jaw betrayed the tension she was struggling to conceal. "This time, I got what I was after. Simone told me where we may be able to find Lebrun. She thinks he works at a boxing gym called *Le Physique*. He might even live in a room over the gym. It seems he was a two-bit boxer at one point, so I guess he still has connections with fighters."

Dave fixed Jill with a look of frank admiration. "How did you get all of this out of Simone?"

"Actually she was very cooperative." Jill quickly recounted her conversation with the former model. "Now I understand what Madame Simenon meant when she said Simone wished the man dead. She certainly has reason to hate him."

"Cici Madison probably would, too, if she were still alive," Dave mused, sinking onto the sofa beside her.

"That's exactly what I thought," Jill concurred. "Now I'm convinced her driving off that bridge was no accident."

Dave nodded pensively. "You haven't actually been to see this gym, have you?"

"Not yet. That's why I came to get you."

"Now let's hold on a minute. Assuming we get past the door of *Le Physique*, do you even know what we're looking for?"

"Sort of. Before I left her house, Simone gave me a good description of Lebrun—not very tall, heavyset, bull neck, mashed-in nose, dark hair."

Dave's mouth twisted to one side dubiously. "An awful lot of guys who frequent boxing gyms fit that description."

"I know," Jill agreed reluctantly. "She did say that he had a tattoo on the back of his left wrist. It's a skull and crossbones with a snake winding through them."

"That seems appropriate," Dave remarked dryly.

Jill nodded, chafing her arms to disguise the shiver rippling through them. "I think we should plan to drop by *Le Physique* first thing in the morning."

"Okay." Dave rose abruptly and rounded the sofa. Although he had not figured out exactly how he would deal with Jill's resistance, he had already decided to undertake any investigation of *Le Physique* alone. She had exposed herself to far too much danger already, and he felt bound to circumvent any further escapades like the solo trip to Simone's farm. "I was just getting ready to have a glass of wine and a sandwich. Would you like something? I bet you haven't eaten all day."

Jill was too canny to be so easily distracted. "You don't sound very excited about our latest discovery."

"I am excited, but I'm hungry, too. How about ham and cheese on a *baguette*?"

"Fine." Jill pushed herself to her feet and followed him to the kitchen. While he assembled the makings for the sandwiches, she selected a bottle of burgundy from the cupboard.

"You must have struck a sympathetic chord with Simone," he remarked casually as he arranged overlapping slices of Gruyère along the sliced *baguette*.

Jill's small hands fumbled with the corkscrew. "I think if she hadn't seen my injury, she may not have opened up. While I was talking with her today, I couldn't help thinking of how radically that one brief accident altered her life. And yet, I guess you could say she's lucky. After all, the person who rigged her car intended to kill her. Just like that man who followed us...." The bottle slipped from her grasp and shattered on the floor. For a moment Jill could only stare at the ruby rivulets curling around her feet. Snatching a kitchen towel, she quickly crouched to blot the mess.

"I'm so clumsy." Jill caught herself in time to stifle the insidious lump in her throat.

Without speaking, Dave knelt and gently took the towel and corkscrew from her trembling hands. "It's all right," he crooned, pulling her up into his arms.

Something in that soft, caring voice tapped a wellspring of hidden emotion within her. "Oh, Dave, will it ever be over? I'm so tired of being afraid, of not knowing when someone is watching me, and what he might want to do..." She choked on a burgeoning sob.

"It will be over," he whispered into her hair with surprising fierceness. "And as long as I'm alive, no one is going to hurt you." When he lifted her, his arms felt so strong, so protective, she could not doubt that he would make good his promise.

Jill rested her cheek against his chest as he carried her out of the kitchen and into the bedroom. He laid her easily on the bed, but when he stepped back, she reached for his hand, unwilling to surrender his warm touch. Dave folded her hand within both of his. "I'll leave you, but only for a moment. Just lie still."

Closing her eyes, Jill released his hand. She opened them again when she felt the bed sink and a cool, damp cloth caressed her brow.

"How does that feel?" he murmured. "Let yourself relax. No one can harm you here. I won't let them."

Jill's eyes fluttered shut, allowing her to retreat into the secure haven his voice was creating for her. As he stroked her head, first with the cloth, then with his own warm hand, she listened to the symphony of scarcely audible sounds around her. Just as the noise from the outside world seemed to fade to an indistinct blur, so were the smallest sounds in the tiny apartment magnified beyond normal proportions. She was acutely aware of the rustle of his shirt against her linen dress when he lifted her and held her to his chest, of the moist caress of his lips on hers.

"I've dreamed of holding you like this, Jill," Dave whispered into her hair. He was rocking her gently now, his strong arm wrapped securely around her. "The other night, when I saw you lying there in the car with your eyes closed, I thought that I might never be able to hold you, never hear you laugh again, never have you touch me. And I knew then that if my worst fear had been true, my life would have been over."

Jill looked up at him and lifted her hands to hold his face steady. "This isn't a dream, Dave." She guided his face down until their lips melded in a kiss.

As they turned in unison, his mouth eased its pressure slightly and then only to discover yet another angle from which to ply hers. She sank back, pulling him down with her. While his lips sprinkled a trail of kisses from her forehead to her chin, his good hand began to slide the zipper down her back.

Jill kept her eyes closed, letting her hands read the contours of his body unaided. She could distinguish the sharp lines of sinew drawn taut down his neck. When her hand ventured inside his open collar, she was startled by the radiant warmth of his skin. Her fingers slid from the firm shoulder to his neck and back again, savoring the contrast of temperature and texture. Loosening another button, she brushed the crisp hair blanketing his rounded pectoral muscle.

When her hand grazed a rough swatch of fabric, she hesitated. Opening her eyes, Jill looked at the rib belt encasing Dave's midsection. "Does it hurt?" she asked softly. Her finger trembled as it etched the line where the bandage cut into his flesh.

"Not when you touch me."

Dave sat back and pulled her upright. He guided her, reassuring her with his own caresses as she loosened the sling and slipped his shirt down his back. In the soft light from the street lamp, she watched the quickening rise and fall of his chest, felt her own breathing accelerate as his hands lifted her camisole to stroke her breasts. Rubbing his cheek against the soft fabric, he teased the nipples into hard points. One at a time, he pulled the straps from her shoulders. She moaned as his tongue traced the curves of her breasts.

When her clothing had joined his on the floor, he stretched on his side and beckoned her to him. Scooped inside his arm, she felt his long leg press between hers. Following the urges of her own body, she encircled his waist with her leg and let him mold her against him. Slowly the wave of passion building within her began to peak, carrying her on its ecstatic crest. She felt Dave shudder, his head thrown back. Then his face sank against her breasts, and he was still.

For a time she stroked his hair, letting her still-heightened senses relish the texture of the thick waves. When Dave reached for her hand, however, she surrendered it willingly. Cupping her palm against his face, he murmured into it. "My sweet Jill." Like a downy blanket wafting into place, a delicious drowsiness settled over Jill. "My sweet love."

When she closed her eyes, she felt a peace she had not known for a long time.

SHE WAS SO BEAUTIFUL in her sleep. Every time Dave's lids grew heavy, he opened them again, just to steal one last look at her. Then he would begin to study her face again: the short upturned nose outlined against the cool street light pouring through the window; the silky dark lashes rimming the closed eyes; the wide forehead with the bangs swept aside to expose the dark widow's peak; the full, sensual lips glistening dewy soft in the light. It was a face he would never grow tired of, one he wanted to cherish and protect forever.

Protect. The word lodged in his mind and refused to yield to less ominous terms. For the past few hours, he had forgotten the danger that lurked outside the close little apartment; he liked to think that Jill had, too. But now as he kept his silent vigil over her, a torrent of disturbing thoughts came racing back into his mind. Outside his door, out in the harsh world of greed and malice and deception, were people who wanted to harm the magnificent woman sleeping by his side.

Taking care not to waken her, Dave climbed out of bed and walked over to the window. *They* were out there now, perhaps not far beyond the gray walls that bounded this tiny corner of Paris. His flesh crawled at the thought of how close one of them had come to destroying his life and Jill's.

Her breathing was even and heavy now, signaling that she was fast asleep; chances were she would not awaken before morning. The bar on the corner was still open; that meant that it was not yet one o'clock. He could probably slip out, accomplish his goal and return without her notice. And just in case she woke up, he could leave a note, say he hadn't been able to sleep and had gone out for a drink.

With extraordinary care, Dave slid open the end-table drawer and pulled out a piece of paper. He had tucked the note under the table lamp and was wrestling his shirt over the cast when the sheets rustled.

"What are you doing?" Jill pushed herself up on one elbow and rubbed her eyes.

Dave glanced at the note, but before he could offer his facile excuse, his conscience pulled him up short. He had once promised Jill never to deceive her again; in light of the intimacy they had just shared that vow seemed more binding than ever. "I was going to sneak out and have a look at the gym," he confessed.

"Without me?" Even in the low light, he could see her dark eyes questioning him.

"Yes. Damn it, Jill! I can't bring myself to lie to you, but there doesn't seem to be any other way of keeping you out of danger. How can I persuade you to let me go to *Le Physique* alone?"

Jill was already pulling on her dress. "You can't, not any more than I could convince you to let me go by myself." When he looked surprised, she smiled. "It works both ways, Dave. When I can't keep an eye on you, I worry about you, too. Come on. We're wasting time." Smoothing her hair into place, she led the way out of the apartment.

In front of the corner bar, Dave hailed a taxi, and Jill directed the driver to an obscure side street in Montparnasse. The cool night air coursing through the open window refreshed them, and put their sense on alert. And they needed to stay on their toes, Dave reminded himself as he paid the cabbie and climbed out a block shy of *Le Physique*.

Loud music and an even louder argument carried from inside a bar situated diagonally across from the boxing gym. They paused in front of the bar's garishly lighted window and surveyed *Le Physique*. Simone had told Jill that Lebrun lived over the place. A row of unlighted windows lined the upper story, gaping down at the street like eyeless sockets; but if Lebrun now slept behind one of them, they had no way of telling.

"Let's check to see if the building has marked mailboxes," Jill whispered at his shoulder.

They cautiously scanned the street before hurrying across to the gym. They stalked the length of the building without finding an entrance to the upstairs apartments, much less a bank of mailboxes. The alley side of the gym looked even less promising, and they were about to backtrack when something caught Dave's eye. Stepping into the alley, he pointed to a shaft of light spilling out of the gym through an open door.

Dave and Jill exchanged solemn looks and then crept toward the door. Gliding into the protective shadows behind it, they waited, listening for sounds of life. The gym remained as quiet as a tomb. Still exercising extreme caution, Dave slipped around the door and found himself facing a dank corridor littered with rubbish. Again he strained his ears to detect any warning sound. He could just make out the faint plop of dripping water from behind one of the corridor's closed doors.

Dave considered himself a reasonably prudent man, but the temptation was now too great. Cutting a glance over his shoulder, he beckoned to Jill and then entered the corridor. A rolled-up carpet lay marooned against one wall. Dave's foot accidentally nudged it, setting off

a chorus of angry rodent squeals. When the racket subsided, he imagined he could hear his own heartbeat,
throbbing dully off the moldy walls.

"Rats," Jill rasped from behind him, but Dave only
nodded.

The corridor was not as long as it had appeared from
the alley, ending abruptly at a steel-clad door. A thread
of light seeped around the edge of the door. On closer
inspection, it was apparent that the door had been
pushed, but had not caught firmly in its frame.

Here was the moment of truth. They were alone in the
corridor; they had found an unlocked door leading into
the gym. What should they do? As if she could read his
thoughts, Jill slid her fingers silently along the exposed
edge of the door. What if they opened it and found
someone on the other side? Dave listened and failed to
detect the slightest sound. He swallowed and looked at
Jill. When she nodded, he eased the door open a fraction of an inch. The ribbon of light widened into a
wedge.

Dave peeked into the room. From his narrow scope,
he could see papers littering the floor. He scooted the
door another handsbreadth and could make out a gray
metal desk with the legs of an upended chair protrud-
ing from behind it. Emboldened by curiosity, Dave
swung the door open.

Even a cursory inspection revealed that the room had
been rifled. The drawers of the file cabinet next to the
desk were hanging out, their folders scattered across the
floor and the jumbled desktop. A few photographs of
boxers in various pugilistic poses still hung askew on the
walls, but most had been ripped down and thrown onto
the floor. As Dave cautiously entered the room, with Jill

close behind him, he could see an open wall safe below an empty picture hook.

His attention was riveted to the open safe, and at first he did not notice the puddle spreading from beneath the desk. Only when Jill gasped and caught his arm did he look down to see the widening crimson circle. With his own blood pounding in his ears, Dave crouched to peer beneath the desk. The man was lying on his back with his arms stretched out beside him, palms up. Whoever had shot him must have used a large caliber weapon, for most of his head was now spattered on the wall below the safe.

"I recognize him, Dave." Jill's shaking finger delineated the mangled skull. "He's the man who startled us when we were in the Montmartre warehouse."

"You're certain?"

"Positive." Still staring at the corpse, Jill took a step forward. Silently sinking into a crouch, she reached to ease the frayed sleeve back from the man's left wrist. He heard her suck in her breath when she revealed the blue-gray outline of a skull and crossbones buried beneath the thick mat of hair.

Dave suddenly caught Jill's hand and stood, pulling her with him. "This isn't a simple break-in, this is murder. Whatever you do, don't touch anything else. We need to get out of here and call Henri as fast as possible." Had they touched anything already? Dave nervously scanned the room, trying to orient himself and quell the insistent nausea building in his gut.

They were retreating toward the door when a glossy photograph, half buried in the debris, caught Dave's eye. "Wait a minute." He caught Jill's icy hand and held her back. Reaching into his pocket, he pulled out a handkerchief and gingerly lifted the photograph.

For a moment, they could only stare at the nude figure displayed beneath the harsh overhead light. This was no soft-focus centerfold, no voyeur's titillation, not by a long shot; this tableau was frankly pornographic, by anyone's standards. But more striking than the obscene pose was the model's pouting face. She was very young. She was wearing absurdly heavy makeup, and she was unmistakably Cici Madison.

Chapter Fourteen

"Your case is as good as solved." Dave's eyes followed Henri as the detective shoved the file cabinet closed and sauntered over to his desk.

When Henri said nothing, Dave shook his head in exasperation. "Don't you see? Lebrun ties it all together. Somehow he got his hands on some raunchy pictures and blackmailed Cici Madison to steal designs from Chausson. She was supposed to make a delivery to that warehouse in Montmartre, just like she had in Milan. But before the big day, she had the accident. Maybe she tried to defy Lebrun, and he engineered the accident. Anyway, he got worried that Cici might have left too much evidence lying around, so he rifled her apartment. When Jill showed up at an inconvenient time, he mugged her. And what did he find in the handbag he took? Madison's calendar! Now if you were a crook, what would you think?"

Henri's sharply defined mouth pulled to one side. "What *would* I think?"

"That Jill knew all about Madison's role in the caper," Dave declared triumphantly.

Henri's fine dark brows rose—whether in interest or skepticism, Jill could not tell. For her part, she found

Dave's scenario overwhelmingly convincing. "That would explain why Madame Petit warned me. Somehow she knew of his suspicions, and realized that he saw me as a threat to be gotten rid of. Just like Madame Petit.''

Snatching up the pack of Gauloises, Henri pulled out a cigarette and lighted it before speaking. "Let me remind you, Mademoiselle Fremont, that we do not as yet have any conclusive evidence linking Lebrun with the Petit murder." He slid onto the edge of the desk and balanced the ashtray on his knee. "Dave's theory is not a bad one, but it leaves a lot of questions unanswered. You say Madame Petit warned you, Mademoiselle Fremont, but she was already dead when that letter was written. Who wrote it?''

Jill paused uneasily. "I don't know," she confessed.

Henri's chin jerked slightly as he took another puff on his cigarette. "Who killed Lebrun?"

Looking into the ice-blue eyes, Jill felt a fleeting twinge of empathy for anyone unfortunate enough to face his interrogation. "I don't know," she was forced to admit.

Henri said nothing, but he smiled as he tapped the edge of the ashtray.

"Look, Henri, we're not pretending to have everything figured out. But if you don't bust that warehouse, you're making a big mistake," Dave warned him.

"What is there to bust? It contains only mattresses." Henri's weary tone reminded Jill of a recorded message.

"That someone planned to ship counterfeit goods in!" Dave leaned over the desk and smacked it with his good hand.

Henri brushed the particles of ash from his trouser leg. "Monsieur Lebrun will not be shipping anything, my friend."

"A petty thug like Lebrun didn't dream up this scheme alone, and you know it," Dave upbraided him. "He was just a cog in the machine—and probably not a very big one at that. Sure, he did the dirty work. Bigtimers usually don't go in for strangling little old ladies and pushing guys in front of trains."

"Or putting a bullet in someone's head?" Henri put in adroitly. His smile suggested that he was not at all fazed by Dave's glowering expression. "You must trust me, my friend, and let me handle this investigation in my own way." He exhaled, drawing two thin streams of smoke into his nose. "Of course, there is every chance that I will uncover an extensive web of crime in the process. We have learned that Monsieur Lebrun was deported from the United States because of some criminal activity, probably drugs or something like that. I have already requested police reports from my American colleagues. Who knows? His death could have been a drug dealer's execution."

Dave shook his head in disbelief. "You have one of the year's biggest fashion counterfeit schemes right under your nose, and all you can think about is dope. I give up."

"You are too clever to do that, *mon ami*." Henri gave him a sardonic smile as he slid off the desk. He held the door open and nodded cordially to Jill, signaling an end to the conversation. As the two Americans filed out of the office, Henri caught Dave by his good arm. He cuffed his shoulder, too lightly for Dave to take offense, too roughly for him to ignore. "You are a good reporter, Dave, but you are not a cop, eh? You should remember that.''

"WE SHOULD HAVE WATCHED her more closely.'' Simone stared into the empty grate, letting the charred stone and ash blur into a shapeless gray mass before her unfocused eyes. Her body felt numb, much as it had in the days when she had appeased its torment with painkillers.

"You cannot watch someone day and night.'' Serge's strong hands fastened over her shoulders and clasped them tightly. "It was not your fault she slipped away.''

Simone's eyes remained trained on the grate. "I know what she is thinking. She told me she was afraid, and she believes this friend of whom she spoke can help her.''

Serge's hands were still. "Who is he?''

"I do not know, and that is what troubles me most.'' She took a deep breath and leaned her cheek against the big hand. "For so long I have thought I had forgotten how to fear, but she has brought the past here with her. I am afraid, Serge.''

Serge's rough hand suddenly cupped her chin and lifted her face. "Forget her, Simone. Let her go,'' he whispered fiercely. "There is nothing you can do.''

Simone's unflinching gaze defied the brooding dark eyes. "I must find her.''

"And then?''

Simone's neck stiffened, but she did not answer.

Serge held her face for a moment, his fingers pressing the delicate bones as if he wished he could mold them after his own will. Then he released her and walked away in silence. She heard the heavy door close behind him. For a time, Simone sat alone with her thoughts. The mantel clock chimed once, the single dolorous stroke of the quarter hour. From the corner, Hercule stirred in his sleep to whine briefly; the huge, wrinkled head looked disquieted as it settled back between his paws.

At last, Simone stood and walked to the armoire. It was an antique, and its veneer doors yielded reluctantly. The dusty scent of old lavender rose from the drawer as she slid it open. Her hands felt among the yellowed linens until they touched something hard and smooth. She pulled the revolver from its hiding place. Cradled in her long hand, it looked coarse and heavy. She held it for a moment, feeling its obscene power. Then she turned and walked slowly up the stairs.

WHEN THEY WERE OUTSIDE the police prefecture, Jill caught Dave's loose sleeve and pulled him gently to a halt. Although he had said nothing, his disconsolate expression testified that he was as depressed by Henri's indifference as she. Jill's face softened, and she gave his good shoulder a quick squeeze. "You ought to go home and get some sleep."

Shaking his head, Dave made a halfhearted attempt to square his shoulders. "Can't. I've got some guy from Customs pinned down for an interview, and after I'm through with him, I need to wander by the office and see if anything's up." He slung his coat over his good shoulder and gave her cheek a quick buss.

Jill smiled, cheered, if only temporarily, by that light kiss. Her world was so full of uncertainty, she reflected on her way back to Tante Yvonne's apartment. Right now, Dave was the only person she felt she could depend on, be honest with, trust. And even her relationship with him was overshadowed by variables beyond her control. As little faith as she had in Henri, she could still hope that he and his detectives might someday solve the case. But absolutely no one could engineer circumstances to keep her and Dave in the same place permanently.

She had left the curtains drawn in Tante Yvonne's apartment, giving the usually cheerful living room a dismal appearance. Jill rushed to the big French doors and ripped back the drapes. But even that sudden flood of sunshine failed to brighten her mood.

She was wandering around the apartment, aimlessly straightening cushions and books when the phone rang. The thought that it might be Dave with some encouraging news to report sent her racing to the desk.

"Hello?" She could hear noise in the background—voices and canned music and things rattling on trays—and she waited a moment before repeating herself. "Hello?"

"Jill?" The woman's voice faltered. "Is that you?"

Suddenly an ice-cold sweat broke out over Jill's entire body, and her heart started to pound. Her head expanded, swelling under the pressure of the blood building in it. "Who is this?" she managed to rasp in spite of the imaginary hand throttling her throat.

"It's Cici." The woman's uneven breathing clouded her words.

Jill felt so dizzy she had to lean against the desk to keep her balance. "Cici! But I thought... You can't..." She knew she was babbling, but what else could she do? If she had not lost her mind, then Cici Madison had phoned her from the grave. Either possibility was overwhelmingly frightening.

"Listen to me, Jill! I don't have time to explain things now." She broke off, and Jill could hear her swallow against the noisy background.

"Where are you?" Jill's free hand plundered the desktop in search of pencil and paper while her ear strained to follow the wavering voice. Could it really be Cici? It sounded *like* her. But dead women don't talk.

"I can't tell you. I'm in awful trouble, Jill. God, I never meant to get Nana and you involved in this mess. I swear it." The young voice cracked.

"I know, Cici," she added, at last overcoming her own aversion to calling this specter by name.

The girl sounded as if she had started to cry. "You're in danger, Jill. There's a man, the one I warned you about in the note..."

"Lebrun is dead, Cici."

"But that can't be!" the young woman insisted, letting her voice rise above its hoarse whisper. "That's not what he told me!"

"Who told you what?" Jill demanded. She was alarmed by the rising hysteria of the girl's tone.

"I can't tell you. I don't know what to do." The trembling voice reminded Jill of a frightened child's. "Oh, God, I'm scared!"

"If you'll tell me where you are, I'll call the police. They can be there in minutes." In the face of the young woman's desperation, Jill forced herself to be calm.

"No! The police will only make it worse. Please don't call them," she implored. "I have to go now."

Jill gripped the receiver in a symbolic attempt to hold on to the distraught girl. "Wait! Don't hang up." Her eyes shot around the room, searching for inspiration. "If you would only tell me what's wrong, maybe I could help you."

"You'd only call the police." The youthful voice had taken on a wary edge.

"No, I wouldn't, not unless you want me to. I promise." If she claimed to have talked with a dead woman, who would believe her anyway?

"You won't tell anyone?"

"No."

The girl was quiet for a long moment. "All right, but I can't talk now. I've been here too long already."

"Then I'll meet you somewhere. Anywhere you like," she added recklessly.

Cici drew in a ragged breath. "Do you know that big movie theater near the cemetery in Montmartre?"

"Cinéma Gaumont-Palace?"

"Yeah, that's it. I'll meet you at the cemetery gate closest to the theater in half an hour." She hung up abruptly.

Thirty minutes was not much time. Jill anxiously checked her watch and then scrambled for her bag and keys. As she was preparing to close the door, she glanced back at the phone. The temptation to call Dave was strong. She had just talked with the central figure in the web of intrigue, someone whom they had presumed dead, but who had come back to life and was about to share her coveted secrets with Jill. Of all the unexpected events of the past two weeks, this was the most bizarre, and she longed to discuss matters with him. But she had promised to tell no one. To betray the beleaguered girl's trust at this point was something she could not bring herself to do.

Out of concern for Cici's misgivings, she told the cabdriver to stop on Boulevard de Clichy, two blocks short of their rendezvous point. The young woman had sounded so skittish on the phone, Jill feared that she would bolt at the slightest imagined threat.

When she reached the terrace overlooking Montmartre's famous cemetery, she immediately spotted a lone figure standing in the shadow of a large mausoleum. The woman's thin shoulders were pressed against the marble wall; although her head was covered by a black silk scarf, the sun sparkled off the wisps of gold curling at her temples. The young woman's position was safely concealed from the gate, but her furtive posture made her stand out to someone at Jill's vantage point. Dwarfed by the ponderous stone tomb, she looked terribly vulnerable. Jill felt a renewed wave of anger at the unscrupulous people—pornographers, counterfeiters, the whole miserable lot—who had taken advantage of that frailty.

Jill was turning away from the terrace overhang to begin her descent to the cemetery when a movement below caught her eye. A man was walking rapidly toward the mausoleum where the young woman had hidden; he had left the path and was stepping across the headstones in his haste. The girl turned as he approached and then shrank back. The man was wearing a tweed hat, and, although the brim was narrow, it was enough to conceal his face. Jill could read his gestures, however, and she knew he was angry. Suddenly his hand flew out, and he snatched at the girl's wrist. The scarved head jerked back, resisting his efforts to pull her along with him.

Still keeping her eye on the prominent mausoleum, Jill rushed to the steps. As she hurried down the walk leading to the street, she could see him dragging the girl by the arm. He was marching her toward the gate, shoving her so roughly that she stumbled. Jill reached

the street in time to see him push her into the front seat
of a silver Jaguar. She heard the powerful engine surge
as he gunned it and then squealed away from the curb.

Jill broke into a run, trying to keep sight of the Jaguar while she frantically scanned the street for any sign
of a policeman. She dared not risk stopping long
enough to telephone; as it was, only the congestion of
the narrow inner-city street prevented the Jaguar from
outpacing her altogether.

When the car turned into Rue Durantin, Jill sprinted
to the corner. The walk was slippery, and she almost lost
her footing. Catching herself on a street lamppost, she
charged up the hill and reached the crest in time to see
the silver car turn into a side street. Jill slowed her pace,
deliberately keeping her distance behind the Jaguar. The
streets were less populated here, making her more sus-
ceptible to notice. She had no desire to confront the
kidnapper; her task was to keep him in sight until he
reached his destination.

At the end of the side street, Jill halted and slipped
inside a convenient doorway. She had been so intent on
following the car, that she had not paid much attention
to where it was leading her. Now, however, she realized
that she recognized this quiet, shady block. The Jaguar
had led her directly to the Mill Terrace warehouse street.
With growing certainty, Jill watched the sports car roll
slowly past the green double doors and then turn into
the alley flanking the warehouse.

Taking care to remain concealed, Jill kept her eyes
fastened on the mouth of the alley. Finally she mustered the courage to make a break for the small corner
newsstand. Not trusting herself to look away from the
alley, Jill plundered her bag until her fingers recognized the familiar shape of a *jeton*. With her lip

clamped between her teeth, she dialed the Worldwide Communications number.

"I'm sorry, but Mr. Lovell is not in," the secretary informed her in a clipped British accent. "May I take a message?"

"Tell him Jill called. Cici isn't dead after all, but she's been kidnapped in Montmartre. I've followed the man who grabbed her to the warehouse. Oh, my God, he's coming out. I've got to go." Jill slammed down the phone and sank back into the protective cover of the kiosk.

Instantly on her guard, Jill prepared to pick up the chase as the Jaguar emerged from the alley. She hesitated when she noticed only one figure seated behind the tinted window. Cici's kidnapper had apparently imprisoned his captive in the warehouse and was now leaving. Jill lingered in the doorway until the Jaguar had disappeared down an adjacent street. Then she dashed across the street and into the alley.

Today, Jill wasted no time appraising the fence before kicking off her shoes. Mindless of the sharp wire that shredded her stockings and left her hands covered with rusty sweat, she doggedly crawled to the top. Swinging her leg over the top of the fence, Jill glanced down at the cold, hard concrete, calculating her fall before she let go.

The warehouse yard was small, making it easy for her to size things up quickly. The high window through which she and Dave had gained access was now securely barred. Gingerly sidestepping a puddle of broken glass, Jill hurried to the single door and silently prayed she would find a way to force it. To her surprise, it yielded to her tug without a struggle. The kidnapper, whoever he was, had apparently left in such haste, he had forgotten to lock the door.

As her eyes adjusted to the warehouse's gloom, Jill recognized the infamous blue-striped mattresses, still stacked to the ceiling in orderly rows. Jill suppressed the urge to call Cici's name and began to work her way along the wall of mattresses. When she heard a muffled rustle from inside the maze, she turned and followed one of the passages. The sound grew louder, more distinct. At the juncture of another passage, Jill peered cautiously around the corner.

Cici tried to call when she saw Jill, but the gag binding her mouth reduced her cry to a pitiful moan. Dashing down the row of mattresses, Jill knelt beside her and quickly loosened the gag.

"Oh, Jill! Oh, thank God!" The young woman was gasping and crying at the same time.

"Cici, it really is you!" Jill gave her a quick hug. "Hold still and let me get you untied."

The ropes wound around Cici's wrists were so tight, the girl's hands had already turned white. After a futile struggle with the intricate knot, Jill remembered the Swiss army knife she carried in her handbag. With a few deft strokes of the blade, Cici's hands and feet were free.

"It's all right, baby," Jill crooned soothingly into the model's tumbled hair as she patted her back. "He's gone now, and we're going to get out of here before he comes back."

Cici brushed a lock of hair back to reveal her puffy, swollen face. "Oh, Jill. I'm so sorry. I never intended for things to work out this way. I'm an awful person."

"No, you're not." Jill gave her abraded wrists a calming shake. "You've made some mistakes, but you can get your life back together."

Cici shook her head. "Every time I try, I just make things worse. For everybody. I didn't want to steal anymore. I *never* wanted to, but I was afraid of what would happen if I refused. I didn't want to end up like Simone." She choked, fighting to hold back her tears.

"Poor Simone! She thought she could help me. It was her idea for me to disappear and come live with her. Her friend Serge is a stuntman, and he set up the car wreck to look like an accident so that everyone would think I was dead. But then Lebrun was after Nana. When Nana told Simone that you had my bag, I knew it would just be matter of time before he was after you, too. And then he found Nana!" Cici broke off and buried her face in her hands.

"It's over now, Cici." Jill smoothed the young woman's tangled fair hair. "Lebrun can't hurt anyone anymore, and I'm going to take you to a safe place."

Cici's shoulders jerked, but she bit her lip, trying to recover her composure. "That's what *he* said!" Suddenly her reddened eyes widened and stared past Jill.

"You should not make promises you cannot keep, Miss Fremont," a hauntingly familiar voice taunted her from behind.

Dropping back on her knees, Jill turned to find Sanford Fielding standing framed between the parallel rows of mattresses. His smile was anything but friendly, and he was holding a gun pointed straight at them.

Chapter Fifteen

Henri was holding out on him, and there was only one way to deal with him. Dave repeated the angry suspicion in his mind as he waited for the Métro to carry him back to the office. He was going to confront Henri the next time he talked with him and demand an explanation.

As it turned out, Dave got the chance to talk with Henri more quickly than he expected. He had just walked into his tiny cubicle in the Worldwide Communications suite when the phone rang.

Dave dumped his attaché case by the computer terminal and grabbed the receiver. "Lovell!"

"Dave, this is Henri. Do you have a minute?" He spoke quickly, as if he had something important to convey.

"Yeah, sure." Dave cradled the phone beneath his chin and unsnapped the attaché case.

"The police report on Lebrun that I requested from the United States arrived on the telex."

Dave frowned over some notes he had taken at the customs office and then tossed them into the trash. "And old Yves was booted back across the Atlantic for messing around with dope."

"Not dope, Dave, pornography."

Dave's hand froze on the lid of the attaché case. "You're serious?"

"Of course I am serious!" Henri sounded impatient, but he paused, just long enough, Dave guessed, to take a puff on a cigarette.

"So that explains how he got that picture of Madison!" Dave was too elated to crow over Henri. His mind was racing, eager for details. "What exactly were the charges? Was he convicted?"

A smart rap on the door frame interrupted his rapid-fire stream of questions. Dave wheeled to find Allison Brinsley, the new secretary, waving a note at him from the doorway. He nodded to her, but his attention was focused on Henri.

"A lot of the charges involved kids, 'contributing to the delinquency of a minor,' nice stuff like that. Too bad the case fell apart once they got it to court."

"Don't tell me the bastards all got off?" Dave frowned and shook his head, trying to avoid the piece of pink paper Miss Brinsley was fluttering in his face.

"A few of the little guys drew light sentences, thanks to Lebrun's testimony. It appears he was able to save his own skin by turning state's evidence. In return for the favor, U.S. Immigration bought him a one-way ticket home."

"What about the big wheels?" In exasperation, Dave snatched the note from the secretary's hand.

"The investors? Ah, yes! You and I, *mon ami*, we know the ways of the world. What are the chances of proving anything nasty about a couple of businessmen and a successful photographer? A few legal technicalities emerge, a few witnesses change their minds, and poof! The case is nothing."

"You wouldn't happen to have the names of those businessmen handy would you?" Dave turned toward the desk, the better to ignore Miss Brinsley, who was still gesticulating wildly.

"Right here in my hand. There was a Perryman and a Noble. That is a good name for someone who profits from dirty pictures of little kids, no? The photographer's name was Fielding."

Dave looked up from the note Miss Brinsley had shoved into his hand and blinked. "Sanford Fielding?"

"Yes. Do you know him?"

In his excitement, Dave tossed the note aside. "Henri, this is *it*! Fielding is living right here in Paris now. He photographed both Madison *and* Simone. We've got our man!"

"Mr. Lovell, *please*!" Miss Brinsley had picked up the note and was dangling it less than a foot from Dave's face.

"Hold on, Henri." Dave cupped his hand over the receiver. "Miss Brinsley, I'm in the middle of a very important conversation. Can't this wait a few minutes?"

The secretary pulled herself up, straightening her narrow shoulders as if she were about to go before a firing squad. "No, Mr. Lovell, it cannot." She nodded curtly toward the note.

Licking his lips slowly, Dave gave Miss Brinsley a skeptical look before examining the note.

3:40. Jill phoned. Cici not dead; kidnapped in Montmartre. J. followed kidnapper to warehouse.

"Is that all she said?" Dave demanded, now thoroughly alarmed.

To her credit, Miss Brinsley did not look in the least smug. "That was her message. She rang off rather hurriedly, said something about someone coming out, and she had to go."

Dave's mind was reeling. Cici Madison had drowned in an automobile accident that both Jill and he had witnessed. She couldn't be alive and in the hands of a kidnapper. But that is exactly what Jill had phoned to say. More disturbing still, she had said that she had followed the kidnapper to the Montmartre warehouse. Dave anxiously checked his watch and then remembered that he still had Henri on the line.

"Henri? I just got a crazy phone message from Jill. She called about twenty minutes ago and said she was on the trail of someone who had kidnapped Cici Madison in Montmartre."

"Cici Madison has been dead for two weeks, Dave," Henri said.

"Yeah, I know, but right now I'm less concerned about who's been kidnapped. I'm worried about Jill. You need to get some of your boys up to that warehouse in Montmartre. Fast."

For once, Henri offered no protest. "We are on our way. *Au revoir.*"

Dave threw the phone down and grabbed his coat. On his way out of the office, he passed Miss Brinsley's desk. The secretary had returned to her post and was now bent over a clipping file, but she looked up as he passed.

"Monsieur Baldin was looking for you. He's still waiting for those expense reports. What shall I tell him?"

Dave held the elevator door for a split second. "Tell him I'm out chasing a woman who's chasing a ghost."

"You should have minded your own business, Miss Fremont." Fielding took a calculated step closer to the spot where Cici and Jill were crouched.

"Please, Sanford! Jill doesn't know anything. I swear. She got my bag by accident, but I never told her anything. Please let her go." Cici had started to cry again, her torn sobs adding vehemence to her plea.

"I can't do that, Cici, and you know it," Fielding told her in a patronizing tone. He was circling them slowly, pivoting around the barrel of the trained gun. "What would she tell her friends? That you and I are playing naughty games in this warehouse? No, my dear, Miss Fremont would spread stories about us, and we can't have that."

"The police are going to find you, Fielding," Jill told him. His mockery had infuriated her, and despite the gun pointed at her she could not remain silent. "When I saw you force Cici into that car, I phoned the police," she lied in an attempt to bluff him. "You're not going to get away with this."

Fielding's pale blue eyes widened knowingly. "Oh, but I will, Miss Fremont. I am not in the habit of getting caught, especially when I am dealing with stupid people." An ugly sneer crept into the low, sinister voice. "Simone was stupid, and she paid for it. She still thinks Yves Lebrun was behind everything." He scoffed. "That man did not have the brains to tie his own shoes unless I told him how."

"You don't have Lebrun to do your dirty work now," Jill reminded him defiantly.

Fielding glanced down at the revolver. "No, I don't. Yves started getting clumsy. He botched your automobile accident rather badly. He outlived his usefulness, and I had to eliminate him."

"You told me you would help me!" The accusation sounded as if it had been ripped from Cici's throat. "When I told you Lebrun was blackmailing me, you said you would get the negatives from him and everything would be all right! And you knew him all along! You put him up to it!"

"My, my!" Fielding drew back, feigning amazement. "You aren't as stupid as I thought. Just a trifle slow. My dear, I *gave* Lebrun those negatives in the first place. But come now, admit it. You wouldn't have been so willing to snitch things from Papa Chausson without a little coercion, would you?" He cocked his head to one side and studied the weeping girl. "No, I think not."

"You're a loathsome man, Fielding. And someday someone is going to make you pay your dues." In her rage, Jill rose to her knees.

"Uh-uh!" Fielding brandished the gun threateningly. "Careful there, Miss Fremont. Just sit back politely, there's a nice girl, and don't speak unless you're spoken to."

Cici had started to shake; her frail shoulders were jerking convulsively. "What are you going to do with us?" she asked between shuddering gasps.

"Well, first we have to fix your hands and mouth again. And we'll have to do the same for Miss Fremont." He gave Jill a cruel smile. "We wouldn't want her to feel left out. And then we're going for a ride."

"You're not going anywhere, Sanford," a cold, deadly voice told him from behind.

Fielding was so startled he glanced over his shoulder. Taking advantage of his split-second lapse, Jill grabbed the Swiss army knife and threw it at his outstretched hand. The knife grazed his wrist, sending the gun spinning across the concrete floor. Clutching his wrist, Fielding stepped back to reveal Simone Nanka-Midou standing in the passageway. Dressed in a black knit tunic and pants, the model seemed to step out of the very shadows, but as she drew closer Jill could see the gun she held in her hand.

"It is over, Sanford." Her perfect face remained free of emotion, as if she were stating a simple fact and nothing more.

"How did you get here?" Fielding stammered. Now that the tables had turned, his demeanor had altered dramatically. A mottled flush had spread from his neck to his pale cheeks, and his left eyelid was twitching uncontrollably.

"I followed you," Simone told him simply. "A man with dangerous plans should not drive such a flashy car, Sanford. It is the sort of thing people remember when one asks them questions. But then you are a stupid man," she added pointedly. "And that is the sort of thing stupid people do."

"Look, Simone. We can work this out." Sanford's watery eyes traveled nervously to the gun. "I can make it worth your while to discuss things."

The gun did not waver as Simone shook her head. "There is nothing I wish to discuss with you, Sanford, nothing that you can offer me. All this time, you have deceived me. I thought you were my friend, that you had helped me in my career. Now I realize that you only wanted to use me, just as you have used Cici. You can offer me money, but you cannot give me back blood and bone and flesh. You destroyed my life, Sanford, and now you must pay with your own."

Jill scrambled to her feet. "Don't kill him, Simone. He isn't worth it. Let the police take care of him."

Simone's full lips curved in contempt. "The police will do nothing with him."

"Yes, they will," Jill protested. "I heard him confess enough to seal his case, and I'll testify. Please don't pull that trigger. You've suffered enough already."

A tremor of emotion flickered on Simone's dark face, but she quickly squared her chin. Lifting the revolver slightly, she braced her wrist with her free hand. "You are a good woman, Mademoiselle Fremont, but it is too late for me. And for him."

"Simone, don't!" Jill lunged forward just as the violent discharge rent the air.

She saw Simone recoil, still clutching the smoking gun. Fielding's hand was pressed against his shoulder, trying to stay the blood trickling between his pale fingers. For a moment, he looked too stunned to move, but suddenly he bolted.

Jill was after him in a flash. Now that he was disarmed and wounded, she felt more than a match for Sanford Fielding, and she was determined that he not get away. She could hear Cici, and Simone running with a limp behind her. She rounded the corner of the mattress wall and headed for the door.

In his headlong flight, Fielding had slammed the door behind him, but he had not paused long enough to lock it. Jill could see his bloodstained handprints on the metal panel as she pushed through into the warehouse yard. He had reached his car and was now recklessly maneuvering it toward the gate.

At least she did not have to scale the troublesome fence again. Hurrying through the open gate, Jill halted long enough to retrieve her discarded shoes before rushing after the Jaguar. "We can't lose sight of that car, or he's gone!" she cried. The other two women had caught up with her; Simone grabbed her arm, helping her hobble along until she had anchored both shoes on her feet.

Once more, the narrow streets of Montmartre were hampering Fielding's progress. He had already cut a corner too closely, scraping the side of the Jaguar against a bricked escarpment. A loose hubcap rolled in a wobbly path past the three women and then rattled against the curb, but Fielding was far from incapacitated. Gunning the engine of the big car, he shot into reverse and then lurched forward.

Suddenly Jill detected a warbling sound in the distance. As she turned to pursue the Jaguar up the hill, she could hear the police sirens drawing closer. The seesawing whine rose to an earsplitting level, just before the nose of a police car jutted from an intersecting street. Another car appeared on the opposite side, effectively cutting off the Jaguar's escape route.

Fielding braked hard and then turned abruptly into the narrow alley to his left. The doors of the police cars flew open and at least a half-dozen men bailed out. She recognized Henri's dashing figure in the forefront, coattails furled out behind him and service revolver drawn. Despite the cumbersome sling, Dave did not lag far behind.

"He turned down here!" Jill shouted and pointed into the alley. Not waiting for Dave and the policemen to catch up with her, she ran down the footpath and swung over the guardrail.

Taking the walkway's direct route had enabled her to descend the hill ahead of the Jaguar. Gasping for breath, she made a dash for the end of the alley. She could hear the sound of metal scraping, of glass shattering on stone as the Jaguar plowed its way through the alley.

Jill's heart was pounding as she held herself back, hands resting on a rubbish barrel as she waited for the car's approach. Just as the nose of the silver sports car appeared at the mouth of the alley, Jill shoved with all her might. The Jaguar's tires squealed as Fielding swerved to avoid the unexpected missile. The can bounced off the Jaguar's fender as the silver sedan spun out of control. The crash that followed was so violent, the surrounding buildings seemed to quake from the reverberation.

Still shaken from the horrendous crash, Jill stepped aside to allow the horde of policemen to charge past.

"Thank God, you're still in one piece!" Before she could turn, Dave had anchored his good arm around her and swept her to his chest.

"Oh, Dave, I was so afraid you hadn't gotten my message. After Fielding cornered me, I knew you were my only hope of bringing help."

Dave's arm tightened around her. "As soon as I got your message, I told Henri and then tore up here as fast as a taxi could take me. When I heard all that cops-and-robbers brake squealing, I knew I had found the action. I'm glad that guy didn't get away. Any idea who he is?"

"Sanford Fielding. Can you believe that?"

Dave chuckled. "Yes, as a matter of fact, I can. I have a lot to tell you. But then I guess you have a lot to tell me." His eyes followed Cici Madison who was fighting her way through the ranks of policemen surrounding the wreck.

Sliding her arm through Dave's, Jill walked with him to the scene of the accident. Cici was screaming; Jill could hear her small hands pounding the side of the battered Jaguar. Simone was tugging at her arm, and the woman was struggling to free herself. Pulling her arm away from Dave, Jill pressed through the crowd.

"It is all right, Cici." Simone spoke softly, trying to make herself heard below the wail of the approaching ambulance siren. "It is time to go now." She slipped an arm around the model's shoulders and tried to guide her away from the wreck.

"No, it's not!" Cici broke free and ran back to the car. Jill caught her as she leaned through the open window.

In spite of her hatred for the man, Jill could not help but feel a glimmer of pity for the broken man lying crushed beneath the wheel. She started when Cici seized his lapels and attempted to rouse him.

"Where are they? Tell me what you've done with the negatives!" she shrieked. "You have them. I know you do."

Fieldings waning eyes narrowed, and the ghost of a smile trembled on his bloodless lips. "No, I don't, Cici," he whispered. "She does."

"Who? Tell me who!" Cici frantically clawed at the lapels.

Fielding's lips parted just as his chin sank lifelessly onto his chest.

"WHO THE HELL was he talking about?"

As Dave stalked past Henri's desk, he eyed the familiar pack of Gauloises closely and, for a moment, Jill almost expected him to grab one and light it up. For the past hour, he had not been able to stay anchored in one spot for more than a minute, constantly pacing the narrow confines of the office.

"Now that Simone's innocence has been established, no women appear to be connected with the counterfeit ring, except for Mademoiselle Madison, of course. At least, no women that we have been able to discover," Henri admitted reluctantly. He consoled himself with a long draw on his cigarette. "Although you did not want to believe me earlier, our investigation has been very extensive, but I feared that you would blow our cover. You were obsessed by that warehouse, my friend."

"With good reason," Dave retorted as he made another pass in front of the desk.

Henri exhaled slowly. "I did not spend months building a case simply to bust a warehouse full of mattresses, Dave. I was only interested in mattresses filled with counterfeit goods. Timing is everything in this business, *mon ami*."

Dave shoved his hands into his back pockets and swung around to face Henri. "Okay, I admit I wanted to jump the gun on the warehouse, but that still doesn't answer my original question. Who is the woman Fielding claimed has the negatives of Madison's porno shots?"

Henri ground out his cigarette with meticulous care. "I don't know." He gestured with his long, slender hand. "I am open to suggestion. Do you have any suspicions based on your own investigation?"

Dave sighed noisily and shook his head.

Jill had been listening in silence to the men's discussion. So much had happened in the past few days, she desperately needed some quiet time to think, to put things into perspective. As much as the complicated workings of the criminal network, she was struck by the profound ways in which so many people's lives had been affected by the counterfeit scheme. Beneath the subterfuge, the cat-and-mouse game of detective and criminal, was a human element. More than by mere greed, the actors in this drama had been driven by fear, hate and a desire for revenge. It was this last thought that now prompted her to speak.

"I have an idea who she is."

When Henri and Dave turned to look at her, Jill got the impression that they had almost forgotten she was there.

"Who?" they demanded simultaneously.

Jill took a slow, careful breath. "I don't have any proof at this point, just a feeling. But I have a plan. And, gentlemen—" she looked from one astonished face to the other "—if it works, we just might have our woman."

JILL LOOKED at the plain black telephone and then up at Henri and Dave. She sighed and flexed her fingers over the phone. "Here goes." She clasped the receiver to her ear and then dialed the seven digits. It buzzed once, twice, then again, and with each ring her nervousness mounted. Her heart was pounding when someone finally answered.

"Hello?"

"Hello, this is Jill Fremont." Jill waited a second to let that revelation sink in. "Do you remember me?"

"I remember you." The icy voice was weighted with contempt.

"Good," Jill shot back. Now that the ball was in play, she was relieved that some of her anxiety had subsided. "I have something that I think you might want."

"What?" the shrewish voice snapped.

"Copies of a calendar that belonged to Cici Madison. I'd be willing to part with it. For a price."

The woman's breathing was audible, betraying her agitation. "How much do you want?"

"Oh, I don't want money." Jill closed her eyes and crossed her fingers. "I want the negatives of those porno shots."

She could hear the woman lick her lips and then swallow. "Very well. You may bring the copies to my apartment. I will be alone this evening, and I will have the negatives for you."

"No," Jill told her bluntly. "We'll do this in a public place, or not at all."

"Where then?" Her tone was venomous.

"Meet me at the Hôtel des Invalides this afternoon at two. I'll be upstairs on the rotunda overlooking Napoléon's tomb. *Au revoir.*"

"Good going!" Dave clapped Jill on the back so soundly that she lurched forward against the desk. "Now we've got her!"

"Not quite," Jill cautioned him. "I still have to get her to talk enough to get something incriminating on tape without arousing her suspicion."

"Do not worry, Mademoiselle Fremont," Henri assured her blithely. "The recorder you will be carrying in your handbag is extraordinarily sensitive and will pick up normal conversation from a reasonable distance. A contingent of plainclothes detectives will be close by. At just the right time, we will close in and spring the trap." His fingers meshed, imitating jaws snapping shut.

Jill tried to hang on to that confidence-inspiring image that afternoon as she entered the cavernous national monument. It had been her idea to stage the rendezvous at Napoléon's tomb, but now she wondered what had ever possessed her to choose such a cold and intimidating spot. Although the place was always full of tourists, it was one of the few landmarks in Paris where one always felt alone. Perhaps it had something to do with the eerie acoustics.

As Jill walked toward the rail overlooking the dead emperor's crypt, she was struck by the way each of her footsteps seemed to echo off the marble floor and carry to the cupola overhead. At the balustrade, she paused to glance down at the monstrous red porphyry crypt. When she looked up again, she spotted Madame Vernier staring across the chasm over the tomb.

Jill's hand traveled instinctively to the shoulder bag resting against her hip and then she caught herself. *Relax. Act natural.* As if there were anything natural about acting as a police decoy! The awful echo of her footsteps followed her around the rotunda as she walked toward Madame Vernier. She stopped short and waited for the woman to come to her.

"*Bonjour*, Madame Vernier," Jill greeted her. Saying "good day" to someone who would have gladly shoved her over the edge of the balustrade seemed ridiculous, but Henry wanted a positive identification on the tape.

Madame Vernier willingly obliged. "*Bonjour*, Mademoiselle Fremont."

"You have the negatives of Cici Madison?" Jill asked, weaving her fingers through the shoulder-bag strap to stay their itch.

"Yes." Madame Vernier opened her black lizard-skin bag and pulled out a folded manila envelope. She shook it slightly, as if she were holding out bait. "I presume you have the copy of the calendar?"

Jill said nothing as she removed the file folder from her bag. In the process, her fingers grazed the tiny recorder, and she winced.

Madame Vernier stepped forward, eager to claim her reward, but Jill held the calendar out of her reach. "What ever possessed you to get involved in a mess like this?" she asked. Her own curiosity infused her voice with a note of authenticity.

"I did not come here to answer questions, Mademoiselle Fremont," Madame Vernier told her coldly.

Jill looked down at the copy of the calendar. "I know, but I'm curious. You're successful, you're beautiful. I don't think you're a megalomaniac like Fielding. What did you have to gain by soiling your hands with illegal dealings?"

For the first time in their brief association, Madame Vernier's stony face revealed a flicker of genuine emotion. "Revenge, Mademoiselle Fremont, simple revenge."

"Against Chausson?" Jill guessed, falling back on her original hunch.

"If I had succeeded in destroying his whole empire, it would not have been sufficient punishment for what he did to me. He thought he could cast me aside like the other women in his life—and there were always women, Mademoiselle Fremont. Men like him never lack for them, even when they are old. Do you know what it is to be humiliated like that, our engagement shattered in front of the whole world? It was in all the papers, Mademoiselle Fremont, there for everyone to read how the great Chausson had turned his back on poor Gabrielle Vernier."

"Was your vengeance worth ruining so many innocent people's lives? Simone Nanka-Midou never did you any harm, nor did Cici Madison. Did you ever think of them?''

A livid flush was spreading up Madame Vernier's taut face, seeping through her flawless makeup. ''They were fools!'' she shrieked. She suddenly grabbed for the calendar. Jill stepped back, almost slipping on the polished marble. She caught the look of astonishment on Madame Vernier's face as Henri and two of his colleagues suddenly stepped in and accosted her.

An echoing patter of applause redirected her attention.

Jill whirled around to face Dave. ''Where were you?''

''Staying out of sight, where I belonged. A journalist's job is to report the news, not make it. Besides, you were the star of today's show.''

''I'm just glad to see the curtain close.'' Jill sagged against his shoulder and then straightened herself wearily. ''I need to entrust this recorder to Henri's care, or the final reviews of my performance may not be so great.'' She gingerly hitched the shoulder bag.

''Splendid, Mademoiselle Fremont.'' Henri added his accolade to Dave's. When he took the bag from Jill, she felt as if a lead weight had been lifted from her shoulder. ''I must say I am quite impressed with your intuition.''

Jill shrugged modestly. ''I just remembered seeing a picture of Vernier with Chausson among Dave's clips. The caption said they were engaged, but they obviously never made it to the altar. Given Vernier's association with so many of the principals in the counterfeit scheme, she seemed a likely candidate for Fielding's mystery lady.''

''She had the negatives.'' Henri held up the manila envelope for their inspection.

"What are you going to do with them?" Dave asked.

Henri's shapely mouth pulled down at the corners and he thought for a moment. "Give them to someone who will never misuse them." He smiled as he handed Jill the envelope.

Epilogue

"Why would anyone want to go to the beach?" Jill snuggled the cotton sweater around her shoulders and edged a little closer to Dave.

"Oh, I don't know. There's a lot to be said for beaches—you know, warm sand, bright sun, blue water. You can find some pretty nice beaches right here in Italy."

Jill shook her head, letting it roll against his shoulder. "If we get the yen for water, we have Lake Como right at our feet. And if we were at the beach, we couldn't have this marvelous fire tonight."

Taking the hint, Dave leaned forward to stoke the glowing embers. "Anything you say, my dear. But frankly, I couldn't have cared less where we decided to go. There was only one thing that mattered to me." He held up a long finger, right in front of her nose. "That you finally manage to have a good vacation."

Jill scooted to one side and rested back against his chest. "I won't argue with that. After nearly drowning, being stalked by a detective, witnessing a murder, and a lot of other things I don't even want to think about right now, I deserve my week in the mountains."

Dave's fingers insinuated their way into the soft hair at the base of her neck. "Never thought your teacher's year in Paris would turn out like this, did you?"

Jill shook her head, relishing the feel of his firm muscle against her neck. "In the future, I'm going to be more careful before I take on any private students." She chuckled and then sighed. "Poor Cici! I'm glad Chausson has decided to take a merciful view of her thievery."

Dave's chest rose beneath her back in a brief laugh. "He should. The information she gave Henri has virtually insured that none of the counterfeit stuff will ever reach the market. After all, it's difficult to be too hard on Cici, given the situation. If she had gone to Chausson or the police, she risked more than having the embarrassing pictures circulated. She could have ended up crippled or dead. I imagine she was glad to get her hands on those negatives."

Jill shifted enough to look up at him. "No, she wasn't, as a matter of fact. When I told her I had them, she said she never wanted to see them again."

"What did you do with them?"

Jill planted her hands on his knees and shoved herself to her feet. "I was saving them, in case Henri needed them as evidence." She went to the bureau and picked up her bag.

"He wouldn't have given them to you, if that were the case."

"No, I suppose you're right." She held up the creased manila envelope. When Dave nodded, she walked back to the fireplace and crouched on the hearth. Pulling the roll of negatives out of the envelope, she dangled them over the flames. When the black celluloid began to melt, she tossed the coiled film into the fire. "It's too bad someone didn't do that five years ago. A lot of people would have been spared a lot of misery." She let out a long breath. "But all's well that ends well."

"But *only* if it ends well," Dave reminded her as he slid onto the floor beside her. "As you know, Ms. Fremont, there are still some loose strings left dangling."

Jill snatched a cushion from the couch and clutched it to her chest, teddy-bear fashion. "You're talking about us?" she asked in a surprisingly tiny voice.

Dave's head moved slowly up and down. "I didn't drop everything to come up here in the mountains, just to say goodbye to you, Jill." His level gray eyes conveyed his unvoiced thoughts.

Jill looked down at the cushion just in time to see Dave pluck it from her grasp and toss it onto the floor. When he enfolded her in his arms, she looked straight into his eyes. "Then let's not say goodbye...ever."

Harlequin Intrigue

COMING NEXT MONTH

#113 DO UNTO OTHERS by Patricia Rosemoor
How many sinners were there at the Osmond Wright
Ministry? Bliss Griffith had to find the answer
quick—if she was to save her sister, who had
vanished. Logan Wright could help, but his father
was the reverend, whom Bliss suspected of foul play.
Their partnership was a dangerous one, for Bliss was
falling in love . . . and time was running out for
her sister.

#114 WITHOUT A TRACE by Catherine Anderson
For genealogist Sarah Montague, finding an
adoptee's natural parents was routine. But the only
clue Michael De Lorio had was the terrifying
nightmare that had haunted him all his life—a
nightmare he feared was a memory of a terror that
was all too real. But as he and Sarah delved deeper
into his past they found danger at every turn. And
their only hope for life—and love—was to rebury the
past and disappear without a trace.

Harlequin Regency Romance™

Romance the way it was *always* meant to be!

The time is 1811, when a Regent Prince rules the empire. The place is London, the glittering capital where rakish dukes and dazzling debutantes scheme and flirt in a dangerously exciting game. Where marriage is the passport to wealth and power, yet every girl hopes secretly for love....

Welcome to Harlequin Regency Romance where reading is an adventure and romance is *not* just a thing of the past! Two delightful books a month, beginning May '89.

Available wherever Harlequin Books are sold.

Coming in June…

Harlequin Presents…

PENNY JORDAN

a reason for being

We invite you to join us in celebrating Harlequin's 40th Anniversary with this very special book we selected to publish worldwide.

While you read this story, millions of women in 100 countries will be reading it, too.

A Reason for Being by Penny Jordan is being published in June in the Presents series in 19 languages around the world. Join women around the world in helping us to celebrate 40 years of romance.

Penny Jordan's *A Reason for Being* is Presents June title #1180. Look for it wherever paperbacks are sold.

Have You Ever Wondered If You Could Write A Harlequin Novel?

Here's great news—Harlequin is offering a series of cassette tapes to help you do just that. Written by Harlequin editors, these tapes give practical advice on how to make your characters—and your story—come alive. There's a tape for each contemporary romance series Harlequin publishes.

Mail order only

All sales final

Janet DAILEY

THE MASTER FIDDLER

Jacqui didn't want to go back to college, and she didn't want to go home. Tombstone, Arizona, wasn't in her plans, either, until she found herself stuck there en route to L.A. after ramming her car into rancher Choya Barnett's Jeep. Things got worse when she lost her wallet and couldn't pay for the repairs. The mechanic wasn't interested when she practically propositioned him to get her car back—but Choya was. He took care of her bills and then waited for the debt to be paid with the only thing Jacqui had to offer—her virtue.

Watch for this bestselling Janet Dailey favorite, coming in June from Harlequin.

Also watch for *Something Extra* in August and *Sweet Promise* in October.

JAN-MAS-1